*The Best
One There*

ALSO BY BRUCE FELLOWS

That Quiet Earth

The Best One There

BRUCE FELLOWS

The Book Guild Ltd

First published in Great Britain in 2021 by
The Book Guild Ltd
9 Priory Business Park
Wistow Road, Kibworth
Leicestershire, LE8 0RX
Freephone: 0800 999 2982
www.bookguild.co.uk
Email: info@bookguild.co.uk
Twitter: @bookguild

Typeset in 11pt Minion Pro

Printed and bound by CPI Group (UK) Ltd, Croydon, CR0 4YY

ISBN 978 1913913 083

British Library Cataloguing in Publication Data.
A catalogue record for this book is available from the British Library.

For Sue

1

Prelude No 1

A RED MERCEDES TOURING CAR WITH ITS HOOD down barrels along a poplar lined road in northern France. The sun's out. The sky's blue. It's after lunch. The driver's in shirt sleeves. His blond hair flies in the wind. He and his two well-dressed young women passengers laugh and shout to each other in German. The car overhauls a farm cart carrying an almost toppling pile of straw. The driver honks at the man at the reins. He pulls the Mercedes out to overtake and sweeps past, honking again and laughing at his passengers as he does. The slipstream of the car snatches lengths of loose straw to swirl away in the disturbed air. The decrepit horse drawing the cart continues its plodding way as the red tourer disappears in the distance. From time to time the car passes not yet salvaged roadside piles of war detritus: a smashed French tank, French and British trucks pushed aside into the ditch to clear the road, the odd abandoned artillery piece.

The tourer continues its joyous way, honking again as it overtakes a short convoy of Wehrmacht trucks until it slows and turns off to the left onto a road that leads up to a barrier tended by two soldiers carrying machine pistols. The car pulls up and the driver slides a Luftwaffe side cap from under a shoulder strap and puts it on.

'Oberfähnrich Murville,' he says.

'ID, sir?'

'In my hut. I was flying.'

The sentry tips his head to his companion, who goes to their tiny shelter and winds up a telephone. He has a brief conversation and puts down the phone.

'Welcome back, sir,' he says, and raises the barrier.

The car goes through and the sentries grin as the girls wave to them.

After a couple of hundred metres, Murville swings the car left and drives towards a group of irregularly dispersed Messerschmitt 109Es that point out towards a large open field that extends to a far distant line of poplars. Ground crews are all over the aeroplanes, patching, refuelling and rearming them. As the men hear the car, faces look up.

Murville gets out, raises an index finger and calls to his audience. 'I got one!'

There are waves and derisive cheers.

'Murville!' It's Krause, the commanding officer, very spick and span in his uniform, standing on the steps of a hut, fifty metres away. 'Get rid of them!'

Murville turns to the girls. 'I've got to be told off now, so I'm afraid you'll have to go.'

He leans over the side of the car and retrieves his tunic, lifejacket, helmet and parachute from the back seat. He dumps them on the grass.

One of the girls has slid over behind the wheel. He bends and kisses her on the lips.

'Thanks for everything and thanks for the ride home.'

The other girl slides over too and stretches across her companion. He kisses her, as well.

'That was the best day I've had in France,' he says.

'Come and see us, Jochen!' one says.

'Yes, don't forget,' says the other.

'If I can wangle a car, I will.'

'Murville!'

He turns. 'Coming, sir! Get going or he'll have me arrested.'

The car starts and swings round in a wide circle. The girls wave and so do most of the ground crews. The car turns right and disappears behind trees back the way it came. Jochen picks up his equipment and walks towards the hut, the staffel office. He drops his equipment on the grass in front of the office and looks up at Krause.

'Who are they?' Krause says.

'General Deichmann's daughters, sir.'

'Doesn't he know there's a war on?'

'He's a general, sir. I got one.'

Krause looks unimpressed. 'Where's your aeroplane, Murville?'

'On the beach at Cap Gris Nez, sir.'

'Above or below the high water mark?'

'Below, I'm afraid, sir. There wasn't any other space and I couldn't glide her any further.'

'Out of fuel?'

'Yes, sir.'

'Idiot!'

Jochen says nothing.

'Wheels up or wheels down?'

'Up, sir.'

'So, now it's underwater.'

'Yes, sir.'

'How many have you got?'

'Seven now, sir.'

'And that's the fourth Emil you've wrecked. One more and you'll be a British ace. They'll give you a medal. I expect Churchill thinks you're his secret weapon. Get out of my sight!'

Murville bends to pick up his things.

'Murville! You're wearing a cap!'

He comes to approximate attention and salutes, bends again and gathers everything up. With his arms full he slouches off past the office. One or two other officers smirk at him.

'And get your hair cut!' Krause calls after him.

In his hut, he dumps everything on the bed, turns and kicks the doorpost. There's a bottle of cognac on the table. He pours a glass and knocks it back. He puts on his tunic and buttons it, checks in a mirror that he's acceptable, and leaves.

In the mess, he goes straight to the piano.

'Anyone mind?' he says to the four officers scattered around, writing letters or reading magazines. A couple look up and shake their heads. He sits, straightens his back, shoots out his hands and plays a piece he was drilled in at the age of twelve by Herr Walter, who taught him so well. Krause fades away and for forty-five seconds he's lost in it, Chopin's *Prelude No 1*.

2

The Golliwog's Cakewalk

BERLIN SEEMS GREY AND DIRTY. IT'S VERY COLD.
Well, it's January still. Perhaps the sun will come out
later. Or perhaps it will snow. He walks fast and has to
throw up the odd salute. It's lunch time. There are a lot
of girls about, often in pairs, arm in arm. It's nice to see
lots of girls again, German girls. He gets many smiles. He
gives many, too. That's why he's walked. He knows he looks
good in the uniform, the tunic, the Iron Cross, the cap at
an angle, his face beneath it, the blue eyes. He knows he's
good to look at.

At their corner the row of lime trees still leads down
their street, just the same as always. Inside their building his
soles slap on the stone steps as he runs up. He rings the bell
and hears feet hurrying down the corridor. The door's flung
open and his mother's there throwing her arms around
his neck. Later, full of strudel and coffee made from the
beans he's managed to get hold of and brought back with

him from France, it's as if he's never been gone. His mother chatters away. He's thin. Doesn't Goering give him enough food? She'll feed him up. He's smoking too much; he'll get a cough, doesn't he remember Herr Schumacher from the floor below, always coughing? It carried him off last winter.

In his room he puts on a pair of old green cord trousers and a shirt too tight on the chest now and gives his mother his uniform to press. She's insisted. It's creased and rumpled from his journey. He has to look his best, a young officer abroad in the capital. He agrees it won't hurt. He takes down *The Red Air Fighter* from its shelf and flicks through the pages. All its lessons are still correct, even if they fly three times as fast now.

In the lounge the piano greets him. He plays the *Minute Waltz* but it takes him longer. He makes a mistake, starts again, has to try three times before the fingers coincide with his memory. There isn't much call for Chopin on the piano in the mess. Songs to sing is what they want, and not Schubert, either. His mother is there when he turns round. Crept in.

'It needs tuning,' he says.

'It sounded all right to me.'

'No, it's out. Get Herr Gold round.'

'He isn't about any more.'

'Dead? He's not old.'

'Not dead. Not around.'

When Ilse gets home, he's just out of the bath. So luxurious.

'Not back ten minutes, Jochen, and you've taken all the hot water. As usual.'

'I left the bathwater, Sis, still warm. You can jump in it now.'

'Swim around in your dirt! Not likely. I can imagine where you've been.'

'Good honest French filth.'

'From good honest French mamselles.'

'Kids, kids!'

'It's all right, Mum, I know she's been dying to see me.'

He pulls her down to sit on the sofa and wraps her in his arms, buries his face in her hair as he's been doing ever since she grew enough hair to bury a face in.

'What time's Bauer home?'

'I've told you not to call him that, he's my husband,' his mother says.

'I can't call him Papa.'

'His name's Rolf.'

'Rolf then, what time?'

'I don't know. The police are so busy these days he's always late.'

'I'll probably miss him, then. Where are we going tonight, Sis?'

'I'm going to bed and hope to sleep. Work in the morning for me.'

But he drags her out for an hour or two around Charlottenburg, the rackety district he's grown up in and still loves. It's more sedate now. When he was a kid there was always jazz floating up from basement dives, many black faces in evidence. Down a flight of steps they share a bottle of hock at a table with a red lampshade.

'Life's not much fun,' Ilse says, 'work, air raid warnings, feeling dirty all the time.'

'And I stole your bath.'

'My present. I've nothing else to give you. And feeling hungry. And Bauer! I don't know how she stands it. He's so uncouth.'

'Dance. Come on.'

A trio do their best in one corner. A few other couples shuffle around, but he and Ilse can dance. They foxtrot a mazy route between and around the others until he feels a tap on his shoulder. A tailored suit, double-breasted, a discreet tie, glasses.

'Share and share alike, Oberfähnrich.'

He looks at Ilse. She gives him a 'what can you do?' smile. He sits down with the red lamp and the hock.

The man clasps Ilse to him. She keeps her cheek pulled back from his shoulder. He doesn't dance well. As they go past his table she makes her 'help!' face at him. He gets another glass from the waiter and as Ilse and the man come by again he stands.

'Whoa!'

Ilse stops and the man is forced to as well.

'A glass of hock with us before we leave.'

Ilse disengages herself and picks up her glass.

'Of course, Oberfähnrich.' The man takes the offered glass and throws the hock down his throat. 'Very refreshing. Goodnight, Oberfähnrich.'

Jochen picks up Ilse's coat and holds it for her to slip on.

The man takes the coat from him and lays it back on a chair. 'We're not going, Oberfähnrich. Just you, I think.'

'I must take my sister home.'

'Work in the morning,' Ilse says, 'the war effort.'

'Oh, you can stay. I'll drive you back later. Let's dance again.'

'I really can't, Herr Heinecke.'

'Oh, Anton, please.'

'Anton. My brother's waiting.'

'Oberfähnrich, leave us. That's a command.'

Jochen laughs. 'Don't give me orders.'

'You should speak more carefully.' He smiles. 'I can make your sister stay.'

'Can you?'

'My brother has a position with the Gestapo.'

'And what do you do?' Jochen says.

'Important work for the Reich. Ilse, think of staying here as part of the war effort.'

'My part in that is being at work on time tomorrow.'

'And yet you're out in a place like this.' Another smile.

'Here with my brother who wanted to dance on his first leave from the front.'

'If I got you arrested, Oberfähnrich, you couldn't do anything about it.'

'Our father could,' Ilse says.

'Rolf Bauer?'

'He's our stepfather. Our father is General Murville.'

'I've never heard of him.'

'You would. And the Führer might wonder, too, why my brother didn't arrive to collect his Knight's Cross from him in the morning.'

Heinecke laughs and stares at Ilse then at Jochen. 'Remember me, Oberfähnrich Murville. I'll remember you. Goodnight.' He turns on his heel, snatches his hat from the girl by the door and disappears.

'Thank you very much,' Jochen says, 'now he'll check and find there's no Knight's Cross announcement.'

'I'm sorry. I've seen him exactly twice. With some friends after work. He's not usually like that. I don't dislike him, but he sometimes has a strange manner. I hope he isn't waiting outside.'

The trio are still grinding away. The people whose attention they caught with their scene are back to their own concerns now. He calls the waiter over and gives him some notes. 'We need the back way out.'

The waiter leads them through the kitchen and up some steps to an alley full of shadows. He tiptoes up to the corner and peers round. A car shines silver under the moon. He goes back and they follow alley after alley on their way home.

Ilse goes to bed. He sits talking with his mother, but he can't stay in. He takes a key. He'll be late. He finds the club again. There are some Luftwaffe officers there now. With them around he'll be safe from Heinecke and the Gestapo brother.

There's a girl. Pale face, haunting eyes. She sits on a stool at the bar, her legs crossed. She has slim ankles. It would be nice to put his hand round one. They talk about school days. She was in Hanover then. Her smile raises one side of her mouth more than the other. Her husband is dead. A panzer commander. He always told her he couldn't be safer than inside all that armour. The tank burnt, she's heard. It was during what they're calling the blitzkrieg. At least she doesn't have a child to bring up on her own in the middle of all this. Is it the end of the world they're living through? Killing, killing, killing! Her hair is dark, no, black. She'd wanted to be an artist but she got married. No, she can't try again. What would she paint with all this going on? Long, slim fingers rise to her face when she takes a cigarette. She doesn't see her family. They disapproved of the marriage. She had tiny parts in a couple of films but that dried up. It's a lonely life. Work, then home, out with a friend, sometimes. She came with a friend but she can't see her around now.

They're drinking whisky. They count the different whisky bottles behind the barman. They should come back and drink them all. They'd have to be quick. They'll be gone soon and getting more won't be easy. Perhaps only from Sweden? If they still ship things like that. Her name is Gerda. Yes, like in the Snow Queen. He's a baby to her. She's twenty-four. She puts on his cap. She looks cute. Luftwaffe caps always suit girls. Her lips are soft. Her lipstick is waxy but surprisingly tasty. She puts some more on for him. Yes. Strawberry, he says. With a hint of elderflower. She laughs. Yes, she'd love him to walk her home but, she whispers in his ear, has he got something?

'Here,' his father said that time he took him out just before he joined infantry school, 'you'll be needing these. You won't catch any nasty diseases and the Reich'll have no more bastards to bring up.'

He put them in his pocket.

'Does Ilse still use Bauer's name?' his father said.

'Mother wants her to and she doesn't care for your name now.'

'I can't think why your mother took up with that man.'

'Why did you take up with that woman?'

'Things happen. You can't predict life. A policeman!'

'A police official, he always says. He's not on the streets with a baton.'

'Still a policeman. Associating with lowlifes.'

'Shh!' at Gerda's front door. She drops her keys and giggles. 'Shh!' him now. They don't bother with a lamp and having to mess about with the blackout.

'Will you be in that club tonight?' she says, when she gets up with the first light coming through the net curtains silhouetting a breast against the window.

'I don't know. I have to see my family.'

'Of course.'

He pulls on his trousers, his boots, slides an arm into his tunic, feels something in the inside pocket and pulls it out. 'Here. Have these. I brought them home for my sister,' he lies, 'but you have them.'

'Silk?'

'I was told so.'

'Spoils of war?'

'I bought them.'

'That's original,' she says with that sideways smile.

'We don't have to be thieves as well as conquerors.'

'They're lovely.' She runs an arm into one. 'Yes. Silk. Are you sure? What about your sister?'

'She can have the next pair.'

She smiles again, her hair tousled from bed, her arm still in the stocking. So attractive, so appealing.

'I'll try to get there tonight,' he says.

He closes the door without a sound and creeps down the stairs. Outside in the early light he looks right and left, has no idea where he is.

He meets Bauer at the door to their building, off to work. Bauer offers his hand.

'Good time?'

'Yes, thanks.'

'Hungover?'

'A little.'

'Your mother was worried.'

'Was she?'

'I reminded her you're in the Luftwaffe and you've faced worse dangers than a night out in Berlin.'

'Yes.'

'So,' Bauer leers, 'good time.' He has thick hands, bushy eyebrows, hair in his ears but not much on his head, a jacket tight across his paunch. He probably eats another breakfast at work as well. Pig!

'I wish I was twenty,' Bauer says. He turns and goes off.

Jochen shaves, then, because he can't empty the tank again, washes all over in a basin of water. He walks his mother to the shops. She holds his arm and they stop often to talk to people, mostly women he's known all his life. His mother sounds smug when she speaks.

'Don't,' he says.

'What?'

'Don't sound so pleased.'

'I'm proud of you.'

'Don't be. It's embarrassing.'

He leaves her to queue. It would be unseemly for a Luftwaffe officer to queue for anything. He stops for a beer to remove the remnants of his hangover, glances at a paper, carries on with his walk. Ahead of him he spots a familiar figure, slightly stooped, in a large grey overcoat and an old fedora.

'Herr Walter!'

The figure stops and turns. It's shocking. He's pale and thin. But the eyes are the same and the smile when it comes is as welcoming as ever.

'Jochen! You look so well. Are you still managing to practise? Your mother wanted you on a concert platform, you know. Beethoven concertos. You could have done it, too.'

'You were always a generous teacher, Herr Walter, but have you been ill?'

'Not yet. It's the war.' Walter pulls the coat away from his gaunt frame. 'Life is difficult.'

'I hate to see you wearing that thing,' Jochen says, though it's been necessary for years. He means the yellow star sewn on the overcoat.

'People might think I was normal otherwise,' Winter says.

Someone shouts at Jochen's shoulder. 'Get away from the officer. Stop bothering him or I'll run you in, you vermin!'

Jochen turns his head at the sound of the voice and holds his arm rigid at his side to prevent it from lashing out at the policeman standing there; red-faced and putting on a show in the high street.

He turns fully to face the policeman. 'This vermin can play Beethoven's *Moonlight Sonata* from memory and so beautifully as to bring a tear to the eye. Can you?'

He turns back to shake Herr Walter's hand but he isn't there.

People start arriving at the apartment at three. His leave has coincided. He's on door duty. He knows most of his mother's visitors: ladies from the church. The husbands are still working, even on a Saturday afternoon. He takes around plates of delicacies. How Krause and his comrades would laugh to see him! But there are probably similar scenes in their own lives that they tell no one about.

'Such a lovely boy,' some say and pat his cheek, 'but then you always were.'

'Oh, lovely boy,' Ilse says, just back from work, 'get me some tea.'

'Get it yourself and take a turn with these plates.'

He plays for them at his mother's request: a Beethoven bagatelle. They talk through it, of course. He feels like a nightclub pianist. He plays *Fascinating Rhythm*. Still they talk. Imagine having to earn a living like this. Years of study and no one listens. But someone does.

'I thought that sort of music was frowned upon.'

He looks up. He opened the door for her but her name is gone.

'Not by me.'

'They said you played.'

She's slim. A cream-coloured blouse, a navy skirt, fair hair pulled back, wide smile.

'Do you?'

'A little. I have to. For the children.'

The school mistress. Of course. Hence the sensible shoes. Still no name, though. Does it begin with a 'K'?

He stands. 'Your turn.'

'No.'

'Yes. Whatever you like. Whatever you're like. They won't hear it anyway. They're not listening.'

She sits, puts her hands out and plays. A Chopin nocturne. Competent. Very nice.

'It's not quite in tune.'

'I know. I told my mother. She's looking for someone to do it. Stand up a moment.'

He rummages under the lid of the stool. 'Do you know this?'

She looks at it. Smiles at the melody laid out there. 'I don't. It looks entertaining.'

'Come on then. Duet. I'll play the left hand, you do the right.'

'I'll make mistakes.'

'No one's listening.'

They share the stool and play together, hips and shoulders touching. He sees her staring intently at the music. She makes no mistakes. He laughs, delighted. She laughs at his laughing and at the humour in the piece, *The Golliwog's Cakewalk*.

'I think this might be frowned on too,' she says.

'All the good things are.'

He gives up on her name and holds out his hand. 'Jochen Murville.'

'Lotte Hofmann.' Long fingers, long clean nails. She smiles at him again.

'I've never met you, have I? I'd remember,' he says.

'We only came to Berlin a couple of years ago. My father got a new post. How long are you home?'

'Till the end of the week.'

'Then back to France?'

'Somewhere else.'

'Aren't you allowed to say?'

'I don't know where yet. I'm being posted. The CO doesn't like me.'

'Doesn't he agree with the music you play?'

'I keep breaking his aeroplanes.'

'Aren't you any good?'

'I'm the best one there.'

'Oh.'

'I can't seem to follow his rules, though. "Cut your hair, clean your boots, don't call the mechanics by their Christian names, read the daily orders!" The list is endless.'

'Shouldn't you read the daily orders? Shouldn't you be smartly turned out as a German officer?'

'You sound like Krause. That's his name.'

'You sound like a spoilt child. How can you give orders if you don't follow them?'

'I wouldn't want to be in your class.'

'I wouldn't want you. Who told you you're the best?'

'It's obvious.'

She laughs, throws her head back. 'You're very arrogant.'

'I'm a chase pilot. If you don't think you're the best, you have no business being a chase pilot. You're just one of the hunted then.'

'How many aeroplanes have you broken?'

'Four. But I've got seven of theirs.'

'That makes three then, really, doesn't it?'

'That's what Krause says.'

'It's just sums. My children could tell you.'

'If you gave me your address, I could write to you.'

'Why would you do that?'

'I'd know someone at home was thinking about me, at least for the few minutes it took to read my letter.'

'Your mother's always thinking about you, I'm sure. And your sister.'

'They don't count.'

'Would you come and talk to my children?'

'What would I say?'

'Tell them about flying. How you got into it. What it's like.'

'Will you give me your address if I do?'

'I'm not going to haggle with you over a school visit.'

That night he tries a different club after all. Ilse stays in with her mother and the wireless. She doesn't want to run into Heinecke again. He has dealings with her firm and she says seeing him at work from time to time is enough.

'You mustn't let him control your life,' Jochen says.

'That's easy for you to say and more difficult for me to do.'

There's another pale-faced girl. Is it the new look or is it rationing? She's an actress. They talk about flying. She took a ten-minute joy ride before the war and remembers it in detail: the smell, the physical sensations. Her remarks are all correct, but they surprise him because flying has become as natural to him as walking down the street and he no longer really notices the things that she remembers. They drink brandy. The club has bottle after bottle and unlike whisky, there'll be no replenishment problems with it. There's a lot around in France to buy or take.

He slips out while it's still dark; leaves some stockings on a chair. He walks and walks. He isn't tired; he slept a little. Perhaps he *is* arrogant, as Lotte said while sharing that piano stool with him. Why can't he just follow orders? But what is the point of having short hair? What does constantly polishing boots achieve? They get dirty again. And he isn't part of a regiment, marching as a whole, where each man has to be the same as the man next to him. He flies an Emil. If anyone has earnt the right to be an individual it's him. And the others in the unit, too. Up there on their own. Responsible for their own fates. Each reliant on his own innate capabilities; eyesight, reactions. OK, he's arrogant. But is he bad to people? Who? The stockings on the chair. Well, she chose to ask him back. Gerda did, too. He's never promised undying love to anyone.

He drinks coffee in a bar; buys coffee and schnapps for a group of railway labourers who pop in on their way to work. They drink his health. He laughs at their jokes. They're horrifyingly crude.

Near home he runs into Frau Schreiber, hurrying to buy the first bread. He walks with her a way. He's looking well, she says. He asks after Bert. They used to play football together. Her face goes stiff. Missing, she says. Nothing's been heard from his U-boat after three months. He's dead. No, he says. Records take time to catch up. There's always hope. The British will have him. He'll be fine. They'll feed him. He'll be back once we've won. But in his mind he's already consigned Bert to the dead. She pats his cheek but doesn't smile. 'You're a good boy. Remember me to your mother.' She joins her queue and he goes home.

'She's in a state,' his mother says, 'and can you blame her? It's worse than getting a death notice to hear "missing". You know he's probably dead but you can't mourn. And it goes on and on and yet one time in a thousand, someone gets another message, "wounded", or a postcard from somewhere and that's the miracle that keeps some people going.'

'I'll be all right.'

'Of course you will,' she says.

Can he come on Tuesday? At three? It's sent from the school. He sends his reply there. To Fräulein Hofmann. On Monday he gets a haircut. On Tuesday morning he polishes his boots. His mother has pressed his trousers again. He hopes he presents a correct enough version of a German officer for her. He takes a tram. His fare is refused. The headmaster meets him at the door. The smell inside: cabbage, polish, bodies. How he remembers it! She's waiting at the door of the school hall. They've got three classes in there! She apologises. The headmaster insisted. Too good an opportunity, she says. She'll ask him some questions. Can he give his replies looking at the children? She talked to them to get ideas for what to ask him. He smiles.

Three classes! She's pulled a fast one. She'll have to let him write to her now.

'Don't be nervous, they're very nice kids.'

'I'm far too arrogant to be nervous,' he says and gets a smile.

Inside the hall, the children stand and, in a ragged shout, greet him, 'Good afternoon, Oberfähnrich Murville.'

He takes off his cap and bows to them.

She motions them down and they sit. There's a chair half turned towards her. Very cosy, as if around a fire.

She starts. Why flying? Birds. He used to watch them a lot. He was envious. He wanted to be up there. When he was twelve, he read Manfred von Richthofen's wonderful book. He's off on his talk. He remembers to face the children when he speaks. He talks to the back of the room so they'll all hear him. He doesn't say much about school where he was always in trouble for being lazy. The Luftwaffe Academy was wonderful, he says, he doesn't mention the drinking, the almost ritual Roman orgy-style vomiting so that they could all start again. Four hours' tuition it was before he went solo; the excitement of being up on his own and then soaring, tumbling flights learning aerobatics, flying very fast and very, very slowly, to control the aeroplane always, learning the art of the air, landing on clouds, all the different colours of clouds at dawn, at dusk, at midday the absolute brightness, like Heaven. The children are rapt. The boys with crisp partings, the girls with plaits or braids curled up around their heads. The boys all want to be him; the girls are all in love with him, he decides. Or is that arrogance?

Finally he says, 'Do you have any questions that Fräulein Hofmann hasn't asked for you?'

A boy stands. 'Have you met Reichsmarschall Goering?'

'Not yet.'

Another boy. 'How can I get to be a pilot?'

'Study hard and pass all your exams.' What else can he say? Except he never did. But he can't say make sure your father is a general and can get you out of scrapes.

A girl asks, 'Are you married?'

'Not yet.'

'Are you going to marry Fräulein Hofmann?'

He laughs and turns to Lotte. She's blushing. Keep the blush going, he thinks.

'Well, I've only just met her, so let's wait and see, shall we? But if I do, you can be a bridesmaid. One more question.'

A boy. 'Are you a member of the National Socialist Party?'

How old is he? Nine, ten?

'I'm a soldier. Soldiers do not take part in politics or join parties. Now, shall we all sing a marching song to finish?'

Lotte stares at him. *Horst Wessel*, she's probably thinking. He goes to the piano.

'This was our favourite during basic infantry training,' he tells the children.

He plays *Muss I denn* and the children and he and Lotte sing along.

'You should have been a teacher,' she says afterwards, but she doesn't give him her address. Well, he can always write care of the school.

The next day a short thank-you note arrives for him. Her address is at the top.

'He trades in metals and pharmaceuticals and, anything really,' Ilse says about Heinecke.

They're in the lounge, side by side on the sofa. Bauer is still at work, or not home, anyway. Their mother has gone to bed. Jochen will go out soon.

'Sweden, mainly. We do a lot of business with him. He comes into the office quite often. He talks. We have to reply. I do the letters we send him. Deal with his account. The first time I met him he was very complimentary. How prompt, how precise I was. It's nice to be told. You usually only hear if something's done badly.'

'He was weird that night.'

'He didn't know who you were.'

'Did that matter? I was who you were with. He's nothing to you. Is he?'

'No. He'd like to be, I think.'

'He sounded as if he thought he was. Be careful of him.'

'Don't lead him on?'

Jochen snorts. 'Aren't there any nice guys around? And younger?' he says.

'You know where all the young men are.'

'I'll have to bring someone home with me.'

'Then the pair of you can go off tomcatting around town and come home with the milk.'

'He's not much of a catch.'

'He's got a job. Money. A car. Not fit for active service so he won't disappear like everybody else. Brother in the Gestapo.'

'Please!'

'Well.'

'Is he honest?'

He stands outside the headmaster's office. Where the naughty boys wait for their punishment. The cabbage and polish smell is there again. There's a portrait of the Führer on the wall opposite. Did he have to adopt Charlie Chaplin's moustache? Was it deliberate? The little man against the whole world?

A sudden clack of sensible shoes in the corridor and the door swings open.

'Oberfähnrich,' she says.

'Fräulein Hofmann.'

'What is it?'

'I've come to take you to tea.'

'What?'

'Your headmaster assured me you have no further duties today.'

She blushes. 'Really!'

'I think he expects you to come with me.'

She stares at him. 'Wait.'

She goes out through the same door. He studies the Führer again. She comes back wearing her coat and hat and carrying a briefcase.

He holds the main door and she exits in front of him. They go down the steps side by side. At the bottom he offers his arm but she refuses to take it. There's a wind and snowflakes whirl in it but those that reach the ground don't settle.

The café he takes her to has mirrors and ornate gold-painted chairs at small marble tables. A feeble-looking waiter takes their order.

'I cannot believe you have done this,' she says. Her face is flushed again but now he thinks it's anger. 'I'm only here because it would have been even more embarrassing to send you away.'

'I apologise if I've embarrassed you. It's more arrogance, I suppose.'

'Is that your habitual excuse? It won't keep working.'

'I wanted to see you. I'm leaving in a few days.'

'What am I supposed to do?'

'Nothing. Just talk for a while. Drink some tea. Eat a cake. Enjoy the occasion.'

'Is it an occasion?'

'For me it is.'

'Don't be silly.'

'It's one of those times I'll remember when I'm where I'm going.'

She sighs. 'I don't want you to remember me.'

'I won't be able to help it. I'm sorry you were summoned like that. But I wasn't sure you'd come if I sent you an invitation.'

'An invitation is the usual thing.'

'Yes.'

'I enjoyed our duet and our chat at your apartment and you were very good with the children.'

'I was, wasn't I?'

'Don't react like that to a compliment.'

'But I agree with you.'

'Idiot!'

'Pax? For this occasion?'

They talk about Chopin, Beethoven and Schubert. She doesn't really know Irving Berlin, Cole Porter, all those American show tune composers. He heard all about them in his teens. There were lots of people still around who remembered the black jazzmen who'd been so popular during the Weimar Republic and quickly forbidden under the National Socialists.

'Have you ever played in public?'

'Only for the children. I get too nervous.'

'Develop some arrogance.'

'Are you going to throw that back at me forever?'

'Forever?

She blushes again.

The tea comes in delicate china cups. There are dainty triangular sandwiches of some kind of fish paste. He doesn't like them but the Luftwaffe has trained him to leave nothing. He thinks the cakes are made from carrot. He insists she goes with him in two days' time to see Furtwängler conduct Beethoven's *Seventh Symphony*.

'You did what?' Ilse says when he gets in and says he took Lotte to tea via the headmaster. 'That's awful! The poor girl. And you think Heinecke's weird! You're as bad as he is. Men!' She's never said that about her twin before. He's taken aback, re-examines his behaviour.

He writes Lotte a note at once. He says his sister has made him understand how bad what he did was, says if she'd rather not go to the concert, he'll completely understand. When he goes out, he walks to her address in the blackout and puts the note in her post box.

Too late he spots Heinecke in the first bar he enters. Heinecke stares at him. He goes over. They stand at the bar. It's like a scene in a western film. Heinecke even has a black hat.

'Where's your Knight's Cross, Oberfähnrich Murville?'

'My sister was confused.'

'She's never struck me as a confused person.'

'Perhaps it was the hock that night.'

'Your father is well-respected, my brother tells me.'

'That's pleasing to hear.'

'But he isn't a Nazi.'

'He's a soldier. He believes that soldiers are the servants of the people and the nation and should not be part of the ruling group.'

'An old-school belief.'

'That's the school he comes from.'

Heinecke turns to the barman. 'Two brandies.'

Jochen nods to Heinecke when the drinks are poured.

'Prost.'

'Prost.'

They throw them back.

'How old are you, Oberfähnrich?'

'Twenty-one. And so is my sister. My twin.'

'Ahh!'

He should say what he thinks. He won't get another chance. 'We've always been close.'

'Of course.'

'I often feel the things she feels.'

'And?'

'She feels uncomfortable with your behaviour.'

'My behaviour?'

'Overbearing and possessive and therefore intimidating.'

'And I suppose you share this discomfort.'

'Yes.'

'You show little sign of it.'

'I'm a German officer. We're trained not to show things.'

'Of course.'

'I would respectfully request that as a gentleman you restrain your behaviour towards my sister. I don't think she appreciates your attitude. She is the daughter of a general.'

'Of the old school.'

'Yes.'

'But I'm a gentleman. You've just said so.'

'So you will know how to behave towards someone in Ilse's situation.'

'Which is?'

'A young woman at work in a country at war with few of the normal protections around her.'

'But I could provide that protection.'

Heinecke is beginning to make him angry. 'Then go about things in the correct manner and don't do things like accosting her when she's in the company of her brother.'

'Come courting?'

'If you have honourable intentions.'

'And if I don't?' Heinecke is smiling now.

'The usual thing is for a male relative to take a hand.'

'You?'

'Of course.'

'Thank you for being plain. Your sister has a plucky champion.' He raises his hat. 'Goodnight.'

He ends up in the whisky club again. There's still some left. What's-her-name is there, he's pleased to see. Dark hair, sparkling eyes: what is her name?

She swings a silken ankle at him. 'These are lovely,' she says. 'You've seen your family, then.'

'Yes.'

'Is your sister well?'

'Very well, thanks.'

'I hoped you'd come.'

The tilt to her face when she smiles is so attractive. Exciting. Her smile encourages his own smile. Despite her sorrow, she manages to seem light-hearted.

She picks his cap up and puts it on, gives him that sideways smile again.

Gerda. That's her name.

He points behind the bar. 'That bottle?'

'Why not?' she says.

As he's leaving her at dawn, he makes a date with her for dinner.

3

Les Adieux

ONE UNREMARKABLE DAY IN LATE APRIL THEY climb from their field at Gazala at two hundred kilometres per hour to meet the British reported approaching invisibly through the haze. The sweat slowly dries on his face. He doesn't mind the Libyan heat, though, because his uniform can be crumpled and his boots filthy. 'There'll be no bullshit in the desert,' Winter said when he reported at Doberitz a month or more ago. Winter had seen him fly at the academy. He'd asked for Jochen when the whole world wanted nothing to do with him. And Dietrich, his academy buddy, was already there, too. It was like coming home.

He peers ahead, up and down, to right and left. They have no radar and can't be homed on to anything. An advance unit radioed back when the British flew over them. He swings the stick over and banks to the right to get a look behind. Nothing. He banks back to the left and peers behind that way. Nothing. He's fallen behind now. He closes the radiator grills and the airspeed nudges up by six kilometres per hour. When he's back in position, two hundred metres to Beck's right, he opens the grills again. The speed drops and the coolant temperature falls by the small amount it has risen. Far away to his left the haze changes tone where the land meets the sea. Five thousand metres directly below him the land is invisible. Wearing his helmet with its headphones, the engine is a distant thrum behind the crackle and static from the radio. His shirt was soaked in sweat by the time he took off and now the small of his back is cold. He pulls down his sleeves. He runs his eyes over his instruments. All fine. The two yellow discs on the oxygen equipment are inflating and deflating as they should to tell him he's not slowly suffering oxygen starvation up here at a height above the summit of Mont Blanc.

He looks at his watch. Any time now. Their course is 85 still. Automatically he thinks 275 home. Glints of sunlight come off Beck's Emil. The sun's broken through. The shadow of the armour plating behind his head lies across the brightness now falling on the instrument panel. Any time now. He checks the tightness of his shoulder straps. Fine. He can't move. He's wedged in like a sardine with his arms against the bottom rail of the canopy. How does Beck manage? He's built like a weightlifter.

'Indians!'

He jumps with shock at the sound of Dietrich's voice in his ears.

'Ten o'clock. One thousand below.'

He can't see anything but that's Dietrich's side.

No, there!

'Got them!' he and Beck yell at the same time.

Stick forward and he tears down with the others towards the British.

Hurricanes? Tomahawks? Who cares?

The British turn, pointing up towards them.

One is growing in size, rising towards him from his left. He fires cannon and machines guns at once. The bullets and shells fly thirty metres ahead of the British machine. The nose with the shark teeth painted on it flies into them. The engine explodes into flame. There's another to his left turning in its climb, turning slowly, to get after him, turning inside him. He cuts the engine boost, lowers the flaps, drops the undercarriage and the straps cut into his shoulders as the Emil seems to shudder almost to a halt in the air. Now he can turn with the Tomahawk and he's pressed into the seat as he does so. The shark-painted engine disappears under the Emil's nose and he fires another short burst. His shots strike the engine as it flies into them and they creep back to the cockpit. Smoke starts from the engine. The Tomahawk turns on its back and dives straight for the earth.

He raises the wheels and the flaps and opens the throttle. He flies in a circle to get a good look around. There are three columns of smoke rising from the ground. He's at two thousand metres now. He pulls the stick back to get to a safer altitude. He can't see anyone else. Where are they all? They can't all have ended up in piles on the desert floor. He flies several more circles as he climbs. Nothing. He's beginning to feel lonely. He glances at the fuel gauge.

Time to go home. 275 he remembers at once and turns onto the course. After ten minutes he feels safe and begins to let down. The ground appears through the haze. He can see the Mediterranean away to his right. There's the panzer camp coming up. He banks away towards the sea. Never fly above a thousand men with guns and nothing to do but get jumpy when a plane flies over. There it is. He lowers the wheels and turns into the wind. He counts the machines. They're all back. He comes in at 140 and sinks slowly, holding the horizon straight. He pulls back on the stick. The wheels and the tail touch and he's rolling now. A little left rudder to stay straight on the ground. With the tail down and the nose up he can't see anything. He slides the side window open and peers out as he taxis up. He switches off the engine and switches on the silence. He pulls out the helmet leads.

Jurg gets the hood up, undoes his straps and helps him up.

He stretches as he stands in the cockpit and then climbs out. He grins at Jurg. 'Two,' he says.

Jurg grins back. 'They thought you were dead.'

'Why?'

'Leutnant Beck said you disappeared.'

'He disappeared.' He jumps down off the wing and pulls his helmet off.

Beck strides up. 'So you're safe.'

'Yes, thanks.'

'Where were you?' Beck shouts.

'Where were you?'

'I was where I was and that's where you were supposed to be, wingman.'

'I didn't see you after we went down on them.'

'You weren't looking or you would have seen the one who got behind me.'

'Oh. But you're back.'

'No thanks to you.'

Winter has come over. 'Come on, lads. Let's go and cool off.'

In the command tent they make their reports. Lehmann got one destroyed. It went straight down. Dietrich hit one but it got away. Beck had to break off his attack when bullets hit his starboard wing. He turned and dived away when there was no help behind him. They look at Jochen. He interprets the look as his turn to report rather than an accusation.

'I got two. Bang, bang. One after the other. Straight down.'

Beck laughs.

'Where?' Winter says.

'Same place as Lehmann's. I saw three columns of smoke.'

'Show us on the map.'

The map is almost featureless but the sides and top are marked with numbers and letters. He does a quick flying time calculation and offers co-ordinates, puts a finger to the map. 'About here.'

Winter looks at Lehmann.

'That's about it, I should think,' Lehmann says.

'I saw Lehmann's going and then another one burning,' Dietrich says.

'We'll send a kübelwagen out first thing,' Winter says.

'Jonny,' he goes on to Beck, 'over here.' The others go to find water and coffee.

Lying on his bed he listens to the final side of Schnabel's recording of Beethoven's *Les Adieux* sonata. How long will those extra-wide discs survive all the moves that are bound to come? Hear them now, while he can. Wear them out before they scratch or break. His forearm is across his eyes to cut out the light. All that genius of Beethoven's! All gone now. Dust and bones.

The music ends. He sits up and takes the needle off, lights a cigarette, lies back again. He's still hot even without his shirt on. Three new piles of dust and bones in the desert now, too. Perhaps just ashes. From who knows where? Canada, perhaps. Or Australia. They come from everywhere to fight for England. Why? England is so far from all those places. What is the compulsion? But perhaps the dead men came from England. From Norwich. The town's name has just popped into his head. It made him laugh once when someone told him they pronounce it Norridge. Norridge! Why? What a language!

He's OK with the thought of the dead men. They don't haunt him now. He remembers the first one, though. Six months ago. That night when he couldn't sleep over what he'd done, kept seeing the Hurricane plunge nose first straight into the Channel and disappear almost immediately. A mother's son and the mother with no body to bury, no way to grieve, no way to bring his life to an end in her mind. Perhaps he had a girl. Perhaps he played the piano, too. Well, no more. And he was responsible. He blows a smoke ring. But he got his head straight finally. It was him or the other. The dead man, the dead pilot, knew what he was doing. He trained to kill. He just didn't. Death is on your wing tip every time you take off. He once heard someone say that. The whole room laughed. But it's true. He stubs out the cigarette in the sand beside his bed. The mothers would never know. Would they hear 'missing in action'? He can't let their unit know. He doesn't know who the pilots are. Dead men give no names. And they'll be burnt up even if the kübelwagen finds them in the morning. Ashes and twisted metal buried in the sand.

Beck puts his head in the tent. 'The boss wants you.' Beck leaves.

He puts his feet into his sandals and pulls his shirt on. He goes to the command tent. They direct him to Winter's tent. He's sitting on his canvas chair half turned from the table. 'Sit down.'

There's an empty ammunition box. He sits. He takes the cigarette Winter offers. He's smoking too much.

'You were at the academy.'

'Of course.'

'What did they say about orders?'

'Obey them.'

'Do you know why you're out here?'

'In the desert?'

'Yes.'

'I was transferred.'

'Because I asked for you. You'd have been instructing otherwise.'

'I heard that. I was very pleased and grateful.'

'Well, you've got a bloody strange way of showing it.'

Winter's tone shocks him.

'Nothing to say?'

'No, sir,' he says after a bit.

'I've just spent half an hour with Jonny Beck. A good pilot. An excellent officer. An illustrious future ahead of him. If he lives. And right now he doesn't rate his chances very highly if you're flying as his wingman.'

'If this is about today, sir—'

'Of course it's about today.'

'Those Tomahawks flew across in front of me. I just fired. I had to.'

'Even though you were disobeying orders?'

'We're supposed to destroy the enemy.'

'You're supposed to protect your leader. In this case Jonny Beck. He destroys the enemy. You only destroy the enemy if they attack him.'

'He didn't destroy anybody.'

'Because someone got onto him. And you didn't get onto them.'

He's silent.

'Well?'

'Make me the leader. Jonny can be my wingman.'

Winter laughs, a guffaw.

'He's a good pilot, but I'm an excellent pilot and I can shoot. I don't think he can.'

'Listen, Billy the Kid, there are other people in the world, other people who can do things. You're twenty-one. You don't know everything. In fact you don't know very much—'

'But—'

'Be quiet! I'm talking. I got you here in this unit because I know you can fly. You can shoot too, but you can't shoot down the whole of their air force on your own, there are too many of them. I'll make you a leader. One day. But not before you've learnt to be a wingman. If you can't be a number two no one will trust you flying as leader. One day when you're leading, that man to your right, whoever he is, will save your life. And you'll buy him drinks and swear to marry his sister or do anything else he wants from you. That's what Jonny would have done today if you'd shot that Englishman off his tail. Instead he came here telling me he didn't want to fly with you again, telling me you're a showboater, an amateur, too dangerous to be let out in an Emil. He got away with it today, but just imagine that he hadn't and that when you put your Beethoven on and lay on your bed you thought about Jonny being gone and realised he could have been here if you'd done your job? How do you think that would have felt? An empty space in the mess. A pile of kit to send home. Guys muttering about you. Turning their backs on you. And Jonny's face in your head looking at you. Think about that.'

He does. Staring at the floor in Winter's tent. Without speaking. Until his eyes fill.

He goes to see Beck. He is abject. 'I've been a cunt, Jonny.'

At first light he is up and shivering. He pulls on a jumper, puts socks and his boots on instead of stepping into sandals. In the mess, he tips some brandy in his coffee. In three hours there's a job escorting Stukas. He can see Jurg and Hans working on his Emil. He goes out to them. They've got the cowling off and their heads inside.

'Anything up?'

'Just checking.'

'Here.' He passes over the brandy bottle.

'Thanks, boss.' Jurg takes a swig and passes it to Hans.

'That's the stuff to give the troops. I thought it was supposed to be hot in the desert.'

'That's just for geography books,' Jochen says.

Hans climbs into the cockpit. 'Wind her up, Jurg.'

'I'll help,' he says. It will warm him up.

He takes the starting crank from Jurg and puts it in on the right-hand side of the motor. Kneeling on the wing, Jurg grabs the handle, too. It's a stiff turn. Two, three times they wind it round together and a fourth.

'OK,' Hans shouts. 'Stand clear.'

He walks ten metres away and then ahead of the Emil to avoid the dust the propeller will blow back. There's an explosion and the engine bursts into life. Flames shoot out of the exhausts and black smoke follows. The smoke clears and they all listen to the engine. Jurg gives a thumbs-up after a minute or so and the engine dies. The propeller slowly winds to a stop. Jurg slams up the cowling and closes the spring catches that hold it shut.

Hans climbs out. 'Are you sure you got two yesterday, boss? You didn't use much ammo.'

'Are you calling me a liar, Hans? I'll have you court-martialled.'

Hans and Jurg laugh. 'Fifteen cannon shells and thirty-eight machine gun rounds,' Hans says.

As he's going in for the briefing, two kübelwagens leave to find the wrecks from yesterday.

They take off at nine. He's on Beck's right again when they see the Stukas. They're at three thousand metres. The staffel swings round in a wide circle above the dive bombers. The Stukas are doing 250, which is too slow for their Emils. They have to weave around a thousand metres above. Winter leads the staffel with his four. Beck's is the final four: Beck and Jochen, Lehmann and Dietrich.

The visibility's good this morning. The faraway sea glints and shines. The desert shimmers into the distance to the right. With their weaving they shouldn't be surprised from behind but British fighters may have climbed high and be waiting to drop on them. He stares up and in front. The sun is a blaze above in the blue bowl of the sky. He tries to lean forward to check his straps are tight enough and can't move.

Good. There's Beck still to his left. The yellow 11 is clear on the fuselage in front of the black cross.

'Indians!' It's Winter. 'Twelve o'clock high. Coming down.'

Beck puts his nose up. Jochen sticks close, pulls full boost. A khaki shape flashes past Beck, and another, heading for the Stukas. Beck banks and follows. Jochen arcs across Beck's turn so that he isn't left behind. Beck is after a Tomahawk. Jochen sees tracers flying all around the Englishman. Ahead he spots a Stuka trailing smoke.

He banks a little to check behind him. All clear. Beck is still chasing his Englishman. The Tomahawk turns on its back and dives. No smoke. No flames. Beck lets him go. He's behind a Tomahawk that's behind a Stuka that's going round in tight circles, very slowly. Too slowly for the Tomahawk, which can't seem to follow him. He ought to slow down! But he doesn't. Beck shoots and the Tomahawk breaks off and dives away. Beck follows and Jochen follows him. There's nothing behind when he banks and twists to look. Beck lets the Tomahawk go and climbs back to the Stukas. There are three parachutes still going down and ten Stukas left.

They fly on with Jochen stuck to Beck's side. There's another attack, Hurricanes this time. Beck shoots like mad at one which trails a little smoke and dives for the ground. Beck lets it go. They stay with the Stukas as they turn out to sea to bomb the three ships they've been sent to destroy. As they circle above, he watches the Stukas drop vertically and sees their bombs throw up spouts of water close by the ships. A Stuka trails smoke and goes into the sea. Black smoke rises from one of the ships.

Back in the command tent Beck claims one Hurricane damaged. Jochen confirms it. The first two could have crashed or could have flown home.

In the afternoon on a patrol Lehmann calls five Tomahawks low down. They fall on them. Beck shoots and the Englishman turns at once. The Tomahawks fly better down low than at altitude. Beck follows in the turn but another Tomahawk appears behind Beck.

'Blue one, break right,' Jochen shouts.

Beck does and crosses in front of Jochen. The Tomahawk follows and fills Jochen's windscreen. He fires and the Tomahawk rears up with the engine burning. It turns on its back and goes straight down. The first Tomahawk is still turning a hundred metres ahead of Jochen. Using the guns has slowed him a little and as he pulls the stick back to follow the turn he can turn tighter and point ahead of the Tomahawk. He aims and fires far in front of it. The tracers arc ahead into nothing but suddenly the Tomahawk is flying into them. There's no smoke, but the Tomahawk pulls up and falls into a spin, going down, round and round, out of control. Beck completes his turn and re-appears to Jochen's left. There are no Tomahawks in evidence. Lehmann and Dietrich appear to their left and they continue their patrol.

'Ten minutes,' Beck says, and after the ten says, 'Home.'

They lose height and flash across the sand and rock.

'How many?' Beck says, his voice ragged through the crackling headphones.

'One,' Lehmann says.

'Saw it,' Dietrich says.

'Two,' Jochen says.

'Two?' Beck says. 'I saw the one that smoked. Which was the second?'

'The one you were after.'

'I saw it,' Lehmann says.

'I wondered where it went,' Beck says.

According to Winter, Beck should now happily marry Ilse. But Jochen wouldn't like that. He'll take Dietrich home to be his brother-in-law. He laughs a lot more than Beck does.

He puts on the last movement of *Les Adieux* and imagines Schnabel's fingers on the keys. When he wakes, the record has finished and the gramophone needs rewinding.

He takes the record off and drops it on the bed. He's rewinding the gramophone when he hears Beck's voice.

'You're awake.'

'I'm awake.'

'Just wanted to say thanks.'

'It's my job. Isn't it?'

Beck comes in. He holds out his hand and Jochen takes it.

'Drinks are on me tonight.'

'Great.'

Beck looks down at the record. He picks it up with his fingers all over the grooves. 'This guy's a Jew, isn't he?'

'Is he?'

'What are you doing listening to this?'

Jochen laughs. 'He's a very great artist, Jonny. There's no one better. Does it matter if he's a Jew?'

Beck looks at him.

'Of course it matters.'

He's smoking in Dietrich's tent when the kübelwagens return. They wander out to see. The four men are hot and dusty. They have owl eyes of clean skin when they raise their goggles. They slurp down water and wash trails in the dust stuck to their faces. They found three crashes, two very burnt up. The third pilot managed a landing of sorts and seemed to have bled to death in the cockpit. They cut the burnt remains out and dragged the other pilot from his seat. They put him on a tarpaulin and towed him slowly behind one of the kübels to the grave they'd managed to dig near one of the burnt planes. They shovelled sand over them and found some rocks to lay on top. It should be clear it's a grave. They cut an identity tag off each body.

Jochen picks one up. Round, with writing on it and a hole for a chain or a cord. His own ID tag is much the same. 'Burgess. LC.' Leonard? Laurence? Charles? 'CE.'

'What's CE?' he says.

'Church of England, I think,' Dietrich says.

Beck laughs. 'The English! Can you beat them? They even have their own church!'

Jochen glares at him. It's not funny. '6.11.18' A year older than he is. '2798248.' Burgess's number. Jochen's got one as well, of course. Just numbers, he thinks. We're all just numbers. He hands the tag back.

In the mess he eats the usual foul meal and then has the drinks Beck buys him. Later he lies in the dark and thinks about Schnabel and Burgess and how he would hate to have Jonny Beck in his family.

Another bright morning. They're at eight thousand metres. He sees them first and shouts them out.

'Indians Two o'clock below.'

Six Blenheims. Bombers. With an escort. Hurricanes? Beck leads them down. The Hurricanes' canopies glint in the sun as they turn and climb to face them. He fires at one as the two groups flash past each other at eight hundred or so k's per hour combined. The four carry on down towards the Blenheims. Beck fires at one from straight behind and dodges away as the top gunner fires back, but anyway, he's too fast and flashes way beyond the bomber. Jochen dives below the Blenheim and loses speed as he pulls up beneath. He fires at the port engine. Bits fly off and he watches them hurtle straight back at him. He's too late to duck but the propeller has stopped them and they've stopped the propeller. There's an awful shuddering in front. He switches off the engine and puts the nose down.

'Blue two, mayday, blue two, mayday,' he calls.

'Got it,' Dietrich calls back.

Where's Beck?

Jochen's at six thousand or so. He's got some speed. He should make it.

'Jochen! Break right!'

He moves the stick over, drops the flaps to slow more and turn tighter and sees a Hurricane go past on his left, turning to follow him but he can't; he's too fast. Jochen reverses bank and the Hurricane appears in front of him and slightly below. He fires and bits fly off the Hurricane's wing and then its canopy. Its nose goes down. Another Emil appears behind the Hurricane, whose engine begins to smoke and flame. It goes down vertically.

He's lost speed and height with all that engineless stunting. He raises the flaps and puts the nose below the horizon as he turns onto 270, roughly parallel with the sea.

'Anyone there?' he says.

No answer. Then, 'We're up above.' It's Beck. 'Keep going. We'll stay up here.'

He glides on, losing height. If he can get back, it might be just a new propeller. If he can't, it'll be another Emil wrecked in the desert.

In the end, he can't stretch it any further. He jettisons the canopy and skims the sand and stones ever lower until he touches at about eighty-five and slides and scrapes along. The straps dig deep into his shoulders. The banging and shaking rise through the seat and up through his whole body. He climbs out and walks through a cloud of dust to wave to the Emils circling above. Then he sits down out of the sun under the tail plane and plays Chopin mazurkas in his head until he falls asleep. An hour later he wakes, stretches and walks around the wreck. This is his fifth dead Emil. He's a British ace now. How much longer can he ride his luck? Any of those five losses could have killed him. Two lives left; if he was a cat.

Winter gives him two days off. He's got a new Emil but Hans and Jurg have to get it ready for him. He drives into town with Fischer, a Stuka pilot who operates from the other side of their field. They sit at a café in the square. They drink coffee and strega. Donkeys and carts pass, women with baskets. The waiter straightens tables, empties ashtrays; strange how life goes on as normal through a war. A column of trucks full of troops drives past and destroys the illusion.

An Italian pilot strolls up and introduces himself. Such a beautiful uniform he has even in all this dust. Giacomo, yes, like maestro Puccini, hates the Fiat he flies. It turns well but it's so slow. It couldn't catch a cold.

Musso should ask Adolf for some Emils. He's from Udine and says up there in the north, past Venice, near Trieste, they're really Austrian. They all go to work up there, he says, they don't just sit in the sun. He takes them across the road to a restaurant he knows for lamb couscous. He longs for proper pasta, but really in Libya, although Libya is Italian, couscous is better. Always eat the dish of the region, he says. His German is passable, good enough, anyway, and better than their Italian so they don't have to resort to English, which would be too much work on a day off. Fischer drives them back carefully as he's quite drunk.

Jochen sleeps it off and wakes to Dietrich dropping letters on his chest. He looks at the top one and sits up, intrigued. 'Oberfähnrich Murville, Luftwaffe', the envelope says. Nothing more. What a postal service! He pulls it open. From Gerda! He's astonished. A letter, even though she didn't turn up that evening they were supposed to have dinner! An hour and a half! He'd given her ten minutes, then half an hour. Something at work? A tram breakdown? Finally he'd paced up and down for a full ninety minutes because it was silly to give her a little time and then not give her enough to get there if she had been delayed. Eventually he decided she wasn't going to show up. She'd stood him up! He wasn't used to it. And now she's written. But she'd hardly even expect him to get the letter with that address.

She's mortified that she couldn't get there for dinner. She'd been looking forward to it and to seeing him all day and then something terrible happened. A friend. She had to take her to a doctor and she had no phone number or address for Jochen and couldn't contact him. Please don't think awful things of her, she says. And she's also suddenly had to move. But she hasn't got a new address yet, so she can't tell him where she'll be. It's a shame he's there, wherever it is he is, and she's here. Seeing him, being with him, those few times has made her more cheerful, made her feel there might be something more to come in life for her. He's given her back her optimism. If he can forgive her, the letter is to say hello. She'll probably see him next on one of those Luftwaffe pilots' postcards they sell. They seem to go like hot cakes. Perhaps they'll meet again one day. One day. 'Look after yourself,' she says.

Her regret and apology seem genuine enough, but why can't she give him a friend's address if she hasn't got one of her own? She must be sleeping somewhere. He reads it again. It's like the start of a mystery story. Someone's disappeared and needs tracking down. But he can't do that out here! Now it's his turn for regret. Gerda with his cap on. She's a doll. He enjoys her company so much. That smile. It's come to mind so often as he's thought about her, replayed their conversations in his head, remembered her body.

He puts the letter back in the envelope and picks up the next. Not thick. He opens it carefully. Lotte. 'I can't get the slow movement out of my head,' she says. 'I can't tell you how much I enjoyed that evening.' He still sees her clearly; her engrossed almost startled look as the power and beauty and surprise of that symphony struck her. She'd never heard it before, she told him, only of it. 'It's one of the experiences of my life,' she says, 'and I must thank you for it. I forgive you for inviting me in that way.' He laughs. He turns the page. Something falls out. A tiny flower. Blue. A forget-me-not? 'When you're next home, perhaps I can invite you to a concert if there's something on?'

He's at seven thousand metres, on his own but far behind the German lines, testing the new Emil. It has that factory smell still. That will soon go. It climbs well. It still needs that touch of left rudder to fly straight. He's at full revs and pulls into a turn to the right. The earth revolves; desert, coast, sea, coast, desert. He keeps an eye out as he turns. Even here, the English are very aggressive. He reverses bank and turns to the left. He turns each way with flaps down, then with flaps and undercarriage to see how slowly he can fly before a stall. He makes a note of the speed on the pad he carries on his knee. Hans can paint a mark on the speedo. He opens up to full and dives six thousand metres. He notes the speed again before he pulls up into a loop. Back over the field, he lowers flaps and undercarriage and flies circles as slowly as he can; his version of an aerobatic display. He lands and taxis over to the range to harmonise the guns.

He and Dietrich drive into Gazala. No Giacomo but they go for the lamb couscous. Dietrich wants to get married on his next leave.

'Another twenty-year-old widow.'

'Thanks very much. She wants to. A lot. And she's twenty-one.'

'Oh, well. There's always the pension. The glamorous widow of an ace.' He remembers Gerda's letter. 'They'll be selling postcards of our widows soon.'

'Cynical bastard. You won't want to be best man, then.'

'Slim chance we'll both be home at the same time. But if we are, you're on. I've got tons of stories for the speech.'

After the couscous, they wander around stalls in the market and he finds half a dozen likely looking records.

He turns after the Englishman. The nose of the Emil begins to slide up on the Tomahawk's nose. He fires. There are flames and then smoke that he flies through. He straightens up and the sky moves from his left to appear above him.

'All clear, Jonny,' he calls.

The Englishman is going down. His propeller is still. They're far from the enemy's lines. They have to take the Stukas on to their target. They're only twenty kilometres from their base so far. He watches his victim's descent, notes his own course, his height, judges his distance from the sea.

Twenty-five minutes later they circle and watch as the Stukas dive and make explosion clouds rise before dashing out of the area. Flying back and nearing home he calls, 'Just checking crashes.'

He climbs, estimating the distance to the sea. It looks about right. He spots a cross shape on the ground and dives to look. A neat belly landing. A man crawls out from under the tail plane. The pilot raises an arm but can't seem to raise the other. He swoops down over him, turns, lowers flaps and undercarriage and flies over just above the speed Hans has marked on the speedo. He rocks his wings, slides back his window and waves. He raises flaps and undercarriage and speeds home.

'I got a Tomahawk,' he says in the briefing room.

'I saw it,' Lehmann says.

'I'm going to get the pilot.'

He runs off for the doctor and an airman to drive the second kübelwagen. Dietrich jumps in Jochen's, too. He drives the course he remembers and after three-quarters of an hour they spot the broken Tomahawk.

The pilot glugs down water. His other arm won't move.

'Shot and broken,' the doc says. He takes off the bandage the pilot has improvised from his shirt and dresses the wound. 'I'll set it when we're back,' the doc says and mimes that for the pilot.

Jochen is in the Tomahawk's cockpit. So roomy.

'Hey, Franz,' he calls, 'you could hold a dance in here.'

Armour plate at the pilot's back and head make for a terrible view behind. Just like an Emil. And the English seem to fly always in threes, not pairs. In their pairs and fours, Jochen and his pals can constantly check behind each other. How does it work with three?

'Jochen Murville,' he says, and holds out his left hand.

The Englishman's right arm dangles, useless. 'Mark Peters.' They shake left-handed.

'Was it you?' Peters says in English.

'Yes.'

'Good shooting.' He and Jochen and Dietrich have looked. Two cannon shells in the engine.

'Kaput,' Peters says.

'Yes.' They all laugh.

On their way back, Peters falls asleep. At the field the doc tucks him up in the sick tent. Jochen visits and writes down Peters' number, rank, full name, and details of his crash and injuries. Peters has a good watch.

'Give it to me,' Jochen says in English.

'No.'

'Listen. Where you're going, someone will take it.'

Peters lets Jochen undo the strap.

Jochen collects all the British ID tags they have in the command tent and writes another note to go with them. 'All killed in action,' he writes. He adds co-ordinates for the graves.

'What are you doing?' Winter says. Beck is there, too.

'Letting them know.'

'This isn't the Great War. You're not a knight of the air!'

'Do you forbid me?'

'Of course he forbids you,' Beck says.

'Jonny!' Winter says, then to Jochen. 'Make sure you bring that Emil back.'

Dietrich goes out to his Emil, too.

'You don't need to, Franz.'

'You can't fly over there without a wingman.'

When they reach the field, Bofors guns open up, popping black balls of smoke at them, and they see men scatter to slit trenches as they swoop across.

The message bag is well-padded to protect the watch. He throws it out when he thinks it will land near a Tomahawk and be noticed.

'Did you strafe them while you were there?' Beck says when they've landed.

'Jonny,' Winter, says and is that a smile? 'Jochen is a humanitarian.'

He takes brandy and his gramophone to the sick tent.

'I took your watch back,' he tells Peters.

He plays one of the records from the bazaar that he's taken a fancy to, *Rumba Azul*. A Latin rhythm with a high wavering vocal sung by a man, and a chorus anyone can join in with: 'Chi qui, chi qui, chi.'

'Again?' he says when it's finished.

Peters nods.

He rides into town with Peters the next day to the clearing station, makes it understood that Peters is a friend of his. A doctor tells him that barring infection Peters should be fine. He takes Peters' address back with him. He will visit after the war. Not Norwich, somewhere in Bridgwater. He smiles at the name, so sensible and direct. The English have lots of towns with sensible direct names: Newcastle, Stoke-on-Trent.

There are letters from his mother and Ilse. No others. But Lotte won't have got his reply yet and she probably won't feel she can just write again without a reply. The spring has come to Berlin. The chill has gone. Frau Schreiber has heard nothing of Bert. It's awful. She's had another Saturday afternoon with her ladies. Fräulein Hofmann played for them very beautifully. She's such a charming young woman. He puts the letter down and plays *Rumba Azul*. Can she dance?

He opens Ilse's letter expecting more Berlin weather. Ilse can rarely think of anything interesting to say but…

she's seeing him! That man! God! What's the matter with her? He's become charming, she says, seems to have changed. He invited her out when he called at the office. It seemed churlish to refuse. She had a nice time. He still can't dance but she gives him a lesson every time they go out. Every time! He's improved no end. Mother likes him! He's called, had tea. He says you spoke to him. 'Thank you, darling brother, dear Jochen.' Oh, God, he's given Heinecke a map and directions to his sister! How can he reply to this?

Another escort flight. They circle above as the Stukas dive down on oil tanks in Tobruk. He spots them above and calls them.

'Indians! Nine o'clock, high.'

'Got them,' Beck calls.

They all turn and climb towards the Hurricanes, specks and then crosses against the blue. Beck fires without result as the Hurricanes tear past then turns after them. There are more coming down, though.

'Blue one, break left,' Jochen calls.

He braces his stomach muscles to keep the blood from draining to his legs as he pulls as tight a turn as he can. His vision begins to blur but the Hurricane is still there. He fires ahead of the Englishman who flies into the cannon shells and mg rounds. The engine explodes. A shape tumbles out and becomes a parachute. He catches Beck up.

'All clear. Blue one.'

There are three other parachutes going down. The oil tanks are burning.

They turn and pick up the Stukas. Beck can't shoot. He shouldn't be leading.

Jochen will never get that Knight's Cross like this, knocking Hurricanes off Jonny's back. He'd never thought of a Knight's Cross before Ilse mentioned it to Heinecke in that club, but now he wants one.

After dinner he feels odd. He leaves the mess tent in a hurry but too late. He grabs a guy rope as he bends and vomits up his dinner. Then he has to run to the latrines to empty his guts. He sips brandy and water and chews some dry bread. He shivers under two blankets but feels better by the morning.

Beck gets a Tomahawk, chases it for two minutes, spraying cannon shells and mg rounds all over it. It goes straight down burning and explodes on the desert floor. When they land, the air commander Africa is there; black leather jacket, moustache, Knight's Cross at his throat. He's talking to Winter, then they have to parade. Jochen slaps Jurg on the shoulder and they both laugh before he saunters over from his Emil to join the line. The commander has a word with everyone, shakes hands.

'How many?' he says to Beck.

'Seventeen, sir.'

He goes on and comes to Jochen and stares at him. 'You're the scruffiest individual here.'

'Am I?' He leans forward and stares down the line. 'Perhaps I am.'

'Sir.'

'Sir.'

'How many?'

'Fifteen, sir.'

'Who's your wingman?'

'I'm the wingman. Leutnant Beck's.'

'How come you've got fifteen?'

'They just fly in front of me. Sir.'

'What's your name?'

'Murville, sir.'

'Well, what do you think of it out here?'

'Very hot. Except when it's freezing cold.'

'What can we do for you here?'

'Find us some girls, sir.'

The commander laughs.

'Or, failing girls, some cold beers would be good. The Italians over there,' he points across the field, 'have got a refrigerated unit.'

'Just keep your mind on the war, son. Don't worry about the Eyeties.'

'Does that mean no beer, then, sir?'

The commander smiles. 'What do you think?'

'I think it's always best to live in hope.'

'You do that. And meanwhile, get your hair cut. You look like some damned Italian yourself.'

The commander is staying for dinner so Jochen tracks down the airman who cuts everyone's hair. They've never spoken to each other before. The man winds up the clippers and runs them up his neck. He tells him to leave the top. The man's name is Gerhard. He's a year older but he's from Berlin and went to a school Jochen played against at football. They try to work out if they were ever in opposing teams. They carry on talking and smoking after the haircut until Beck finds him and glares at him.

'Murville, the commander's buying drinks.'

'Goodo. See you around, Gerhard.' He gives him the remains of the pack of cigarettes and slaps his back.

'Friend of yours?' Beck says as they walk off towards the mess.

'We were almost at school together.'

'Another Berliner.'

'Yeah. It's nice to run into someone from the old town out here.'

'What's his name?'

'Gerhard.'

'No. The name you should be using.'

'Look, Jonny, if I'd played football against him, I'd have called him Gerhard.'

'You're not playing football. You're in the Luftwaffe.'

'Is he not in the same air force as me?'

'You're an officer and he's an airman.'

'He'll call me "sir" when he needs to.'

'Will he? How do you know?'

'Because I'll call him Lang and use the imperative. That's how he'll know it's an order.'

'You get away with murder.'

'Loosen up, Jonny, and maybe you would, too.'

Winter calls him into the command tent.

'What do you think I've called you in for?'

'Jonny's been telling tales, I expect.'

'What?'

'No?'

'No. You can lead a pair from Sunday. General Moeller asked me when I was going to do it. I explained to him about following orders. Do you know what he said? "The kid can shoot. Let someone else look after *him*." Lehmann's going on leave, there's a new guy arriving on his transport out. Jonny can have him. Dietrich will be your wingman.'

'Shouldn't Franz take Lehmann's place?'

'Don't you want to lead?'

'Of course, but Franz?'

'He's OK with it.'

He takes a bottle to Franz's tent.

'I can't shoot like you, Jochen. I'm as bad as Jonny.'

On their final flight together, he and Beck get a Tomahawk each. No parachutes. Walking back from the flight line, Beck puts his arm around Jochen's shoulder.

'We were a good team,' he says.

Team? One-man band.

'Good days,' Beck says.

He can't work Jonny out. One moment he's a stuffed shirt, a Nazi ramrod and the next he's getting all misty-eyed over some imaginary cock-eyed relationship he seems to believe he's enjoyed with Jochen up there in the sky.

'Yes,' he says.

'Now you've got your own pair. Good luck and remember all I've taught you.'

'I'll do my best.' Wait till he tells Franz.

Beck passes him a flask of water. They drink a litre after every flight. Winter's orders.

'Prost!'
'Prost!'
He has to run for the latrines.

'What are you doing that for?' Dietrich says.

It's just after dawn and Jochen is doing sit-ups on the floor of his tent on a length of old tarpaulin he uses instead of the carpet he can't get hold of.

'Stomach muscles for turns. If you tense them up you stop the blood going to your legs.'

'Does it make a difference?'

'Not much, but staying conscious for an extra fraction of a second can be enough. Try it.'

'I hate doing exercises.'

'They might save your life.'

He finishes and jumps up. He pulls a cigarette from Dietrich's breast pocket, takes the cigarette from Dietrich's mouth, lights his own and then hands Dietrich's back to him. 'I wonder what's for breakfast.'

They leave, laughing at the idea that there might be anything for breakfast other than awful coffee, bread and a hard-boiled egg.

After half a cup of coffee and a mouthful of bread, he stops. He's fighting the urge to run for the latrines. No good. He stands and things seem to sway, but then he straightens up. When he's finished at the latrines and he's pulled his shorts up, he finds he needs to tug his belt past the final hole. He needs a hammer and a nail to make a new one.

'You look godawful,' Dietrich says.

'I'm fine,' he says, but at the command tent Winter grounds him.

He sleeps. Winter flies as Dietrich's wingman. They get a Tomahawk between them.

At lunch he keeps down an egg and a glass of water. He insists he's fine. He's got some colour back. He leads Dietrich off. Over Tobruk, the Stukas are about to start their dives when Hurricanes tear down after them. Beck has seen them and called them. Jochen sends one off in a spin with a smoking engine. The pilot jumps. The tail comes off the next Hurricane and the pilot jumps, too. The third explodes when Jochen's fire moves back from the engine to the fuel tank. He sees no parachute.

'Red one, break left,' he hears.

He throws the stick over, closes the throttle and winds down the flaps. A Hurricane appears in front of him making a turn that's much too wide. The Emil's nose creeps up the length of the Hurricane's fuselage. As it passes the cockpit, he fires a short burst. The Hurricane's propeller stops. The nose goes down as the pilot tries to glide for home. Jochen fires again and the engine starts to burn. The pilot jumps. Jochen winds up the flaps and opens the throttle.

'Thanks, Franz,' he calls.

'My pleasure, maestro,' he hears.

The Stukas are dashing for home. There are no more English around.

'Home time,' Beck calls. They all turn. There's one Stuka missing.

On the ground again, as the propeller winds to a stop, Jurg opens the canopy. Jochen is as white as a sheet.

'Help me out,' he says.

Jurg undoes the straps and pulls him up under the armpits. He guides Jochen's foot onto the wing and Hans grabs him as he's about to fall off. On the ground he hobbles round to the other side of the Emil, drops his shorts, squats and empties himself out.

'Sorry, lads. Get me a shovel, Jurg!' He's leaning against the wing, buttoning up his shorts with his eyes closed.

'I've got it, boss.' Jurg shovels sand over the mess and the flies already landing.

Hans supports him as he moves away from the Emil. Two airmen run up with a stretcher.

He wakes as it's getting dark. There's someone in the tent.

'Who's that?'

'Me,' Dietrich says. 'Just packing your bag. You're out of here when the transport arrives.'

4

The Girl with the Flaxen Hair

H E'S ASLEEP ON THE SOFA WHEN ILSE COMES IN from work and wakes him.

'Had a hard day?' She mocks him to his face, but he heard the shock and concern in her voice when she was talking to their mother that first evening he got home: 'He's skin and bone!' He pulls himself up and makes room for her. She sits and he slides down and rests his head on her shoulder. She speaks, but he's already back in that vibrating old Junkers flying up the length of Italy playing cards with the Hauptmann of Stukas.

'I'll make some tea,' she says, 'if we've got any.'

He hears that but then his head is down again and in the white Italian hospital where everything is so clean and they feed him rice and the sisters are in white too and wimples with ends that flick up like wings and bounce as they flit around. He pulls himself up again. He's been lying here all afternoon. He rubs his hands over his face.

'The dead man wakes!' Ilse says as she walks back in. 'Where's Mother?'

'Gone to queue for something.'

'What?'

'Whatever they've got.'

'I saw Lotte Hofmann. She asked after you.'

'What did she say?' He realises he sounds excited.

'Jochie, we all ask after everyone's brothers.'

'But did she say anything?'

'I told her not to call. I thought you might prefer to see her when you look a bit more human.'

After dinner he has more energy. Bauer is not back. He's late as usual. Probably eating his second dinner, he thinks. His mother and Ilse are pickling beetroot. Someone had a glut and his mother took them off his hands. He goes through the music in the piano stool. So many pieces. So many evenings and Sunday afternoons he would practise to be ready for Herr Walter's next lesson. On top is *The Golliwog's Cakewalk* that he played with Lotte that January afternoon. He lifts them one after the other. Mozart, Chopin, Bach, Schubert, Satie and another Debussy, *The Girl with the Flaxen Hair*. That'll do.

It's not a piece he knows well but that's fine. He could work on this and do a proper performance. The piano's been tuned. His mother found someone. But it's not quite there; it's not as Herr Gold would have prepared it.

When he's played it, he plays it again.

Ilse puts her head round the door. 'Twice, eh?'

'I like it.'

The next day he gets a haircut; on the top too this time. The day after, he cleans his boots and rubs a cloth over his Iron Crosses. He goes out in the afternoon. At a café he has a large cake and what passes for coffee with milk. From where he sits he can see the main gate. To pass the time he reads *The Sorrows of Young Werther*, which he's managed to avoid in his life so far. It may be great literature, everybody says so, but what a weary willie old *Young Werther* is. When he sees her, he slides the book into his tunic pocket.

He gets up and crosses between two trams to follow her as she turns the corner. He walks quickly and, when he's three metres behind her, calls out, 'Fräulein Hofmann.'

She spins round. There's a smile and surprise on her face and she blushes.

How delightfully maidenly, he thinks.

'Oberfähnrich Murville.'

'Leutnant now.'

Winter told him as he was lifted into the Junkers in the darkness at Gazala.

'Congratulations. What a surprise that you should see me.'

'A surprise if I hadn't. I've been waiting across the road for you to come out for an hour.'

'Really? You could have sent a note.'

'But that would have meant a day's wait while you answered.'

She blushes again.

'Can I buy you tea?'

'I'd like that. But no sandwiches.'

'No. Weren't they vile?'

'I didn't like to say.'

Suddenly they're walking down the road, chattering about anything that comes to mind as if they've known each other for years; smiling at each remark the other makes. In the tea room at the marble table amongst the mirrors they giggle when the waiter has gone off nonplussed at their refusal of the sandwiches.

'May I see you this evening?' Jochen says.

'To do what?'

'Anything.'

'I have to help my mother.'

'Are you working tomorrow?'

'Of course.'

'Be ill.'

'I can't do that.'

'I'll meet you after school then.'

'If you want to.'

'What will I do till then?'

'Eat potatoes, or you'll blow away.'

Gerda isn't in the club. Why did he think she would be? He'd wanted to answer her letter. Things to tell her just seemed to spring up in his mind, as if he was talking to her at the bar. But that was months ago. The barman, an old man, doesn't know her.

'We get a lot of pretty girls in here.'

He has a Johnny Walker. There are only one or two bottles left now. The girl he talks to doesn't like whisky. She has schnapps. She tries on his cap but she doesn't look as cute as Gerda. She asks if he wants to go back with her. He says yes because he can't help himself.

'Shhh!' she says when they've climbed the stairs. 'Don't wake my daughter.'

'Where is she?'

'In the next room.'

He can't do it. Not with the daughter next door. He should have had more to drink. He stuffs some money into her hand and creeps down the stairs again.

Back at the club he has another Johnny Walker. There's just a hum of conversation. The band is resting. He wanders over with his drink and sits at the piano. 'May I?' he says. The regular pianist shows him 'be my guest' with his open palm.

He plays *Ain't Misbehavin'* in the style of Fats Waller. The pianist smiles. When he starts *Lady Be Good*, the manager hurries over. 'Leutnant, I'm sorry, but I must ask you to stop. Someone might report us.'

The pianist smiles again. Jochen picks up his cap and leaves. At home he eats a large piece of cake. There aren't any potatoes.

The Reich has invaded the Soviet Union! He reads papers all morning in various cafés while he eats cakes. The army is sweeping all before it. It's the Führer's masterstroke. There are maps with arrows and names of Russian towns. The Russian losses are enormous, the German, negligible. Since they are going forward, losses will be killed or wounded and not missing. As he reads, he remembers conversations with his father, the general. How to invade Russia was always a discussion question at staff college, he said. The best overall solution was thought to be: don't do it. Remember Napoleon. At least have no other opponents if you hope to succeed. Perhaps the British backed by their Empire don't count. After all, the British are safely penned up across the English Channel and tucked away in North Africa and the Greek Islands. Might Stalin surrender before the snow and ice arrive? Why would he? He has thousands of miles to withdraw into. Wasn't there a treaty? Perhaps treaties with Russia don't matter. Hundreds of Russian planes have been destroyed in the air and on the ground. He's not surprised; he remembers their shapes from aircraft recognition pictures and silhouettes as well as their technical details and performance estimates. They have dumpy little Polikarpov monoplane fighters and biplane dive bombers; target practice for the lads out there in their Emils. No. It must be Friedrichs they have and that must be why they've been waiting for Friedrichs so long in the desert.

He sees a placard outside a cinema and goes in: the first newsreel from the new front. It must have been rushed back. There are a few burning tanks and huddled groups of Soviet prisoners being bossed about by smiling German troopers with machine pistols. What he remembers most, though, as he goes to meet Lotte, is the horses pulling wagons, pulling field pieces, bearing laughing German officers. So many horses! He's shocked. It's like Napoleon's invasion a century and more ago. Where will the fodder for the horses come from in December when Russia is burning? He'd like to talk to his father, which is not something he often thinks.

'What is it?' Lotte says.

'We've invaded Russia.'

'I heard. I thought you'd be pleased. All the old men in the staff room are.'

They walk, sit on a bench. He talks about being a twin and his father leaving and his stepfather. She talks about her mother, once an actress; her father, a doctor, and her sister nearly a doctor herself now, always studying, always busy.

'I fainted at a dissection,' she says when he asks whether she hadn't wanted to be a doctor, too.

She asks him tentatively if he would like to call round after dinner for coffee; they still have a little left. He asks what time and says he'll polish his boots. She says she tried to get tickets for a concert, Beethoven again, a piano concerto, but she was too late, sold out. When he leaves her at her door, he catches a tram to the concert hall.

'Coffee!' Ilse says when she's taken her coat off. 'Be careful. It's a slippery slope.'

'Ha, ha!'

'You'll have to give up your girls.'

'What girls?'

She gives him a look. 'Where else would you be till the early hours of the morning? Every morning.'

'Clubs, bars, music.'

She laughs. 'Mother worries. I'm surprised she hasn't said anything.'

'It would be too embarrassing for her to talk to me about girls.'

'Would it? I know Bauer has told her a couple of times not to.'

'How do you know?'

'You know how the sound carries in this apartment.'

'What did he say?'

'You're a young man risking your life every day, for the nation, for all of us. It's a terrible strain. Does she want you not to have that experience when you could die at any moment? Blunt, eh?'

'I didn't think he was as bright as that.'

'He's right, then? That's why you do it?'

'I don't want to talk about it.'

She comes closer and puts her palm on his chest. 'Jochen. You should be honest about it. We all know you could be dead tomorrow. It's a horrible thought, but you can't escape it. You only have to look at the boys in our classes. They're beginning to drop, aren't they?'

He looks down at her, takes one of her hands, about to kiss it and say, 'I'll be fine,' when he notices a large bruise on her wrist.

'Where did this come from?'

'Oh, Anton did it.'

'What?'

'He had to grab my arm and pull me out of the way of a truck that came out of nowhere round a corner.'

'Did he?'

'Yes. It was a close call.'

'Are you sleeping with him?'

She steps back and slaps his face. It stings. 'How dare you say that to me? I'm not one of your tarts. How could I ever be married when the time comes if I've done something like that?'

At the Hofmanns' he rings the bell and puts a hand out to lean against the side wall. His fingers slip into a narrow gap. He peers at it in the darkness and can just make out what looks like one of those slots that Jews put prayers in beside front doors. Then Lotte's there and her smile sweeps away the discovery. In the apartment, her mother flirts with him. He glances at Lotte; she's smiling. He goes along with it. Frau Hofmann still has a figure, would be glamorous in different clothes. He can imagine her when younger in an English comedy film entering through French windows with a laugh and a tennis racket. He likes her; Lotte in twenty-five years' time.

Lotte's sister, Anna, is plainer than Lotte, darker, no flaxen hair. She smiles and laughs over coffee and surprises him when she asks if he's ever blacked out in a turn. She's read about it. He explains about his exercises and tensing his muscles to keep the blood longer in his upper body as his weight doubles or trebles in a turn. She leaves them to get back to her books and then go to bed. She has to be at the hospital by six in the morning.

He plays chess with her father. The coffee long finished, they drink brandy. He sees the end coming but doesn't seek to avoid it and nods when her father explains his errors to him. He and Lotte are left alone finally and he remembers the prayer slot.

'Was this a Jewish house before you moved here?'

'We had it well cleaned.'

'I didn't mean that. Where did the people go?'

'The man resigned or was told to leave his post when the new laws came in, I believe. Father took over from him.'

'Your father took his job and then his house!'

'Jochen! The position was vacant. Father applied and got it. And the house was vacant, too. It was very convenient.'

All over Germany like this? Many convenient houses. He's silent.

'Jochen?'

'I've got concert tickets,' he says.

'How?'

'I asked to see the manager and told him I was going back soon. I said my girlfriend was distraught at not getting tickets so now I wanted to impress her.'

'Girlfriend?'

'I said fiancée.'

'You're a proficient liar, Leutnant.'

'Where's the lie?'

'Fiancée.'

'Don't be angry. You should know I let your father beat me, or rather didn't struggle against it.'

'I know, he told me.'

'Oh, dear.'

'He likes you, he said.'

'Do you?'

'What do you think?'

'I think, yes, but I should still watch the arrogance.'

She laughs and says, 'Six o'clock?'

'Yes. What will I do till then?'

'Potatoes!'

Back home he writes a note to Frau Hofmann thanking her for coffee and an enjoyable evening. It's what a well-brought-up young man should do. He posts it on his way out.

Gerda isn't at the club and there is no more whisky. He drinks brandy alone. The band plays dance tunes. Then a singer comes on. He watches her in the mirror behind the bar. Not young but not old. Not a great voice but not a bad one; gravelly, seductive. Blonde hair pulled up, a long black dress, décolleté. After her songs, half a dozen of them, she sits at a table near the band. The bass player and the drummer go to the bar; the pianist continues quietly and smiles at Jochen as he goes over to the singer's table. He's guessed and brought her a brandy and soda.

'Thirsty?' he says.

'Thank you.'

'You sing very well.'

'I know my limitations.'

'Are you with the band?'

'With the band?'

'Are you married to one of them?'

'Not likely! This is my first date with them. They're not bad.'

'I've heard worse.'

'Are you any good, fly boy?'

'In the air?'

'Where did you think?'

'I'm very good.'

'You all say that. Kurt said that.'

'Kurt's dead?'

'September last year.'

'Over England.'

'His Emil dived into the sea, they said. Went straight to the bottom, I guess.'

'Were you—'

'Married? Yes. God knows why. He wanted to, though, so I did.'

She slides a hand under his medals and lifts them. 'Two Iron Crosses. One for five victories, the second for ten. Kurt had two, as well. He was terribly proud of them. Are you proud of yours?'

'I'm pleased to have them. It's a sign. For other people.'

'It's the next one you want then. The Knight's Cross.'

'Yes.'

'That's for thirty or forty, isn't it?'

'Fifty now. Probably seventy or eighty in Russia.'

'Are you going there?'

'I don't know.'

'Wrap up warm. I'm on again.'

'Good.'

'I'm done in half an hour.'

She wakes him with her weeping. She's turned away from him with her face in the pillow. He pulls himself up and her too as he wraps his arms around her and across her breasts. Her face is towards the window. There's a little light from the dawn through a crack in the shutters.

'I'm sorry.'

'Kurt?'

'I can't help it sometimes. I try to shut him out but he just slips in.'

'Don't explain.'

He rubs his face in her hair. She cries again but then slowly the crying subsides.

'Are you feeling any better?'

'A bit.'

'Good. Look, where's the bathroom? I'm bursting.'

She laughs one of her gravelly laughs. 'Down the corridor on the left, but there's a bucket in the corner. Go behind the screen if you're shy. Kurt never was.'

He scorns the screen but turns his back for Renate's sake as he pees into the bucket. What a relief!

He climbs back into bed.

'God, you're bony,' she says. 'You need feeding up.'

He looks at her.

'Not by me. Find someone without a history.'

The art gallery is cool after the streets. It's odd to be filling in time, waiting for six o'clock, when the army is rolling over the steppe and Friedrichs flash across the skies searching for prey. There doesn't seem to be any painting on view that was done after 1900. He remembers as a kid seeing strange, exciting-looking pictures. Bright-coloured shapes, women with three faces. He remembers some names, too. Picasso, Modigliani, Mondrian. They were entertaining pictures. Things you could stare at and laugh about with your friends. Here there seem to be a lot of knights in armour and pale maidens with long hair; high, bleak mountains. It's all very Wagnerian and Wagner gives him a pain in his bum. He goes through room after room searching for the pictures from his youth but without luck. He collects his cap and leaves.

He saunters the streets without occupation, beginning to feel a little guilty. Everyone he passes seems to have a purpose, a duty; a delivery to make, a queue to join, an office to hurry back to.

He turns a corner and recognises the street. Dr Feinstein lives down here. Number 20? Yes, there's the huge lime tree. He hasn't seen Feinstein for two years, three years? He was always so friendly and kind; their family doctor all through his youth; chickenpox, mumps, athlete's foot. He was going to write a letter of recommendation to the academy for him, but at the last moment, Bauer found someone else to do it. He runs up the steps and pulls on the bell. After an age, a middle-aged woman in a housecoat appears.

'Is Dr Feinstein at home? I'd like to see him for a moment.'

'Who?'

'Dr Feinstein. He lives here.'

'Wait a moment.'

She turns away; the door hangs open. He pushes it a little and puts his head inside. The vestibule looks exactly as usual: dark panelling, a chandelier, a Persian carpet on the parquet floor. He hears steps and brings his head out.

'No. No one's ever heard of him. Good morning.' She closes the door in his face.

On the street he looks up at the house; definitely the right one. He has an idea. Herr Walter lives not far away. Jochen went there so often he could find the building in his sleep.

A cleaner, an old lady in black, silver hair, is kneeling at the door scrubbing the top step.

'I'm calling to see Herr Walter. He has rooms on the third floor.'

'Go on then.'

He goes past her and takes the stone steps inside two at a time. There's a rackety old lift but he never used it before so he doesn't now.

He rings the bell. He hopes he isn't interrupting a lesson. But if he is, he'll just sit and wait.

The door creaks open as it always did.

The face of an unknown man stares at him. Too old for the army, bald, a moustache, a stiff upright collar, a rather shabby grey suit. An unusual-looking pupil for Herr Walter, but it takes all sorts.

'I'd like to see Herr Walter. I don't want to interrupt you, though. I'll just come in and wait.'

'Oh, will you? Go away.'

'But I want to see Herr Walter.'

'Never heard of him. Now, go, before I send for the police.'

'But he lives here.'

'I live here. This is my apartment. There is no Herr Walter.'

The door shuts on Jochen and he turns and walks slowly down the stairs.

On the floor below, a front door is open. An old man in a cardigan is banging dust out of a doormat.

'I heard your conversation,' the man says. 'Walter's gone.'

'Where?'

'I don't know.'

'Why?'

'Why? Where have you been? The moon?'

A letter has arrived when he gets home. His father's in Berlin. He'll call round before dinner tomorrow. Could they all find time to see him? He tells Lotte on their way to the concert.

'So I won't be able to meet you after school.'

'I'll have to find my own way home. I hope I make it.'

'I'd rather see you.'

'Silly. You must see your father.'

'It's always the same. He speaks and we all jump.'

'That's fathers.'

He paid the gallery price for their seats but they're shown to the second row of the stalls on the left where they will have a good view of the pianist.

'What did you pay?' Lotte whispers.

He explains. 'The manager said he always keeps a handful of seats for last-minute VIPs.'

'VIPs?'

'He said his nephew's in Russia and he can't do anything for him, but he's pleased to be able to for someone else.'

As the music begins, Lotte squeezes his hand for a moment then takes hers back again. He watches her applaud with gusto at the end. As they rise for the interval and shuffle towards the aisle, the man next to him, thin, fortyish, a dark double-breasted suit, says, 'Home on leave, young man?'

Jochen turns to him. Does he know him? That face.

'Yes, sir.'

'Good to see one of our young warriors taking in some culture. Did you enjoy it?'

'I always enjoy Beethoven but I would have taken it at a slightly slower tempo myself.'

'A musician.'

'I play a little.'

'You and your young lady must join us for some refreshment afterwards.'

They've reached the aisle. Jochen turns to Lotte, who has been listening. 'Jochen, I must get back afterwards. I'm good for nothing in the morning if I don't sleep. My class will run riot.'

Jochen smiles. 'Another time, perhaps, sir.'

The man's companion speaks. His wife? 'Are you a teacher, my dear?'

Lotte nods.

'This is splendid,' the man says. 'A hero and a teacher; each with a love of Beethoven! This is Germany!'

'Come with us now. We have some spritzers waiting,' the man's companion says.

Lotte smiles.

'We'd love to,' Jochen says.

'What's your name?'

'Murville, sir. And this is Fräulein Hofmann.'

'Goebbels,' the man says.

Bauer is there, too. To proclaim his interest? Jochen opens the door. His father claps him on the shoulder on his way in.

'You still need to put some weight on, boy,' he says.

He's smart, a pressed uniform; of course, he's a general; he has a servant to himself. He pecks Jochen's mother on the cheek. He's very correct.

'Herr Bauer.'

'General Murville.' They nod.

Ilse allows him to peck her cheek too. Then she folds her arms across her chest and waits.

'I found myself in Berlin and wanted to see you all. I'm off in two days' time. Who knows, it could be the last time.'

'For a general, father?' Ilse says.

'No one's safe, even in the rear lines, these days, Ilse. I wanted to see my family again to have a picture of you in my mind.'

'Your family?'

'Ilse!' Jochen says.

'If anything does happen, there will be a little money for you, Jochen, and you, Ilse, and for you, too, Christa. With your permission, Bauer.'

Bauer nods.

'And if you have time, perhaps I could take you both out this evening,' he says to Ilse and Jochen.

'I'm afraid I have an appointment,' Ilse says, and as if on cue, the bell rings.

She goes off.

'I'll come,' Jochen says, and Ilse walks in with Heinecke. He's in his sharp suit.

'Father, this is Anton Heinecke. Anton, this is my father, General Murville.'

The general nods.

'My brother speaks highly of your reputation, General,' Heinecke says.

'That's kind. Your brother is?'

'Georg Heinecke of the Gestapo.'

'I'm afraid I don't know of him.'

'We should go, Anton. A cinema, Father.'

'Of course.'

Heinecke helps her on with her coat.

'She won't be late, Frau Bauer,' Heinecke says. They leave. Jochen sees Bauer and the general give each other a look.

'It's supposed to be good here,' the general says as they hand their caps in at the door.

A table is suggested for them but the general points to one in the corner and leads the way to it.

'We'll have the rabbit and bring a bottle of claret,' he tells the waiter after a quick survey of the menu. 'Is that all right?' he says when the waiter's gone. Jochen laughs.

'What?'

'Nothing,' Jochen says.

'Keep an eye on that man.' He means Heinecke.

Jochen laughs again. 'I'll do my best from the far side of the Med.'

'Have a word with Bauer. I could tell he doesn't like the look of him either.'

'I thought you didn't like Bauer.'

'I don't, but I'd trust his instincts with Heinecke's sort. And he'll be on our side for your mother's sake. What does Heinecke do?'

'Buys and sells things, Ilse says. Often through Ilse's firm. She sends him bills and import licences and so on.'

'Just enough official stuff to cover his tracks, I expect. Black market. What does she see in him?'

Jochen tells him.

The waiter arrives and opens the wine. The general sniffs the cork and nods.

The waiter pours and they drink.

'Not bad,' the general says. 'Listen, I know it's a tall order, but keep an eye on Ilse. She hasn't had your exposure to the world. And women get carried away by sentiment.'

He nods.

'What do you think about this Russia business?'

'A leutnant doesn't think.'

'Of course he does, he just doesn't speak.'

'I only know from papers and newsreels.'

'And?'

'We seem to have a lot of horses.'

The general pours more wine. 'You can eat a horse.'

'And then you can't move your guns. Well, I expect they'll die quickly anyway when the fodder runs out.'

'There'll be a plan.'

'Will there?'

'I very much doubt it.'

'You always said, "If you want to invade Russia, think very carefully about it and then don't do it."'

'What do I know? I'm just a soldier.'

The rabbit arrives and they eat. The general chews and looks at Jochen. 'If my orderly served me this I'd post him to the front line.'

'My guys would wolf it down and ask for more. But then they're already at the front line.'

The general calls the waiter over. 'Send a beer and a plate of this out to my driver. He'll be asleep in the Mercedes parked across the road.'

They eat in silence for a few minutes.

'Listen,' the general says eventually. 'I'll be very surprised if I get back from this little jaunt because I won't feel able to get on a Junkers at the last minute while my regiments are stuck there. I asked about winter clothing and there isn't any. They said it would be all over by then.'

'Why are you telling me this?'

'So you're warned. Think about yourself a bit.'

'I'm a junior officer. I can't, can I?'

'Just don't join the circus. Keep your distance. When the English and the Americans turn up, and it's all over, then you'll just be a German soldier.'

'Instead of?'

'One of the clowns.' He waves the empty bottle at the waiter. 'Who's your CO?'

'Hauptmann Winter.'

'I knew a Winter. Good man. Killed at the Sambre-Oise Canal near the end.'

'His father.'

'How old is your Winter?'

'Ancient. Twenty-five?'

'Ancient! Cheeky bugger, what does that make me then?'

'Pre-historic.'

'Listen to his advice.'

'I do.'

'Good. How's your girl?'

'What girl?'

'The schoolteacher.'

'How do you know about her?'

'Your mother writes me little notes.'

Jochen stares at him.

'Surprised? Yes, the ogre likes to know about his kiddiwinks. How was the coffee?'

'I expect you know already.'

'What does her father do?'

'A doctor. Her mother was an actress. Her sister's a medical student.'

'A looker, your mother says.'

'She didn't say that.'

'She said, "A very charming and attractive girl."'

'Well, she is a looker and so was her mother before her.'

'Good. You need someone you're happy to look at. And make sure she's got an arse you're happy to watch climbing stairs for the next fifty years.'

'Is this your advice for a happy marriage? Why didn't you take it yourself?'

'I did. Your mother fulfilled the requirements. There were other things that happened. None of them her fault. I was a fool. I can say that now. My advice would be, marry properly or not at all. In other words get rid of all the other women. I wish someone had told me that when I was your age. Are bottles getting smaller?'

He waves the bottle at the waiter again.

'Sorry to come over all fatherly. I wanted to say that. I may not have another chance. Well, seen any good films recently?'

'What?'

'Isn't that the kind of thing people say over dinner?'

'No one's ever said it to me.'

'You don't move in the right circles.'

'I went to a concert and met Goebbels.'

The general laughs. He can't seem to stop.

'What's so funny?'

'Haven't you heard that song the English sing?'

'No?'

'I heard some English prisoners sing it after Dunkirk. Sparky lads, obviously. There was a hauptmann wanted to shoot them on the spot. I stopped him.'

'How does it go?'

The general is quite drunk but he hasn't lost all sense. 'Come closer.'

Jochen leans in and the general sings into his ear in English:

'Hitler has only got one ball,

Goering has two but very small.

Himmler has something sim'lar,

But poor old Goebbels has no balls at all.'

Jochen laughs loudly and one or two people look round at him.

'Very good. Unfortunately, his wife said they've got six children.'

'Poetic licence.'

'He wanted to get our photograph taken, Lotte and me, "the ace and the schoolteacher, lovers... of Beethoven".'

The general is suddenly serious. 'Don't! Don't get dragged in! Do you want a picture like that all over the country? It's not fair to the girl, is it? Stay out of the circus.'

'The circus again. So Hitler's a ringmaster.'

'If only. He's more like the clown whose trousers keep falling down. There is no ringmaster.'

'Goering?'

'A sea lion juggling balls on his nose.'

Jochen thinks about that for a moment. 'I wish you hadn't said that. I'll keep seeing it. Do all the higher staff share your opinions?'

'Only us old-school army types. The younger men have all come up with the Reich. They haven't seen their regiments shot to ribbons yet.'

He waves the waiter over. 'Have you got anything with strawberries?'

'Yes, sir.'

'Bring it, and better bring another bottle while you're at it.'

'I thought I could drink,' Jochen says.

'Make hay while the sun shines. I'll be drinking looted vodka soon enough. Can't stand vodka.'

The strawberry dish arrives and the bottle.

'I didn't think you could make strawberries unpalatable,' the general says.

'Not up to the generals' mess?'

'I know, your guys would wolf them down and ask for more. This'll wash the taste away.' He pours more wine. Jochen puts his hand over his glass. The general throws the wine down his throat and pours another. He stares into the distance. Imagining the steppes?

'What about the Jews?' Jochen says.

'Vermin.' The general's eyes are beginning to glaze, his speech to slow.

'You don't believe that.'

'The clowns running the circus say they are. It must be true.'

'Where have all the Jews gone?'

'All gone.'

'I know that. I can't find Dr Feinstein or Herr Walter. And Herr Gold isn't around.'

'All gone.'

'Where?'

'Where do vermin go? Down the cracks to hide. But you're never very far from one.'

'What are you saying?'

'All gone.'

'Where?'

'All gone.'

Jochen waves to the waiter. 'Get your wallet out, Father.'

The general does so from the third pocket he tries. The wallet falls on the table. He fumbles and fails to pick it up. He breathes out heavily and pushes it across to Jochen. Jochen pulls out notes to cover the bill. As he does so, a snapshot falls out face down. He picks it up and turns it to put back. The general has his eyes closed and his elbow on the table with his chin resting on the heel of his hand. Jochen stares at the picture. His mother has a copy in a frame: Jochen and Ilse at his academy graduation.

'Come on.' He pulls his father up by his elbow and slides the wallet into a tunic pocket.

'Where are we going? Nightcap!' the general says. 'Thank you, my dear,' he says to the girl who hands back their caps. He can almost walk.

Outside, the general insists Jochen gets in the car and directs them somewhere for a brandy. Jochen guides them to the whisky club.

Renate is singing as they enter. She gives him a smile between songs. There is no sign of Gerda. Tomorrow is Renate's last night. She has a month of dates to come in Hamburg. She sings *Komm zuruck* and joins them when she's finished.

'That was charming,' the general says, 'thank you.' He orders her a brandy and drops a handful of notes in front of Jochen. 'Put those in your pocket and buy yourself a drink when you think of me. If you do. Now get me out to that car.'

The general shakes hands with Jochen rather formally and Jochen hands him over to his driver, who helps him into the back.

'He seemed all right, for a general, and I've met one or two,' Renate says when he goes back with her from the club after her show has finished. 'Just remember to have that drink when you think of him. Are you all right?'

'Yes.' He's silent for a few moments. 'I may never see him again.'

'What?' Ilse says the next day when he tells her about the photo and their mother's notes to the general. She turns her face to the window. 'Why couldn't he just be a normal, proper father?'

'So he isn't an ogre,' Lotte says that evening, when he goes round to lose at chess again.

'Well, even ogres care for their baby ogres, I expect,' Jochen says.

The day after that, while he's stretching his legs and wondering where to have his mid-morning cake, still part of his building-up process, he sees Gerda cross the road in front of him. He is sure, definite. She looks strangely shabby, but it's the same pale face, and he calls to her. She half glances round but keeps her eyes to the ground.

'Gerda! Wait!' he calls again, but she hurries on, not looking up. He lengthens his stride to catch up but she turns down a narrow side street and when he gets there, no one is in sight. He walks slowly down the street, examining names on doors, looking up at windows but without result.

Neither he nor Ilse has quite recovered from her slap to his face. He has made no mention of it since and nor has she, but they are restrained with each other in a way they have never been before. She is a good Christian girl, a believer, who follows the Church's rules, and he knows he should never have accused her of such a thing; of fornication.

One late afternoon when she gets in from work and their mother is still out in a queue somewhere, he pulls up a chair to where she is sitting at the table sipping a cup of acorn coffee.

'Ilse, I want to apologise for what I said about you and… Anton. It was cruel and wrong. I said it without thinking in reaction to the sudden thought that some… man had hurt my dear sister, who is the most precious person in the world to me.' He takes her hand and kisses it. 'Please, forgive me and let us be as we were together.'

They look into each other's eyes.

'Jochen,' she says after a few moments, 'I'll forgive you, but I don't think I'll ever forget that you said that to me.'

Their mother returns and he says no more, which is for the best, he thinks.

The next morning he's up early and leaves the apartment at the same time as his stepfather.

'This is an honour,' Bauer says.

He tells Bauer about his and his father's anxiety over Heinecke. They sit on a bench in a small park where young mothers walk their toddlers.

'He's always charming when he comes to the apartment, but he's definitely shady. I could tell your father didn't take to him. I'll keep an eye on him. He trades very much on his brother being Gestapo. It wouldn't surprise me if he had some other connection there, too, something unofficial. Just having a car is suspicious, of course. He must have a connection to get the fuel. I'm just a pen-pusher, Jochen, not a great man like the general, but I'll do my best.'

At the cinema he and Lotte watch another newsreel. The invasion is going swimmingly. At an airfield, Friedrichs land and taxi up. Their pilots jump down, pull off helmets and reveal blond hair, laugh and chatter to each other, wave their arms about, one hand behind another, showing how each got an Ivan. He spots no one he knows.

'Is that what it's like?' Lotte says.

'Yes.'

'They all look like you.'

'I suppose we're a type.'

On the screen, the sun beats down on marching German soldiers who grin for the camera as they pass. Hordes of dishevelled sub-human-looking Russian prisoners with bowed heads shuffle by on their way to camps where they will work for the Reich, the commentary says.

'Is this good?' Lotte says.

'The sun's out and we have a lot of horses.'

'And?'

'Have you heard of Napoleon?'

'That was a century ago.'

'The winter's the same.'

'Surely they'll have thought of that.'

'Oh, yes.'

In his mind, Hitler's trousers fall down and a ball bounces on Goering's nose.

The pianist smiles when he comes in. There's no Gerda and the whisky is long gone. He drinks brandy and sends drinks to the musicians. At their break, he goes over. The pianist is tall and thin. He wears a dinner suit, shabby, but fine for the dim lighting in the club. He must be sixty, a lined face and silver hair.

'Give us a tune, Leutnant?'

'Not tonight. I don't want to get you closed down. It would be nice to listen to Renate. Is she coming back some time?'

The pianist's face changes. His eyes widen. 'Haven't you heard, Leutnant?'

'What?' he says, knowing what's coming.

'In Hamburg. The club took a direct hit apparently. It was her first night there.'

He turns and walks from the club up the steps and into the blackout. He stops and kicks a wall. It jars his foot and his ankle. He can still hear her laugh and her gravelly voice: 'There's a screen if you're shy'; 'Find someone without a history'; 'I try to shut Kurt out but he just slips in.'

He walks on trying to imagine her together with Kurt again in Heaven, but all he sees is the pilot strapped into his Emil deep underwater on the bed of the Channel and the singer with her unforgettable voice blown into pieces by a British bomb in a Hamburg cellar.

He's home early. Ilse is still out; with Heinecke, his mother says. Bauer is not back.

'Do you mind if I play?' he says.

'I'd love it.'

He sits and plays the piece he's practised and learnt over the past few afternoons.

He plays chess with Dr Hofmann and then the doctor pops off to his study. Anna is already at her books and Lotte's mother, unusually tactful, disappears into the kitchen.

'Is it too late to play?'

'Only for people who can't play properly,' Lotte says.

'I've been practising something. I think it's ready for an audience.'

He draws up the stool and gets comfortable, shoots his hands out well clear of his cuffs. Lotte sits on an upright chair to his right but out of his line of vision. He looks ahead. This is like years ago getting ready to play for Herr Walter.

He starts. The piece is slow but sometimes fast, then slow, with a melody that emerges and haunts the ear until it fades only to reappear a little later. He stares ahead but sees nothing. The emotions he has endured over the past few days swell inside him: the revelation that his father cares in his own way; the sight of Gerda the other morning; his reconciliation with Ilse but his continuing anxiety over Heinecke; the army perhaps heading for disaster in Russia; Renate buried in pieces under the Hamburg rubble. When he finishes, he knows those feelings have somehow emerged in his playing.

He sits still for a moment feeling wrung out before he turns to Lotte, about to say, 'Well? Any good?'

She's gazing at him. Her eyes are pools and when she blinks the tears spill out and run down her cheeks.

Someone clears a throat behind him. He swings round. The doctor, his wife and Anna stand at the door, having clearly been attracted by the music. As they turn to leave, Anna is smiling, the doctor is nodding and Lotte's mother blows him a kiss.

'What was that?' Lotte says.

'Debussy. *The Girl with the Flaxen Hair.*'

He really needs to be around some aeroplanes. He takes the tram to Tempelhof. He has his cap and his Iron Crosses and they wave him through at the gate. There's the airfield breeze, the smell of oil and fuel. Junkers tri-motor transports shine in the sun in the distance, and there's an Emil in the circuit coming in but it's not an Emil; rounded wingtips, no struts under the tail plane, no dip on the engine cowling down to the spinner. It's sharper than an Emil, more threatening. It's beautiful. It's a Friedrich, the first he's seen. He wanders over when the propeller stops. He salutes, although the pilot has no uniform when he gets out.

'Murville,' he says.

'Wendel.'

'First one I've seen. It's beautiful.'

'It is, and the answer's no.'

He laughs. 'To what?'

'Your question. You all want to take one up. There's a conversion course, I'm afraid. Three weeks per staffel.'

'Not even round the circuit?'

'No, but come and stick your head inside and have a look.'

He does and asks questions for twenty minutes.

'Buy you a drink?'

'Thanks, but no time. I'm late now. Good luck when you're back out there.'

Wendel ambles off and Jochen is going towards the mess when he hears his name called. He swings round. An officer, also a leutnant, is limping towards him from a flak emplacement.

'Harri!' He hasn't seen his old school friend for eighteen months. 'What happened? Or is it just to get sympathy?'

'I met Wendel,' he tells Ilse that evening, 'the guy who set the speed record in a 109 before the war. And Harri Hahn's coming round to say hello this evening. But look, he lost half a leg, so don't stare. He got blown up behind his gun in Poland. Now they've given him a flak unit in Berlin when he wanted to go to Russia with his guys. Be nice to him.'

5

Petrushka

FINALLY OUT OF THAT VIBRATING JUNKERS transport that's brought him across the Med he makes his way in the dark to his tent. There's a lamp alight. Dietrich is there.

'Jochen!'

If they were French, they'd embrace and kiss cheeks. They shake hands.

'Just tidying up for you.' Dietrich has a record in his other hand. 'We've been playing them. None broken.'

He drops his bag on the bed and digs out a bottle. 'Nightcap?'

'Why not?'

Lehmann comes in having heard the voices. Then Berger and Vogt. It's a party. He hears the news. Schmitt's dead. Koehler's missing in a Hurricane fight. Winter's promoted. Beck has the staffel.

'Talk of the devil!' he says as Beck puts his face through the flap. 'Have a drink, Jonny. Congratulations.'

In the morning, he wanders up to the tent from which Winter now commands the three staffeln in the gruppe. He offers his cigarettes around.

'More girls than here,' he says when Winter asks how Berlin is. A couple of NCOs are clacking away impressively on typewriters, each using several fingers of both hands. Flies are circling to land and they all flap away at them.

There's crackling from a wireless set in the corner. It's tuned to the frequency of today's operation. No voices. They're keeping good radio discipline. They would, Beck's in charge.

'Indians!' Dietrich's voice, his eyes are renowned in the staffel. 'Ten o'clock low.'

'Got them,' Beck calls. 'Come on.'

'Hurricanes!' Another voice. Vogt?

There's laboured breathing. Sounds of machine guns and cannon. It's tense, very tense to listen to. Jochen is twitching. He wants to be up there.

'Red one, break right.'

More sounds of guns and breathing.

'Blue two, break left. There are two behind you. Keep turning.'

Jochen lights another cigarette. Winter takes one from the packet without speaking. He holds it close to his lips but doesn't move to light it. The typing has stopped in the tent. The NCOs are concentrating.

'Blue one, break left.'

'Got one.' Vogt's voice.

'Saw it.' Dietrich.

Then an explosion.

'Who was that?' Beck again.

'Horst! Horst!' Dietrich's voice. 'Horst!' Shouting. 'Get out, now! You've got flames underneath the engine. Bale out now! Horst! Horst!'

Only crackling now, then, 'Anymore?' from Beck.

'Can't see any.'

'Two Stukas going down. Three, four, five chutes.'

'Horst?'

'Nothing.'

'Did you see him hit the ground?' Dietrich.

'No.'

'No.'

'There's the target, dead ahead.'

Jochen leaves. How does Winter stand that every day? He collects some things from his tent and wanders over to his Emil. Hans and Jurg are clearing out sand filters.

'Morning, lads. Goodies from Berlin.' He tosses each a large pack of cigarettes, two hundred in each.

Jurg and Hans grin.

'This is from my mother for you two. Don't share it around.' He hands over a tin.

'Made with her own fair hands?' Jurg says.

'I saw her do it. I told her what a hopeless pair of useless shits you two are but she wouldn't have it. She seems to think you keep me alive.'

'Mums! You can't fool 'em, can you, boss?' Hans is pulling at the lid of the tin. 'Biccies! Terrific.' He grabs one and takes a bite. 'Butter! Is this her ration?'

'Don't ask me. I'm just the delivery boy.'

'Have you missed us, boss?'

'Yeah, like I missed that dysentery when I was over it.'

Hans and Jurg laugh.

'Twenty minutes and she'll be ready.'

'I'll be back, then.' He turns to go. 'Oh, Oberfähnrich Berger seems to have gone in.'

'Chute?' Jurg says.

'Don't think so.'

'Which one was he?' Hans says.

'Tall bloke. Arrived the week before the boss went off.'

'Oh. Poor sod.'

'Yeah, poor sod. OK, boss, we'll get cracking again.'

'Don't forget to check the seat.' Others have been flying his Emil. They might be taller or shorter than him.

'First thing I did,' Hans says.

Later he's strapped in with the engine running ready to check out his Emil and Jurg is about to jump off the wing to let him go when they hear the pom pom pom of the light flak at the edge of the field.

'Get off!' he shouts to Jurg as Jurg shouts 'Get out!' to him. He pushes at Jurg, but Jurg has reached in and switched off the engine. A brown blur flashes past firing machine guns. Jurg punches the quick release on his straps and pulls him up from the low seat. He follows Jurg off the wing and runs after him to dive on top of Hans in the trench fifteen metres away. He peeks up over the top of the trench. Tomahawks are buzzing about above the field shooting everything up. A couple of Emils are burning. The shark teeth are clearly visible painted on the noses of the British planes. Jurg pulls him down. Where are Beck and the others? They should be back soon. They could catch them all. But they'll be almost out of fuel and ammo. There's a horrifying noise of machine guns and bullets striking metal and hitting the ground and a terrific roar as a Tomahawk flashes over them. Then the sound is of engines receding. They peek up and the sky is empty. The flak has stopped. There's a distant crackle of flames from the burning Emils, three of them now. Others are emerging in cautious fashion from nearby trenches.

'Why did you switch off?' he shouts at Jurg. 'I could have got off after them.'

'You'd have been too slow and too low. You'd be burning on the edge of the field now.'

From the trench nothing seems wrong with the Emil but from close up there's a hole in the hinged-up canopy and a hole on the other side of the fuselage. A cannon shell. Hans lays his forearm across from hole to hole. His arm is ten centimetres away from the seat back; about where the middle of Jochen's chest would have been.

'See that,' Jurg says. 'You owe me a drink.'

'I wouldn't have been there if you'd let me take off. It only hit the Emil because you dragged me out and it was still standing there.'

Jurg looks at Hans and shakes his head.

His Emil needs a new hood and a patch so he borrows Dietrich's to get his hand in again. He walks around it. Everything's there.

'Fuel, guns, radio?'

Franz's mechanic nods. He helps him with his straps. The cockpit is the same, of course, but different. The paint is scratched in different places. There's no white mark showing the lowest speed he can do. He climbs away from the field and at two thousand metres turns back. Over the field he's at four thousand. He does a loop, several rolls then tight turns at maximum speed to see what he can take. He clenches his stomach and when his vision begins to grey and contract, relaxes the turn. He'll have to start his exercises again properly. It's been weeks. Plumes of smoke rise from the field where the latrines were. It gives their presence away but the British clearly know where to find them anyway. The alternative is to burn them out at night but then fires are visible. You can't win. He turns over and flies upside down for a while. The land is above him. There aren't really many more features than in the sky.

Two shadow crosses pass on the earth high above him. He flips over and dives. He's three kilometres from the field. The other planes are very low. Black bursts appear in front of them. Hurricanes. On the field, men are running for trenches. He's dropping on the British like a hawk. They haven't seen him. They don't seem to be firing at the Emils on the ground. The flak has stopped with him closing in. The second Hurricane is two hundred metres ahead. It fills his sight and he's about to shoot when the canopy of the leader slides open and something falls from it. Jochen pulls to one side and throttles back. He flies alongside the leader. He rocks his wings and waves to the pilot. The Englishman waves back. Jochen pulls away and flies a circle as the Hurricanes hare off back to Tommyland.

Beck is incandescent.

'Why didn't you shoot?'

'I tried, Jonny. Nothing happened.'

'Your guns failed? I'll put those jokers of yours on a charge.'

'Franz's jokers.'

'His then.'

'It wasn't the guns. It was my thumb. It wouldn't let me murder them.'

'Your thumb! God in Heaven! I don't know what you're doing in a uniform!'

'Me too, sometimes, Jonny. What did the note say?'

Dietrich is holding it.

'Koehler's a prisoner. Burns, left arm amputated. But doing well, it seems. He's on his way to a hospital in Alexandria.'

The Stukas are below. What strange crow-like aeroplanes they are. Who would even think they'd fly?

They reach their target without any interference. Where are all the Indians? Are they off on some raid of their own? Or caught on the ground refuelling? The Stukas tip over one by one through the black-bursting flak, plummeting on ships in Tobruk harbour, their sirens screaming though he can't hear them, just the background throb of the engine and the static in his ears. He looks all around for those Indians through the shiny glass of his new hood. Hans and Jurg worked half the night to get his Emil ready, to put on that almost invisible patch beneath the cockpit rim.

They turn into the sun to make for home. It's a milk run. One Stuka trails smoke but is getting ever closer to home, just a few more minutes.

'Indians! Three o'clock high!'

They all turn and climb on full boost towards them; specks and then crosses against the blue. He fires at a Hurricane coming straight at him. No time for clever manoeuvres. There's a thud that shakes the Emil. The machine slows with the thud and the recoil from firing the guns. The Hurricanes are past and turning back for them as the Emils turn down again after the Hurricanes. He tenses his stomach and holds the turn as his vision greys.

'Red one, break right!' Franz calls.

He reverses his turn and spots a Hurricane dropping in behind an Emil, number eleven in yellow on its side, which is behind another Hurricane.

'Jonny, break right!' he shouts. He has no time to watch. Another Hurricane crosses three hundred metres ahead of him. He pulls the stick back and over to the right. Nothing to see through his sight but his nose has moved ahead of the Englishman. It feels good. He holds his thumb down and counts; one thousand, two thousand, as he's trained himself to do. The Hurricane flies into the bullets and shells. Smoke pours from its engine but he has no time to watch.

'Jochen! Break left!' He does. Is Franz still there, after all this?

He cuts the throttle and lowers the flaps as he turns. A Hurricane shoots past and immediately goes into a right-hand turn as he sees his danger. Smoke appears across the windscreen. It's rising between his legs.

'You're on fire, Jochen!' Franz calls. He raises his flaps and opens the throttle. He pulls the stick back to gain height. The engine stops. He glances down. The fuel gauge shows empty. A long fight at the end of a mission.

He won't get back.

'How are we doing, Franz?'

'All cleared off.'

'I'm getting out in a tick.'

'Do it now. You're near enough. And you're brewing up nicely.'

Winter's had good entertainment today. Probably standing there with a cigarette halfway to his lips.

'OK. I'm going now.'

He pulls the toggle and his new hood flies off. He checks he's got the quick release on the straps and not the parachute release that's pretty well underneath and bangs it with the heel of his fist. He unclips and pulls off the oxygen mask and drops it and pulls the radio lead out of his helmet. Jump or fall? He turns the Emil onto its back and pushes his feet on the floor as he feels himself going. The slipstream snatches at his shirt and something bangs his calf but he's falling away looking down at the ground. He looks up for his Emil starting its final descent, lovely neat patch and all. This is his sixth life. He pulls the cord. Over the wind he hears the flap and the crack as the silk pours out and the chute fills with air, stopping him short and jerking him upwards between the legs. He's sailing, swaying and looking all around. An Emil circles. Franz.

Probably calling out, 'Chute open,' and reading out the map co-ordinates in case he doesn't get home either. Winter can light that snout now.

When they bring him in after four hours' sitting under his parachute, he slaps Franz on the back and says, 'I don't know how you do it. That was twice you called me.'

'I've got to get my sister off my hands somehow.'

'I propose.'

'You know I haven't got a sister.'

'Ohhh.'

'My auntie's only thirty. You could be my uncle.'

He apologises to Jurg and Hans.

'It was the shiniest canopy I've ever had.'

There's no Emil for him yet so he sleeps, rubs his calf, badly bruised probably from hitting the tail plane on his way out, listens in at the command tent, writes letters and puts on records. He brought *Petrushka* back with him. He plays it a second time. He loves the way it turns from merry to tragic. Stravinsky. A top guy, he decides. Jewish? No idea. Russian? Yes. But not a commie. He left years before, didn't he? Is *Petrushka* permitted? Not a clue. Who cares? He wishes Beck would come by and he could say, 'Oh, it's from a ballet.' Jonny is scornful of ballet. All the men are poofs. Yes. All those athletic men with huge strong thighs and enormous wodges of genitals, with their hands all over women all day, are poofs.

There are shouts and loud laughs from nearby. One shout becomes almost a scream. He's at his tent flap by now. Jonny Beck runs past towards the command tent, minus his cap. What's up? It can't be serious or they wouldn't be laughing. He strolls over. Vogt and his guys are standing over a dead snake. Not very big. An asp, not a cobra. Of course, they're dangerous if they bite you but they're usually much more scared of people and slither away fast. Anyway, one of Vogt's guys has flattened it with a spade and it's head is half cut off. Vogt is grinning and shaking his head.

'Jonny's got a phobia,' he says.

Beck's peaked cap lies nearby, blown off during his fast escape. Jochen picks it up and scoops the dead snake up in it. He carries the cap to the command tent. Beck is sitting there on an ammo box, smoking a cigarette.

'No cap, Jonny? You'll get sunstroke. Here. I brought it for you.'

He offers the cap. Beck reaches out to take it, sees what it contains and jumps up with a shriek. He runs out. The cap falls and the snake spills out on the ground. There's a split second of alarm on Winter's face that turns at once into a grin.

There's a new Emil in Benghazi so he drives there with Hans and Jurg. They sing and natter all the way. Jurg misses his wife and his three year-old daughter. He's five years older than Jochen. He's a fan of marriage.

'You don't have to go out, spend a fortune and wonder if you'll get lucky.'

'I'm worried it might be like going to the same place on holiday every year,' Jochen says.

'I've never been on holiday.'

'Jurg's right about marriage,' Hans says, 'but make sure you choose and don't get marched up the aisle with a gun in your back.'

Jochen and Jurg laugh at Hans although neither asks if that was his experience.

He tells them about Renate, blown up in Hamburg. It shocks them.

'First night!' Jurg says, as though dying on the second night would have been fine.

In Benghazi he buys them dinner. They find a table in a corner and he tucks himself into the darkest part. He'll happily argue with anyone who disputes their right to eat with him but shouting matches like that are a real fag, especially in the hottest part of the day. They have a beer each. He's got to fly back and they've got to drive and before that check the Emil over to make sure it's safe for their boss to get in.

For some reason, he talks about Lotte.

Hans sucks his breath in through his teeth.

'What?' Jochen says.

Jurg answers for him. 'Doctor's daughter, teacher, plays the piano. Girl's like that. Well, I've never known one but with a girl like that you need to do the right thing, boss.'

'He's right,' Hans says. 'Your name would be mud if you messed her about. General's son and all! Watch your step! Don't muck your life up.'

'Have I got a life? Doing this?'

'You're the best one there.'

'I know that,' Jochen says.

'Modest, too,' Hans says with a grin.

'Assume you'll live,' Jurg says. 'It won't hurt.'

They find the coast road for the airfield but after two kilometres come upon an open car with the driver's door wide open and a woman waving to them. Jochen pulls up in front of the car.

'Please. Help. *S'e fermata la macchina. Non so che cos'e successo.*'

She wears a tight blue silk dress to her knees that just manages to hold all of her in, sandals with high heels and a wide brimmed white sun hat.

Hans already has the bonnet up.

'Fan belt. We've got one in the back, Jurg.'

'Wait!' Jochen says. 'Sure?'

'About a fan belt?'

'OK, OK. You two get off.'

'Get off?'

'Yes. Get off. I'll fix this and she can drop me at the field.'

Jurg gives Jochen the fan belt and a spanner and he and Hans drive off.

Jurg fits the fan belt and slides the spanner into the leg pocket of his trousers. Then he trots fifty metres back down the road and picks up the broken fan belt, which he's spotted. He stuffs it in a tunic pocket. He's got a use for it.

'*Tenente Murville,*' he says. '*Jochen.*'

'*Ah, tenente. Piacere. Mi chiama Claudia Pietrosanto.*'

She's an opera singer. He's already recognised her from a poster in Benghazi.

He tells her he needs a lift. She understands eventually and swings the convertible round on the empty road and drives towards the airfield.

He loves his new Emil. Hans has painted his number, '14', on the side, nineteen victory bars on the rudder, and the slowest possible speed on the speedo. The engine purrs like a kitten. No baling out, no belly landings in this one, he tells himself.

They see nothing for two days. The English are on holiday. Then on a patrol one morning, he gets two Tomahawks.

'Seven cannon shells and twelve mg bullets,' Jurg tells him.

That evening they come across five Hurricanes but can't catch them. He shoots one down at four hundred-metre range.

'How do you do that?' Dietrich says.

'I don't know. It just feels right,' he says.

He catches a lift into Benghazi that evening. Claudia has a concert. He isn't there when the truck leaves to come back. In the silence just before first light a few wake as a car pulls up at the gate. Over the sound of the idling engine comes a woman's laugh. A door slams and the car drives off.

A little later those near Jochen's tent hear him curse.

In the morning, he's distraught.

'I sat on *Rumba Azul*,' he tells Dietrich. 'I'd left it on the bed.' It was his favourite record. He played it when he woke up and a couple of times most evenings.

Two days and a Tomahawk later he's playing it again.

'I thought you sat on it,' Dietrich says.

'I got another one.' Jochen is dancing around the tent and joining in the chorus, 'Chi qui, chi qui chi.'

When the record stops, the message written on the label is clear to read, '*Caro Jochen, con amore, sempre, Claudia.*'

There are letters. He reads Lotte's first. It's nearly the end of her summer. School starts soon. She's in the country at a camp with lots of her children. They walk and help with the harvest during the day. She wears shorts and has gone brown in the sun. There's only the river to wash in, so she wears her hair in braids or coils around her head. At night they sing songs around a fire and then she sleeps and dreams of him. He reads it again immediately.

The weather is good in his mother's letter. Oh! Harri has called several times. He chuckles. That evening when Harri turned up was awkward at first. He was out of breath from the stairs. Naturally, with only one leg. They drank tea, rattling cups in saucers. How long was he in hospital Ilse asked after a silence. 'Months,' Harri said, 'then they finally told me to hop it.'

Jochen couldn't help it; the remark was so unexpected. He guffawed.

'Jochen!' Ilse said.

But Harri was laughing, too. 'It's all right,' he said, 'don't be delicate. Losing a leg is terrible but I'm still here. Four of my guys aren't.'

After that, conversation was easier.

'Still playing the joanna, Jochen?' Jochen played *Fur Elise*. Harri applauded.

'Give us a song, then, Harri,' Jochen said.

'Oh, yes,' Jochen's mother said, 'you used to do solos at school, didn't you?'

'Well, what? I'm a bit rusty on drawing-room songs.'

Jochen rummaged through the stool. 'What about this?'

Harri looked at it. 'Well, if you like. Here you are,' and he passed it back to Jochen.

'Oh, no, I'm not accompanying a man with a peg leg singing a love song. Ilse, you do it. You've played it before.'

After a protest, she glanced through it and looked up to see if Harri was ready. He nodded. It was delightful. She played well. Of course, Jochen knew she did; she just wasn't as good as him. And Harri could sing, though he'd never had training. *Dein ist mein Ganzes Herz*; terrible old schmaltz from *Das Land des Lächelns*, a musical play from their youth. Franz Lehar. So was Harri round there serenading every evening or weekend he had off from his battery of eighty-eights? That would be a turn up for the books.

No weather in Ilse's letter; straight to the point. 'The more I see of Harri, the more I realise that Anton is not really very nice. Harri is always laughing despite his injury and always seems to see the good side of everything and everyone but Anton is always highly critical and only seems to laugh at people's misfortune. Even when something seems good, he's got some disparaging remark or other ready. By the end of the evening I'm feeling miserable. I'm going to tell him tomorrow when I meet him that I don't want to see him anymore.'

It's happened by now. She's done the deed. Good old Ilse! He can't wait for the next episode.

Dietrich spots them as usual and they tear down. The Hurricanes climb towards them. They all shoot as they pass and then they're in a turning fight. The Marylands below go on in their tight formation while the Hurricanes occupy the Emils. Jochen gets three, one after the other. The final one explodes and he flies through the pieces. It sickens him but Dietrich shouts, 'Break right!' and he does and forgets the explosion. They're full of excited chatter in the command tent. Dietrich got one, Beck, one, Vogt got two. Seven with Jochen's three.

After a moment Jochen says, 'Useless.'

'We slaughtered them,' Beck says.

'But those bombers went sailing on. I don't expect the guys under that lot thought we'd done well.'

'We can't ignore the fighters. They'll just knock us down if we don't fight them. What can we do?'

'I don't know. But however many we shoot down, the English just keep sending more up.'

'We're completely outnumbered, Jochen,' Winter says. 'One Geschwader we've got out here. 140 Emils. God knows how many Tomahawks they're shipping over from the States every day. Anyway, a drink. You've got twenty-five now.'

He lies on the bed and listens to *Petrushka*. He blows smoke rings. He remembers the Hurricane that exploded; a man blown to pieces in the air right in front of him. He should have asked Jurg if they had to clean any blood or flesh off the propeller. Revenge for Renate blown up in Hamburg? Revenge isn't something that particularly interests him. And how many Tomahawks do the British ship in? They shoot them down at will but there always seem to be just as many around the next day. Thank goodness a Tomahawk is a bit of a carthorse compared to their Emils or they'd be slaughtered. He falls asleep and wakes up remembering the fan belt he found on the road.

He creeps into Beck's tent where he lies sleeping and gently lays the fan belt on Beck's chest and bare neck. Outside he lights a cigarette. Anyone who passes he signals to wait around quietly. Near the end of his cigarette there's a shriek from inside the tent and Beck runs out tearing his shirt off. The fan belt seems to have slipped down inside it as he jumped up. Finally the shirt is off and Beck has thrown it from him and started running off towards the parked Emils when he notices the officers all around, some bent double with laughter. He stops and sees Jochen grinning.

'What have you done, you bastard?'

Jochen picks up the fan belt and waves it around. 'Such a shame Jonny doesn't appreciate fan belts, they make such rewarding pets.'

'Very funny. Just wait, Murville, just wait.'

The next morning, they've all just landed from a fruitless patrol when Winter calls out.

'Listen a minute. No more flying today. New orders just in. We're off home tomorrow to convert to Friedrichs.'

There's a moment's silence while they take in the news and then there's whooping and cheering and caps thrown in the air. Jochen grabs Dietrich and jumps around with him.

'Party!' he shouts. 'Everyone to my tent.'

They all turn to move off.

'Stop. Reports first.'

They all turn again for the command tent but Winter stops Jochen.

'Listen,' he says, 'you've just missed a friend of a friend of yours. An Italian general was here to horse whip you for annoying his great friend the opera singer.'

'Claudia.'

'I don't want to know her name. I told him Luftwaffe regulations forbade horse whipping and anyway, you'd just left for Germany. Have a bit of dignity, do.'

Autumn in Germany, just outside Munich. Sausages and beer that spills out of steins as the waitress's bosoms threaten to out of their blouses. Grass, cows grazing, reds and golds beginning on the trees in the valleys, great pines higher up, their green almost black, mountain tops jagged against the sky.

He imagines them, him and Lotte, her long legs brown from days in the sun in her shorts, hiking in the summer through all this green; picnicking by a stream; joyously nattering non-stop over dinner as they always seem to about he never knows what afterwards, her smile that paints the day, always opposite him across the table; coddled in their inn bed by a down quilt.

But he can't do that in his usual way, can he? Not with Lotte, doctor's daughter and teacher, who plays the piano.

Lectures, diagrams, new features on the Friedrich compared to the Emil mean a session or two in the classroom, straining to keep eyes open as motes spiral in shafts of sunlight through high windows. Note-taking; Beck has an exercise book, he writes assiduously; Jochen a slip of paper he takes down one or two speeds and crucial facts on.

Friedrichs are in short supply so they take turns to play with them. It's sleeker, with a lovely streamlined nose; a shark of the air. It's 500 kilos heavier and doesn't turn as quickly as an Emil but it's faster and flies higher and further. The cockpit's still cramped with the same up and over canopy and the glazing bars like an apartment window. There's the same narrow undercarriage that needs concentration on take-off and landing and there's still no view to the front on the ground with the tail down and the nose up. But it's faster. That's the important thing. All chase pilots want a faster aeroplane.

They go up in pairs, different pairs each time. They fly towards each other and turn and chase. It's strange to do this with a European landscape below again; valleys, hills, grass, trees. Always, after a minute or two, Jochen sees his opponent framed in his sights and calls out, 'Franz,' or, 'Paul,' and makes a farting noise into the oxygen mask. They call back, 'OK, got me,' and break off to fly away and then back to try again. No one minds losing to Jochen. He has faster reflexes, an impossibly delicate touch and a mind like a calculating machine. They don't think they'll ever meet an Englishman as good.

No one minds but Jonny Beck. One day Jonny turns tighter than ever before, as tight as Jochen. Jochen's vision begins to go and he pulls out and up into a fast climb towards the sun. As his speed bleeds off, he turns to dive back down on Jonny out of the dazzle. Below him, Beck falls out of his turn and into a spin. Jochen puts the stick straight down and dives after Beck.

'Jonny!' he calls. 'Jonny! Jonny!' again and again. But Beck won't wake.

Jochen catches up and turns in a wide spiral around the spinning Friedrich.

'Jonny, wake up, you useless fucker! Jonny! Jonny!'

There's nothing he can do but shout and watch as the Friedrich flicks round and around from eight thousand metres down to two thousand and seems about to drill a hole in a Bavarian field when the spinning stops, the nose points straight down and then pulls up. Jochen accelerates past Beck and leads the way home.

As they walk back to the mess, Jonny says, 'I'm not a useless fucker.'

They're given a week to themselves and they spread out across Germany. Dietrich's route lies through Berlin but he won't stay the night. Jochen leaves him at the station waiting for a train that will take him to north to the Baltic coast and his fiancée.

Ilse looks exhausted, dark around the eyes as if she isn't sleeping but more than that, under strain. He's seen comrades with that look when they need a break.

'How's Harri?' he says.

'Gone.'

'Oh. Argument?'

'He was posted to the Ruhr.'

'When?'

'A month ago.'

'That's a pity. Isn't it?'

'Yes. I'd got used to having him around. And he seemed to like to call and go out sometimes. Do you know he can dance after a fashion?'

'Can he? How does he know if he's standing on your foot?'

She laughs. 'I yell.'

'That's better. A laugh.'

'I don't feel much like laughing.'

'He'll get some leave sometime.'

'It's not Harri, it's Anton.'

'Didn't you speak to him?'

She tells him.

The scene is vivid in his mind. Ilse stops their walk and makes Heinecke sit and listen. They're on a bench in the park near their apartment, where Jochen sat with Bauer and they talked about Heinecke. It's a Saturday. Early evening. Still light. It's an alien setting for Heinecke in his sharp suit: surrounded by grass and gravelled paths, trees beginning to turn, dog walkers, and children running around. Heinecke's presence seems to threaten the normal people around them.

'Anton,' she says, 'I'm afraid I can't see you anymore.'

'What?' His gaze is intent. Behind his glasses, his eyes are wide. Perspiration appears on his upper lip. 'I don't understand.'

'I'm wasting your time. You're very nice but that's not enough to continue seeing you. It's not fair on you to carry on. I can never be to you what I think you want me to be.'

'Don't be silly. You're my young lady, as people would say. I'm your young man, though,' he laughs, 'not so young, of course.'

'I'm not, Anton,' she says, 'and you're not. Look. We'll be friends. When you come to the office, we'll smile and chat and make a joke or two and then you'll leave with your business completed and if we happen to meet somewhere, we'll be pleasant with each other and then say goodbye and move on.'

His face shows puzzlement, incomprehension. He grabs her wrist as if she might run from him. 'Don't tell me what I will do! Never do that! Only I will decide what I will do. And I will not stop seeing you.'

She stares back at him. She takes his wrist in her hand to break his hold on her but she can't. 'Let me go, Anton.' She means her wrist.

'Never!'

She doesn't think he means her wrist and she's suddenly frightened.

'Very well,' he says, 'we'll marry. I was going to wait to ask you but I can see it will be best to marry now. We can do it tomorrow or we can wait a little if you want to plan a celebration.'

She stares at him as if she finally sees him. 'You're mad. I'd never marry you. You're the last person I'd ever marry.'

'You'll never marry anyone else.'

'I will. I've met someone,' she says in desperation. Her mouth runs on with her. 'He's proposed and I've accepted. He's a soldier and he's everything you aren't.'

'Be quiet.'

'He's kind and he sings and he makes me laugh.' She's describing Harri. He hasn't proposed, though she thinks he might.

'I'm sure he got Harri posted,' Ilse says.

'Does he even know who Harri is?'

'He finds things out. That's what he's like.'

'Look. If I was running flak batteries, I'd post Harri up there. He's good and that's where the raids are. He's been doing nothing in Berlin for months now.'

Ilse's haunted eyes flick around. 'You don't know him.'

'He's a civilian.'

'His brother's Gestapo. He's probably connected. He's a snake. He follows me . I catch sight of him sometimes. If I'm out with one or two of the girls, I'll see him somewhere in the room.'

He grabs her shoulders, pulls her to him.

'Get off, Jochen!'

'Give me a hug.'

'I'm all right.'

'I'm not.'

They cling body to body, her face in his chest, his face in her hair.

'What can I do?' Bauer says.

'Talk to him.'

'I have. You know the expression, "talking to a brick wall".'

'Isn't there a law?'

'No.'

'Can't you threaten him?'

'Be a thug?'

'Why not?'

'I can't. His brother. The Gestapo out-thug the police.'

'Don't do that!' he says when Ilse says she's going to Vienna to escape Anton.

'The company will transfer me. Mother's keen. She says they'll never bomb Vienna.'

'Ilse!'

This is like a knife in the kidneys. He spends his life protecting himself but how can he protect his twin, his other half, when he's back in Africa?

There's no sign of Heinecke. Does he really expect to see him around in the blackout? The whisky club still has no whisky and only the pianist is there playing. He smiles. Jochen sends over a brandy. No Gerda, of course, and no one else there interests him.

Someone runs down and says there's been a siren. He goes up to have a look. It's a clear night. Berlin has good stars now there's a blackout. He hears a single aeroplane, two engines, Jumos. A night fighter, a Junkers 88. Searchlights cut the black. Swords of light. The stars are gone with the new brightness up there. Guns open up; distant dull cracks. Are they all deaf? Do they do no training? The poor devil in the Junkers is probably lost and now he's shitting himself with flak coming up.

People hurry past as he stands on the corner gazing up. The fearless, glamorous leutnant taking a professional interest, he imagines them thinking. He glances round at approaching hurrying heels. A pale face in the dark; her height, her build:

'Gerda!' He grabs her arm.

'Let go! I have to get home.'

'Gerda! Gerda, stay a moment! I must talk to you. Where have you been?'

'Let me go! My name's not Gerda.'

'Of course it is.'

'I don't know who you're talking about, sir.'

'Sir?'

'Don't make a scene. Please. It's too public here.'

'Come and have a drink.'

'I can't do that. Look, there's an alley just here.'

They turn off the street and into deeper darkness. A door opens and, 'Careful!' comes a shout as someone hurries past them and light floods the alley momentarily.

The woman is clearly Gerda but even paler, thinner and very poorly dressed in a coat too large, as if it belongs to someone else.

'Let me go!'

'You'll run.'

'You'd easily catch me. I've had no dinner for two days.'

'Let's go and eat then.'

'I can't.'

'Why not, Gerda?'

'I'm not Gerda. I'm Ute. You can check my papers.'

'Gerda!'

'Ute.'

'What's happened? Let's go to your place and you can tell me.'

'I haven't got that place anymore.'

'Gerda. Ute, I've been worried about you since I saw you that day.'

'Speak more quietly. Someone might hear.'

'So?'

'Shhh! Nothing can hurt you but it can me.'

'Well?' he whispers.

'I had to run. I was told to report but I ran.'

'Report?'

'Don't betray me. Let me go soon. Promise.'

'Betray you?'

'Promise.'

'Of course.'

She gives that sideways smile of hers. 'Jochen, you lovely boy, I'm a Jew.'

He laughs. 'A Jew!'

'Shhh!'

'Called Gerda?'

'Ruth. My real name is Ruth. But now it's Ute. On the papers I have now. I'm Ute. Now let me go as you promised. Give me ten minutes, please, before you report me.'

'Stop it! Your husband? The panzer commander.'

'He didn't care.'

'I don't care either.'

'Don't you?'

'Of course I don't. If you'd reported when they said, what then?'

'A train, I think. I had to report at Neustadt Station.'

'To go where?'

'I don't know. No one's ever come back.'

'How do you live?'

'I have a room.'

'Where?'

She smiles again and shakes her head.

'And money?'

'I work at a laundry.'

'Around here?'

'I change trams nearby.'

The all-clear sounds. He realises he hasn't heard the Junkers or the guns for some time.

'Can't I buy you dinner? You'd be safe with me.'

'Where could I go with you looking like this?'

'Do you change trams at this time every evening?'

'Don't look for me, Jochen. It's too dangerous. Perhaps even for a hero of the Reich. I'm a war widow but I was still on their list.'

Her logic frustrates him but he's persuaded. Perhaps he can watch out for her another time and not speak. Could Bauer help? Bauer and the Jews: how does he feel? Of course they've never spoken of them.

'I must go.' She pulls away.

What can he do?

'Wait!' He, dredges his pockets for coins and pours them into her hands, pulls out his wallet and empties it on top of the coins.

'Thank you. But not this fifty,' she says. 'It's too big. I could never spend it. Someone would smell a rat.'

'Keep it. It might get you out of a spot with the right person. And listen, if you're desperate, get a message to me.'

He tells her his address. 'What is it?'

She repeats it to him.

'But you'll be at the front.'

'I might not be. I'm here now.'

She strokes his face. 'Darling Jochen, stay alive,' she says, and is gone.

'You haven't seen her? You've been home three days.' Ilse's off to work but has stopped with her coat half on to stare at him. 'What's the matter with you? Have you finished with her? Aren't you even going to tell her?'

'It's complicated.'

'Is it?' She pulls her coat on properly, grabs her hat. 'I thought she was something to you. You learnt that piece for her in a week. She told me she wept. She said her family all think you're a great artist, just like mother does. Her sister says you're a very interesting case, an artist-warrior with great depth of feeling. Feeling! How wrong can you be? I've got to go.'

He talks as he follows her out, hopping as he pulls on one boot after the other, grabs his cap at the door, patters down the stairs beside her. 'It's not that easy.'

'No?'

'Lotte needs to be married and I've got no business marrying. I'd just be making another widow.'

'Perhaps you should let her decide that.'

'Would you do that? If it was just for a few weeks, perhaps?'

She leans back as she pulls the heavy front door open.

'Jochen, if he was the right boy, what choice would I have?'

He's waiting when she comes down the school steps. Lotte's surprised to see him; there's delight on her face, her voice is excited. They take tea; they find a concert for the next day. Over the few days left to him, they walk out, play the piano, chatter. He plays chess with her father, answers her sister's questions, flirts with her mother. When he leaves Berlin, though, he's made no mention of marriage and despite waiting a couple of times, hasn't managed to see Gerda again either.

Back in the desert it rains and their new Friedrichs need manhandling around in the cloying mud. Jurg paints '14' in yellow on the fuselage sides behind the cockpit. Hans paints the victory bars on the port side of the fin, twenty-seven of them.

The next morning it's drier. Dietrich as usual calls them out.

'Indians! Nine o'clock low.' A dozen Tomahawks glinting in the sun.

Beck leads them down and immediately the enemy moves into a line astern formation that becomes a wide circle so that each machine can protect the one in front.

Jochen pulls up to observe the circle but Beck dives onto the tail of a Tomahawk and is at once hit by the one behind. He breaks away as a thin trail of smoke comes from his engine.

'I'm with you,' Lehmann calls, and the pair turn for home.

The Tomahawks continue in their slow circle and Jochen studies them from five hundred metres above. A defensive circle; 110s used it against Spitfires over England. The Tomahawk pilots must be really rattled.

'Stay up here and watch my back, Franz,' he calls.

He puts the Friedrich's nose straight down, picks out a target and waits till the wings with their roundels fill his sight, the cockpit at its centre. He squeezes the trigger on the joystick and the Friedrich slows as his three guns fire. The bullets sparkle all around the cockpit, on the wings and the fuselage. Jochen tears through the formation too fast for any of the Englishmen to hit him.

'One!' Franz calls in his ears, and he's pushed hard into his seat as he pulls the stick back and converts the dive into a zoom that brings a second Tomahawk into his sight, this time with roundels on the pale blue underside of its wings. He fires again; sparks all over the Tomahawk and smoke from its engine. The guns' recoil slows his climb till he's almost down to the painted mark on his speed dial. He banks to the right in a very slow turn and finds a third Tomahawk approaching head on.

'Two!' he hears Franz call. He fires again before the Tomahawk does and its engine explodes into fire. He puts the Friedrich's nose down and heads for the ground.

'Three!' Franz calls.

He sees two parachutes. He turns to check behind and glances at his map to check the position of the chutes. He sees Franz tear through the British formation and a Tomahawk start to fall trailing smoke.

'Four!' he calls to Franz.

Over the field he rocks his wings three times as he tears across before turning to land. He and Franz taxi up and then leap out cock-a-hoop. They dance around together. As he's draining his water bottle afterwards, he sees Beck watching him from beside his Friedrich. The cowling is open and his mechanics have their heads inside.

'All right, Jonny?' he calls as he lights a cigarette. 'Three!' He points at Franz, 'And one!'

'Good for you!' Beck calls back and puts his own head under the cowling.

Japan has attacked America: a Sunday-morning surprise in the Pacific. What does it mean?

'They'll need all those Tomahawks themselves,' Lehmann says.

They fly patrols, high in the blue as usual, the coast a line of white surf edging the azure Med far below, sand and scrub stretching away endlessly, frighteningly, into Africa. He breaks a defensive circle again: dive, fire; zoom, fire; turn, fire. Three more; a repeat performance. Franz has called them out and gets another as he dives after Jochen. Beck copies his dive and gets one but takes hits to the wing on his zoom and breaks away.

The RAF impresses Jochen.

'Every day they come out and we knock down three or four but they're back the next day.'

'Then we can knock down some more,' Beck says.

'But how do they do it? Day after day. The same number of them?'

They escort Stukas bombing Tobruk. As the bombers pitch into their dives, Hurricanes jump them. The Friedrichs jump them. The Hurricanes turn; the Friedrichs turn after them, flying in great arcs above the smoking town. Squashed into his seat, he holds a tight right-hand turn behind a Hurricane. He closes the throttle a little and fires ahead of the Hurricane, which flies into his stream of shells and bullets. The Hurricane burns.

In his ear: 'Jochen, break left.'

He tips the stick over and reverses his turn, closes the throttle a little more and sees a Hurricane shoot past followed by Franz giving it a good hosing and fires himself far ahead of the Hurricane chasing Franz. It flies into his fire, turns over on its back and goes straight down.

They circle to pick up the Stukas. Five parachutes going down, one drifting through a huge column of black smoke, one Stuka missing, one Friedrich trailing smoke, number seven. Vogt. He lands first and they see him jump out quickly as the engine is sprayed with foam.

Winter is there with news: the Reich has declared war on the United States.

Jochen imagines his father receiving the message in his HQ and burying his face in his hands. He grabs his water bottle.

'Who's next? The fucking Martians?' He leaves the command tent, walks to his own tent and flops on the bed. He has no energy even to put on a record.

It rains. The mud clogs them up. They can't get off for two days. He plays his record of *Petrushka*.

'It's ballet music. By a Russian,' he tells Beck as he's been waiting to. 'It always reminds me of you. It's about a puppet.' Beck says nothing.

Early one morning he takes off alone just to be up. From five thousand metres he spots the shadow of a lone Tomahawk below him. The pilot is awake and he banks to the right just as Jochen is about to fire. They turn and twist above the desert. The Englishman is good but the Tomahawk won't allow him to get away. Eventually one turn is a little late and he remains in Jochen's sight long enough. Shells hit his engine, which smokes instantly. The Tomahawk noses down and Jochen pulls up. They are far over British territory. The Tomahawk makes a wheels up landing not far from a road. Jochen flies over and rocks his wings. The Englishman waves to him and starts walking towards the road.

He's got a stomach pain. He goes to bed shivering and pulls blankets on top of himself. He must be allergic to the desert. He's always ill out here. He sips water, can't eat anything.

Christmas Eve. With his greatcoat round him, he shambles over with bottles of brandy for Jurg and Hans. He drinks a toast with them and stumbles back to bed. He wakes and for a moment imagines he's back home. Somewhere nearby a group is singing *Stille Nacht*.

Franz comes in. 'You're off again, you lucky bastard. The boss has been on the radio about you. Athens. We've got a hospital there now.'

From the window, apparently, the Parthenon is visible in the distance but he doesn't see it for a week or more, not until he's almost recovered from all the conditions he's been diagnosed with: malaria, jaundice, amoebic dysentery, gastroenteritis. He's standing gazing out across the ancient city, trying not to scratch the skin rash he also has, when an orderly enters and comes over to him carrying a message sheet.

6

Pavane for a Dead Infanta

THE DOCTOR'S BEEN. HIS MOTHER'S FINALLY asleep. He reads the two letters. Vienna is lovely; many beautiful buildings. It seems far away from the war. You can still get sachertorte. She's sharing a room with a girl called Johanna. Johanna has a gramophone. They've been to the cinema. She's good company. It's a good office; very nice people; old men and girls as usual, of course. She's fallen on her feet.

He stares through the lace curtains at the street and the windows opposite. Down there is the pavement and the road. He has only to open the inner windows and then the outer ones and he could splatter himself on the stones below.

He turns away to the room; the table with its brown chenille cloth and empty fruit bowl, the small table with the lamp on it near the stove, the glazed doors to the kitchen, the Persian rug, the sofa and its cushions. Darkness is seeping in and over everything but he doesn't move to put on a lamp. He looks around again at the room and the worthless, useless crap in it. He has an urge to pick up a chair and smash it against the wall, to rip the tablecloth to shreds, to hurl the fruit bowl to the floor. What's the point of any of this? He should have asked the doctor for something for himself. He could use a drink. But he can't go out. He can't leave his mother.

When will Bauer be back? He'll be having a dinner somewhere. Has Lotte heard? There's no note from her. He should tell her. He goes over and leans on the piano, runs his fingers along the veneer on the top. He can't play it, though. Too noisy. And what would he play? It would sicken him to play.

His hand drops and bangs against something at his side. He's still wearing his pistol. He undoes the belt and slings belt and pistol onto the sofa. He throws himself after it. He grabs a cushion and hugs it then chucks it away from him. His mind is whirling. When they were young, even before she became the gymnast she was later for a couple of years in school, she would turn cartwheels as he watched from the sofa, wonderful straight circles she'd turn with her weight on her hands then back on her feet, upright again. In this room! Hide and seek they'd play in here, too, and all around the flat, build dens with cushions and blankets from their beds, eat their snacks cosy under the roof of blanket.

The dark has arrived. He should do the shutters ready to keep the light in. In a minute. Who will mock him now? No more tinkling laughter at his expense. No more laughter! How can anyone ever laugh again?

He stands eventually and moves from shutter to shutter, closing out the night. He catches his hand on the hook on one of the shutters. It hurts. Good. A feeling! But he doesn't cry out. He sucks his finger and goes back to the sofa, his feet knowing the way even in the pitch black.

There's the sound of a key. The door opens. A click and light floods the room. He throws his arm across his eyes.

'You're sitting in the dark, boy!' Bauer goes over and puts on the lamp by the stove, goes back to the door and turns off the big light. 'Where's your mother?'

'Asleep. The doctor came. He gave her something.'

'Thank God for that! I didn't think she'd ever sleep again.'

Bauer puts the bottle he's carrying on the table by the sofa. He goes into the kitchen and comes back with two small glasses. He pants and grunts over the cork until it comes out with a pop.

Jochen smells the brandy from where he's sitting. He takes the glass from Bauer's podgy hand. Bauer throws his brandy down his throat, sighs loudly and pours himself another before Jochen has lifted his to his lips. Jochen drinks his in one go as well and puts the glass down. Bauer refills it, takes a sip from his own glass.

'I was on the phone to Vienna for an hour. I may go there tomorrow if I can leave your mother that long. They sent photos. I've seen some things in my time but... They don't prepare you. Not if it's one of your own.'

'Did she know what was happening? Did she suffer?' he says.

Bauer stares at him. 'How much do you want to know?'

'Everything. Tell me everything. She's my other half. Was.'

'She knew. She suffered.'

'Can I see the photos?'

'No.'

'Why not?'

'Use your loaf, son. I can barely look at them and this is the kind of thing I deal in every day.'

'But I won't know what happened to her.'

'I'll tell you what I know but I won't let you see those pictures.'

Jochen nods. He downs his brandy and tops up both glasses.

'A dog walker found her in a small park. She was lying on her back. She'd been raped and then strangled. Her clothes were all in disarray as you might expect.'

Jochen buries his face in his hands. 'Shall I carry on?'

Jochen nods.

'She'd been struck about the face and head, though the bruises hadn't had much time to emerge. Her face was bloodied. They found her shoes about ten yards apart in the street as if she'd been running and one had come off and then she'd kicked the other off to run quicker. There was dried blood under the fingernails of her right hand, so there's someone still walking around with scratches on his face.'

'So was it just someone who came across her? Some random man?'

'Or someone who knew her. Someone following her.'

'Who did she know in Vienna?'

Bauer shrugs. Jochen sips some more brandy.

'What can we do?'

'Wait. They sounded like they know what they're doing over there. They're happy for me to visit. They said I can bring her back.'

'I'll come.'

'Stay with your mother. I'd like to get back to the office for a couple of hours if you can stay. Do you need anything?'

'I wanted a drink but you've brought some.'

'Leave me a drop for when I get back.'

The doorbell rings.

Jochen looks at Bauer.

'That'll be Fräulein Hofmann, I expect.' Bauer huffs up from his seat. 'She's been every day,' he says at Jochen's surprised look. 'Usually brings some food.'

'Come in,' he says as he swings the door wide. 'I have to go but,' he tips his head to the room, 'he'll look after you.' He pulls the door to behind him.

Lotte is hugging a large pot. She has a surprised smile.

'I didn't know.'

'No. Let me take that.'

She shakes her head and takes the pot straight through to the kitchen. She comes back and stands before him. 'Jochen. This is so terrible.'

'Yes.'

'I didn't know if you would get leave.'

'The doctor told me to go and said he'd sort the paperwork out.'

'Are you ill again?' She sounds horrified.

'I was in hospital in Athens.'

'What are they doing to you out there?'

'Trying to kill me.'

She gives a little laugh. 'Will you kiss me?'

He looks into her eyes. 'I can't.'

'No.' She kisses his cheek instead. 'Your mother's asleep, I suppose.'

'The doctor gave her a pill.'

'When did you eat?'

'I don't know.'

She takes off her coat and hat, takes him by the arm and walks him into the kitchen, pushes him down at the table. She moves around the cupboards and drawers, never hesitating, as if the room is her own. She lays a bowl of soup in front of him and puts a spoon into his hand. 'Eat,' she says.

He turns his head to look at her. Who is this girl navigating herself in their kitchen so easily?

'Eat,' she says again when he doesn't move.

The soup he scoops up has what he knows is a delicious smell. There are small pieces of cabbage, carrot, potato, bacon. The surface is oily. Steam is rising from it. He raises the spoon. It stops near his lips.

This is life. Sustenance. It's supposed to keep body and soul together. But why bother? Body and soul separate so easily and soup won't keep them connected.

His head droops over the bowl. He slides the spoon back into the soup and stares down at it. Something plops into the liquid, a tiny splash. And another.

'Jochie!' She grabs his shoulders and pulls him to her. His head lies on her breast and he weeps.

After a while she pulls him up from the chair and walks him out of the kitchen to the sofa. She sits in a corner and pulls him to her again.

Eventually, she struggles up, pushes him off. 'I have to go. It's late.'

'I'll come,' he says at once.

'Stay with your mother.'

'I can't let you go on your own.'

'I'll be fine.'

'I know, but I can't.'

At Lotte's insistence, he writes a note for his mother in case she wakes. He leaves Lotte at her door. He can't face her mother and father, her sister.

He walks home. He crosses the road twice when he makes out the shapes of lone women ahead of him and passes them on the other side of the street. What an anxiety it must be for any girl with an imagination to hear male footsteps approaching behind her in the dark.

There are noises in the apartment when he comes in. The lavatory flushes. Water runs. Surely she's not awake.

'I remembered you arrived,' his mother says as she walks in. She's in a dressing gown.

'The doctor said you'd sleep for twelve hours.'

'Did he?' She's pinning her hair up. Bits still stick out but she's finished with it.

'Come in here.' He takes her into the kitchen and lights the heat under the soup pot.

She leans over the pot and sniffs. 'Nice. Lotte?'

He nods.

She gives him a serious look. 'Don't go breaking her heart.'

He doesn't answer. He ladles soup into a bowl and puts it on the table. She sits down, sips a spoonful. She pushes it away. 'It's lovely but I can't.'

She's bowed like an old lady but she isn't forty-five yet. Her hair has no lustre. He suddenly is aware of the grey. Her face is pasty. Dark bags sit beneath her eyes.

'You should sleep some more.'

'Wisdom from the boy. You should have that soup.'

'Go back to bed and rest. Get some energy back.'

'What for?'

'Tomorrow.'

'What's happening that I'm interested in?'

'There'll be things to do.'

'Will there?'

'Bauer wants to go to Vienna if you're fit to be left on your own for so long.'

'Don't call him that.'

'Rolf.'

'He came back?'

He nods. 'Do you want a brandy?'

'You know I hate it. He loves me, you know. He's a funny old stick but he loves me.' She stands and pours herself a glass of water. 'I'm going to lie down.'

'Is there anything I can do?'

'Eat that soup,' she says, and walks out but stops at the door. 'Play me something, but not before you've eaten. Nothing jolly. Slow. It's just you and me now, son.'

He pulls her bowl towards him, picks up the spoon. It's good soup. He said Lotte made it but probably it was her mother while Lotte was at work. She carried it all the way though. On and off the tram. It counts as Lotte's.

Ilse! He hasn't thought of her for… several minutes. Is this how it happens? The brain latches on to something else. He looks at the soup. Some unimportant thing crops up, your appetite takes over, your body reasserts itself and the object of your pain fades.

But only briefly. He puts down the spoon. There's soup left but he can't eat any more. Ilse is going down a street in the darkness with a man's much heavier feet behind her, walking quickly then running as she runs. She half stumbles, a shoe comes off, she staggers on a little then stoops to grab the other shoe and pluck it off and drop it. The pavement is hard and rough beneath her feet. She feels her stockings tear. Her breath is coming in gasps. Her bag is over her shoulder and clutched safe under her arm. What is there inside that could be a weapon? Her keys! But she'd have to open the bag and rummage, impossible while running. The feet are getting closer. She tries to speed up. The cold air tears at her throat. She has pains in her chest. Hands are on her shoulders and he pulls her to a stop. She tries to swing her bag but he bats it away. She rakes her nails down his face. 'Bitch!' he cries out. What voice is that? Jochen in his mind has no idea. She wants to scream but he hits her twice in the face; awful, shocking blows. Pain as she's never felt it before. It's stunning pain. He hits her again. She begins to collapse. He drags her onwards. Her knees scrape on the pavement but at once she's on grass. He rolls her over onto her back. No! she thinks, and drags her nails down his cheek again. He punches her and her mind begins to close down.

At the kitchen table, Jochen has his hands over his face. He won't imagine any more. It's as if he's woken himself from a dream too vivid to endure. He goes into the other room and the piano. He opens the stool. She told him to play. Nothing jolly. He finds Ravel. It's appropriate. Too appropriate? Can he? Nothing jolly. Something slow. He opens the music and sight reads it. It's not a piece he knows very well. *Pavane for a Dead Infanta.*

He reaches out his hands for the keys and brings out those first sounds. How do they manage to pluck melancholy from a handful of notes, these guys who compose? A dead infanta. A princess? She was the princess of this family, that's always been clear to him, just as he is the prince. He plays through to the end. Not many errors. If he ever plays it again, he'll remember this evening. Perhaps he'll never play it again, though. He leaves the piano. No sound from his mother's room. He imagines her silently weeping.

He's hungry again. In the kitchen he eats more soup, finds some bread to dip in it. He goes back to the sofa and has another brandy. He will live his life now without Ilse. Who will tell him what to do, be his conscience? But that's too melodramatic. Who will laugh at him, be angry with him? And she will never have a life. He's beginning to move from shock and pity and despair to anger. The man who did this, the man who stole her life, what kind of animal is he? What does a man get from such violence?

What pleasure can there be? Will they catch him? Are the Viennese police competent? They'll execute him, he supposes. If not, he'll seek him out and do it himself. His decision is sudden and certain. He'll put a bullet in the man's brain. It won't bother him. He's killed enough in the past few months. Somehow he'll get in to see the man. He could say he wants to forgive him or persuade him to repent of his crime, his sin. And then he'll pull out a pistol. Let him see it, recognise what's coming, know his fate before he drills a hole between his eyes; a clean red hole that ends in a massive excavation at the back of his skull as the vicious, cruel and perverted brain spews out and splatters across the wall behind him. They can do what they like with him afterwards.

It won't solve anything, of course, won't cure any of this pain. She's gone. There'll be none of her children to play with. No husband to drink a nightcap with at Christmas. No aged parents to bury together. That'll be his job; on his own. But, of course, he'll be dead long before that, doing what he does. So, who will bury his mother? Bauer? His heart will already have seen him off the way he eats and drinks. How will it all end? He'll never know. He reaches for the brandy, sees how far down it is and gets up for a glass of water instead. He should go to bed. But he wouldn't sleep. He stares at the wall and starts when there's a knock on the door.

It's his father.

'You got leave, Jochen. Good. How are you?'

'Terrible.'

'Yes.'

He takes the glass of water from Jochen's hand and drinks it down. He pours a large brandy into Bauer's glass.

'Leave some for Bauer.'

'I've got another in my bag.' He throws back the brandy. 'Is Bauer here?'

'He went back to work.'

'Where's your mother?'

'In bed.'

'Asleep?'

'I don't know.'

The general spins his cap onto the sofa, pulls off his greatcoat and throws it to Jochen. He strides towards the bedrooms. A door opens. 'Christa,' Jochen hears then the door closes behind the general.

He comes out half an hour later.

'She's in a terrible state.'

'You're fine, I suppose.'

'Don't be so damned stupid. I'm ill with it all but it doesn't show. I've had years of disasters and tragedies, remember. This is just the worst. You were both babies in my arms, don't forget. What's Bauer told you?'

He passes it all on.

'I wish I had that bastard in front of me now.'

'You'd have to take your turn.'

The general pours another brandy.

'There's some soup.'

'Who made that?

He tells him.

'Good girl.'

'Do you want some?'

'I couldn't eat.'

'Where are you staying?'

'There was no time to organise that. I'll have your room.' He pats the sofa. 'You can sleep here.'

When Bauer returns, he and the general talk and finish the brandy. Jochen pulls off his boots and stretches out on the sofa.

He wakes to the sound of shutters opening. His father's greatcoat lies over him. The general looks round.

'How the young sleep!'

The general is cleanly shaven. He looks a little drawn but nevertheless fresh.

'Bauer's left for Vienna. Get ready. Breakfast.'

They stop at the nearest place. They have cheese, ham, rolls, apple cake, coffee; and brandy in their second cups.

'I've changed my mind about Bauer. He apologised to me, said he should have taken better care of Ilse.'

'It wasn't his fault.'

'I told him that. He said he'll chase the bugger down and shoot him himself if necessary. You were ill again.'

'I must be allergic to the desert.'

'If it happens again, tell Winter to get you sorted out properly. You're no good to anyone ill. Don't come back an invalid from all this.'

Jochen laughs.

'What?'

'I won't be coming back.'

'Don't start talking like that.'

'Father, their aeroplanes aren't good enough but they keep coming. We shoot lots of them down but they nibble away at us. When they get Spitfires out there, we'll be swamped.'

'Stay alert and do your duty then.'

'Of course. Russia?'

The general leans towards him and speaks softly. 'We've shot our bolt. We suffer from a grand strategist. The humble guys from the staff college would have concentrated on one objective. We were given three to get at once.'

'The horses?'

'Undelicious stew. How's that girl, the singer we heard?'

'I thought you were out of it that night.'

'Not quite.'

He tells him.

'No one's safe, are they?' He shakes his head and tut-tuts. 'What a waste. Such an individual voice.' He's silent and stares through the window. 'Look, I must get back. I told Bauer I'd get your mother to eat something.'

He goes to pay the bill and buys more apple cake. 'Carry this for me.' He puts the package with the cake into Jochen's hands.

Jochen smiles at him.

'My Prussian training,' his father says.

He leaves his father at their door. He can't spend the morning sitting up there doing nothing, thinking about Ilse. The air is raw. There's still snow in corners that the sun doesn't reach. He passes the spot where he met Gerda. Where is she? Is she still free? Have they put her on a train to... where? He passes a few officers, gives and takes salutes where necessary, nods to other leutnants. He sees only one ordinary soldier, limping, arm in arm with a girl. Convalescent leave, about the only sort non-officers seem to get.

A truck passes him at speed, honking its horn to clear its path ahead. It screeches round the next corner and by the sound, brakes sharply and stops. He speeds up his stride and turns the corner himself. The tailgate is down and an SS trooper with a machine pistol held across his abdomen guards it. Three others stand behind an SS leutnant who is hammering on a door. There's a civilian with them. It looks just like... it can't be. His back is towards Jochen but it must be; the hat, the suit. The leutnant steps aside and one of the troopers raises his boot to the lock. On the second kick, there's a splintering crash and the door swings open. The SS men disappear inside, led by the leutnant. The civilian follows and as he goes in he turns his face a little and shows his right cheek to Jochen. It *is* him.

Jochen goes to the trooper guarding the truck.

'What's happening?'

'State's business, sir. I can't say more.'

A crowd has formed; old people and housewives in the main. He moves his gaze from one to another. There's expectation in their eyes, excitement in their voices.

'Look!' someone shouts. A trooper emerges from the smashed-open doorway and stands to one side. There's a collective grunt of satisfaction from the crowd as a young woman comes out clutching a bundle under her right arm. A small girl who looks about six grips her left hand. A trooper, machine pistol at the ready, follows a metre behind them. The woman and the girl have their eyes cast down but the woman looks up for a moment to see where they're going. He studies her face in that instant. She isn't Gerda. As she moves her eyes down again, she sees Jochen. He would smile but in this context, a smile would be pure mockery.

'Dirty Jews!' a woman shouts. 'Good riddance!' someone else calls. The pair walk across the pavement to the truck. 'Another one!' comes the cry as an old man comes out of the building. He stumbles and the trooper behind him nudges his machine pistol into his back. As he approaches Jochen the old man trips on a raised paving stone and sprawls on the ground at Jochen's feet. A laugh erupts from the crowd. The man's glasses have fallen off. His hand pats the pavement in front of him. The glasses are just beyond where he can reach and possibly see. The man's face is by Jochen's foot. There's a shout of, 'Kick him!'

Jochen bends, picks up the spectacles, grasps the man's forearm and raises him to his feet then passes the glasses back to him. The man threads the wire arms behind his ears and turns to Jochen. There's so much shouting that Jochen can't make out any individual calls. The man takes in Jochen's face and gives him a very dignified almost imperceptible bow of the head before he's pushed on by the machine pistol in his back.

'You should be ashamed of yourself!' he hears. 'Jew lover!' 'That's too good for them, you should have kicked him!'

He's sickened by the scene and ashamed. He wants to flee but feels he must witness all the horror of what's happening. The woman lifts the girl up into the truck and climbs up herself via the steps cut into the tailgate. As she reaches the bed of the truck, the trooper below flicks up her skirt with the barrel of his machine pistol. The crowd laughs as her stockings and underwear are revealed. She vainly tries to hold her skirt down as the trooper swings the barrel again. He grins at the crowd. Jochen imagines grabbing the weapon and smashing it into his face. The woman takes the girl's arm and moves further into the truck out of reach of the trooper. Meanwhile the old man is struggling with the steps. The trooper pushes him out of the way, leaps up himself then reaches down to grab the old man's arm and drag him up by brute force. The old man rolls on the bed of the truck and sits up. To the laughter and applause of the crowd the trooper wipes his hand on his tunic in an exaggerated way to remove all trace of Jew from it and then flops onto one of the benches and takes out and lights a cigarette. A second trooper climbs up and joins the first. The third swings up the tailgate and secures it as the SS leutnant turns to Jochen.

'You're too soft-hearted, comrade.'

'Where are you taking them?

'Somewhere cosy where they can work for the Reich instead of sabotaging it.'

'That old man's a saboteur? And that little girl?'

'The worst kinds. One has knowledge to pass on; the other a brain to remember it. Good luck at your front.

Don't be too soft-hearted with those Russians or those English.'

He pulls himself up into the cab and slams the door. With screeching gears and a cloud of black smoke from the exhaust, the truck moves off. Jochen lights a cigarette and loiters for several minutes but Heinecke doesn't emerge.

He writes to Harri. He doesn't know if he and Ilse were writing but he'd want to know anyway. If he is writing, there'll be letters piling up unanswered on Ilse's Vienna doormat. He keeps it simple and sends it via Harri's mother, whose address is in their book.

He tells Lotte as much as he thinks she wants to know about Ilse. She turns pale and puts a hand to her cheek.

His father has to go back to the Eastern Front. He's only granted himself five days' leave and his journey will be difficult. There's a formal handshake at the door.

'"Break an arm and a leg," you say, don't you?'

'Yes. You, too.'

He listens to the footsteps down the stairs and then goes in and closes the door. He'll write and tell him about the funeral.

His mother is up and tidily dressed. Not recovered, enduring. He leaves her with two friends who've come to sit with her. She has to offer refreshments and they've brought a cake. She can't insist they partake without her. Soon it's just crumbs on her plate. They're going through photo albums as he pulls the door to.

How can she bear it?

He can't be too late and the blackout isn't a good time for walking. He goes down the stairs to the whisky club. He has a beer and sends brandies to the band. There's no Gerda/Ute/Ruth and no one else who'd look cute with his cap on. In any case his mood has changed since he heard about Ilse. When the band breaks, the pianist beckons him over. He pulls a chair next to him and says, 'Make something up.' Jochen does. The pianist repeats it with a little change and they're off extemporising for several minutes until they notice the manager waving a finger at them from behind the bar.

'Don't let's give him a heart attack, he pays the wages. Not bad. You could do this if you ever want an honest job. Afterwards.' He puts out his hand. 'Otto.'

'Jochen.'

'We call you "The Kid".'

Jochen laughs. 'I suppose I am.'

'How's the general?'

'All right. He's in Russia.'

'I was there in the last one. I was glad to see the back of it. I wish him a safe return.'

'Thanks.'

'How's the widow?'

'I haven't seen her for a long time.'

'We haven't seen her in here, either. Lovely laugh, I thought.'

'Yes.'

'There's a girl just like her round by me. Same face. No laugh, though. Very pale. I'd have said it was her except for her clothes. She looks poor. The widow never looked poor.

And she scurries around in shadows. As if she's frightened to be seen. The widow walked as if she owned the world, as if she didn't mind whether she arrived anywhere or not.'

Should he talk? Is it safe for Gerda? He can't help himself. 'I saw her briefly. I think her circumstances changed.'

'That could be it.'

'She was embarrassed, I think. Didn't really want to be seen with me. Thought it might be difficult for me, I think.'

'She might think that. She's a nice girl.'

'Have you seen her again?'

'Once or twice,' Otto says.

'Have you spoken?'

'I didn't want to put her on the spot. And I don't even know if she recognises me. Why would she? I'm just the pianist.'

'Could you give her some money from me?'

'Are you sure you want to do that? There's an obvious reason these days why her circumstances might have suddenly changed. Think about it.'

'I have.'

The band are taking their seats.

'Tell her to give you a message for me if she needs to.'

Otto looks anxious. 'These are dangerous times for all that sort of thing.'

'Please.'

Jochen goes to the bar and begs an envelope as the band starts up. He finds a corner table and writes a message on a page from a waiter's order book and signs it 'J'. He puts the message and most of the contents of his wallet into the envelope. Between numbers he slips the envelope to Otto.

'The gangster's just come in,' Otto says. Heinecke stands by the door surveying the room. Covering most of his left cheek is a large surgical dressing.

Heinecke catches his eye and nods towards the bar. He joins him there.

'Brandy?'

He shakes his head.

'I heard about Ilse. Through her old office,' he says when Jochen stares at him. 'Awful. Tragic. Please accept my condolences.'

Jochen nods.

'Do you know that we were seeing each other for a while?'

He nods again.

'If we hadn't stopped, perhaps it wouldn't have happened.'

He manages to speak. 'What have you done to your face?'

'Flying glass. My own fault. Too near a window during a raid. I was visiting my sister. It was my niece's birthday.' Why is Heinecke saying so much? He goes on. 'She's a sweet thing. I bought her ballet shoes. I don't think she's any good but all girls want to be ballerinas, don't they? Did Ilse?'

He shakes his head and says, 'I saw you the other morning, helping to kick in a door and drag away some dangerous enemies of the state.'

'Just some help I'm able to give our authorities from time to time. I saw you too from a window. Giving aid to that Jewboy.'

'I was brought up to help the old.'

Heinecke smiles. Or is it a sneer? 'Are you sure you won't have that drink?'

'I have to get home. My mother.'

'Of course. She must be distraught. Such a terrible thing. Please give her my deepest sympathies.'

He waits up for Bauer.

'We checked him, of course. He was in bed for five days over the period. Gastric flu, the doctor said. He even had a sick note for the dates, though I didn't know why. He doesn't work for anybody.'

'Did you ask him more questions?'

'When my chap found out about the illness and saw the note, he didn't bother. And he didn't mention his face, either. We'll have another go in the morning. I wish he didn't have that Gestapo connection. If he's out rounding up Jews that connection is quite plain.'

Now he has a face to put on the animal bearing down on Ilse, has a figure to see chasing her, a recognisable voice to hear shout, 'Bitch!' as she claws at the cheek. In bed, he re-watches the scene endlessly.

The burial is awful. He and Bauer hold his mother up. It's his first family funeral. There is no feeling behind the grief of a long life well led, of achievements to be noted and remembered. There is nothing but the grief.

Afterwards he walks Lotte home. He talks to her about Ilse. How important she was to him.

'She was there all my life. She always knew how I felt. She got on my nerves and I got on hers. We'd fight and tell each other to go away and five minutes later one of us would be calling out, "Where are you?" I was jealous of her. I thought she was my mother's favourite and she thought I was the favourite and she was jealous. If one of us achieved something we only wanted to hear the other's opinion. She'd say things like, "Yeah, good, but it was easy for you. You didn't have to work at it," and that was the message I remembered, not my mother saying, "Wonderful, darling."'

'Did she always tell you what she thought?'

'Always. She told me I was an arrogant show-off.'

Lotte laughs.

'She told me to see you that time when I didn't for three days.'

Lotte stops. 'Weren't you going to?'

'I don't think I was.'

She takes her arm from his. 'Don't feel obliged!'

'Whoa!' He tells her about the conversation in the hall, as he pulled on his boots, on the stairs, at the front door; about his doubts, his proximity to death and why he couldn't marry anyone. And that Ilse said she'd have no choice but to marry if it was the right boy even if it might only be for a few weeks.

'So, Lotte,' he says, 'marry me.'

She gazes into his eyes. She looks very serious. 'This is fifty years if we're spared, Jochen. Are you sure this isn't all mixed up with your thoughts about poor Ilse?'

'Oh!' He smiles. 'You don't want to. It's not me, then, the right boy.'

'Of course it's you, but am I the right girl?'

'Yes. Ilse just made me understand that it was all right to think of you in that way and not to worry about the future.'

'Look,' she says, and talks. She asks him to wait and think. To be certain that he wants to marry her. Is he ready? He's young and even if he isn't aware of his glamour as a Luftwaffe expert, she is. If he gets another medal, he'll be all over the papers. Girls will throw themselves at him. What will he do?

'I won't be in a queue,' she says.

7

Rondo alla Turca

HE'S THREE KILOMETRES FROM THE STRIP AT FIVE hundred metres and just about to lower the undercarriage when a voice screams in his ear, 'Hurricanes in the circuit!'

He slams open the throttle and bucks ahead.

'They're gaining on you, Jochen! Two of them. Two more above.'

He cuts the throttle and lowers the flaps, makes a half turn to the left. Two Hurricanes rocket past him. He slams up the throttle and raises the flaps, straightens up his Friedrich to the right. The left-hand Hurricane is directly in front of him. He fires at once. Bits fly off the tail plane. The Hurricane is still there. He fires again. Smoke and then flames come from the engine. The Hurricane pulls up and climbs. He puts a few more rounds into its belly and puts the stick over to starboard to seek the second. It's in a turn to port to come back at him, crossing in front of him. He fires a hundred metres ahead of the Englishman and the Hurricane flies into the rounds. The engine sheds pieces of cowling and the propeller stops. The pilot puts his nose down. Jochen flies at top speed away from the field and then pulls into a climb, looking for the two above. They're coming down after him. His speed bleeds off as he rises. He flies at the leader. They both fire. The Hurricane is square in the middle of his sight. He must be square in the middle of the Englishman's. He feels hits on his starboard wing. The Hurricane explodes. He flies through smoke. Firing the guns has slowed his Friedrich even more and it's about to stall so he converts the stall into a turn and dives after the fourth Hurricane now way past him. He takes a long-range shot at it, at least three hundred metres, first pulling the nose up to give the shells some trajectory to fly the distance. It feels right. The Hurricane starts a trail of smoke that marks its passage back to English land.

'Any more for any more?' he says into his mask as he turns the Friedrich to get a good look around. There's a Hurricane belly-landed in the corner of the field and a parachute spread out on the ground. A kübelwagen is hurrying to each.

'All gone, I'm afraid.' It's Winter's voice.

He taxis up, swings the nose round to point towards the strip and switches off. Jurg is on the wing at once helping with the canopy and then his straps.

'Jesus, boss! You're shit or bust, you are.'

He grins. 'Anyway, everything was fine,' he went up to test out his Friedrich after his six weeks away, 'but you'll need to check the starboard wing. I felt a couple of hits.'

There are pilots gathering around as he jumps down. They slap his shoulder; someone gives him a cigarette.

He reports at the command tent.

'Good shooting,' Beck says.

Later he learns he's caught up with Beck, who went past his score in his absence and has thirty-nine victories. Well, with those three today, so has Jochen.

There are two extra for dinner; Jochen's RAF guests. One, a sergeant, is very quiet. Just says thank you when given things. The other, Kendall, a flight lieutenant from Kenya, has his left arm in a sling. Jochen cuts his meat for him and plies him with drink. Kendall's family has a coffee plantation. He went to England before the war to join the RAF.

'You chaps have had it, you know,' he says, 'now the Yanks are in. Wait till all their factories get going.'

'Propaganda!' Beck calls down the table. 'German factories are the finest in the world.'

'It's like driving a bullock cart,' Kendall says when Jochen asks how he likes flying a Hurricane. 'Spits are much better.'

The sergeant glares at Kendall. 'He thinks I shouldn't be talking to you,' Kendall says, 'Thinks I'm spilling the beans. Telling you secrets,' he says when Jochen looks at him with a blank expression. 'I don't really know him. He's usually in the sergeants' mess.'

Jochen asks Kendall to write a note saying he and the sergeant are safe and prisoners and that the other pilot is dead. Early the next morning, he takes off with the note accompanied by Dietrich as a kübelwagen leaves with

Kendall and the sergeant. At the British airfield, he drops the note by a line of Hurricanes. On their way back he sees a glint below them. Two Tomahawks going home low.

'All clear above,' Franz says.

A dive and they line up behind their victims. Jochen pulls out to the port side to get a deflection shot at the engine. Flames start at once and a figure tumbles out. A chute opens. He pulls up to watch Franz, who is turning with the other Tomahawk. Half the Tomahawk's tail flies off and it starts going down. The pilot emerges, gets stuck at first but then the Tomahawk starts a spin and he shoots out. Both parachutes are falling behind British lines. They circle to check the sky then climb and go home. He's ahead of Beck again.

There are two letters for him. One from Lotte and the other, oh God, is from Ilse! For a moment he imagines her cold hand somehow writing to him from the grave. He has to sit down. Then he looks at the postmark. The day she died. He can't open it yet. He lays it on the bed next to him. He opens Lotte's. It has a formal tone as if she's stepped back from him a little. Well, she turned him down. She clearly has his number, clearly sees through him. If he wants her, he'll have to change or lie to her forever.

Ilse's letter isn't thick. He slides it out. One sheet. The writing is a mess, scrawled, done in a hurry. To catch the post? He's here, she says! In Vienna. Heinecke! She was looking in a shop window and saw his face with his glasses reflected next to hers, like something in a nightmare. When she turned she saw his back walking away from her. It was the same dark brown overcoat with the wide shoulders and the collar raised. The grey fedora, tipped at a slight angle, the shiny backs of his always-shiny shoes. What can she do? He's followed her! She hasn't escaped! Help me, Jochen! Tell me what to do!

He's in anguish. Why did she write it? What did she think he could do from Libya, all that distance away? Even if he'd been in Berlin, he'd have been too far away. Why didn't she ring Bauer, go to the police or speak to someone at her new job? Did she imagine they'd take her for a hysterical female? No. Ilse could always present herself calmly, would have done even if frightened out of her wits. Anyone who heard her would have done something. Had she told Johanna, the girl she shared with? They could at least have stuck together. There was some safety in numbers.

He looks up. Dietrich is standing there.

'What's happened? Are you ill again? You're as white as a sheet.'

'I've had a letter from Ilse.'

'But—'

'Yes.'

He tells him all about it.

'But what can you do about this guy?' Dietrich says.

'I don't know. Does everyone know about Ilse?'

'The message about her came here first. Even Jonny said, "Poor bastard!" There was a discussion about whether to send it on with you so ill but Winter said you had to know.'

They have to go and fly. There are Stukas to escort. Hurricanes attack again but Jochen is leading a four, high above everyone, in a Friedrich he's borrowed from Wolfie Klein.

'Indians! Ten o'clock low,' he calls, and they fall like an avalanche on them.

His first goes down in a spin gushing smoke and he shoots as another labours round in a turn that is much too late. He sees his shells hit around the cockpit and it turns on its back and dives to the ground.

'Two,' Franz calls out.

He glances round and sees past the ironwork of his canopy a hump-backed shape sliding in behind Franz.

'Franz, break right!'

Dietrich turns immediately and Jochen continues the turn he's already started. The Hurricane has seen him and Jochen cuts the throttle as the Hurricane slows and turns with him. His Friedrich is not as agile as an Emil, won't turn as tightly. He pulls the stick into his crotch, tenses his stomach muscles to keep the blood from draining into his legs and fights the greying of his vision. He sees a chance and presses the trigger on the control column. The Hurricane's fin and rudder disappear in pieces. The pilot has lost a lot of control and Jochen fires again into the rear fuselage. Holes appear. Perhaps control wires have been destroyed. He imagines the other pilot suddenly having no pitch control. The Hurricane turns upside down and a shape falls out, dropping and dropping, almost gone from sight until a thin white ribbon appears and then the full chute opens.

'Three!' Franz calls. 'Thanks, maestro!'

He has three days in bed. Muscle and joint aches and a headache: sand-fly fever, the doc says. He takes aspirin and drinks chlorinated water. On the fourth morning he declares himself fit again. He plays *Rumba Azul* as he drinks his coffee.

They catch a dozen Tomahawks before they've dropped their bombs. Beck gets one and then the Tomahawks form into a defensive circle. Jochen shoots four of them out of it inside five minutes. Two parachutes go down. In the afternoon he gets another in flames and one that belly lands. He notes its position. He reports and goes back to his tent. To stop his thoughts about Ilse, he puts on a Mozart piano sonata. He closes his eyes and follows the pianist's fingers in his mind. He gets up to turn the record over and wind the gramophone, lies down again, closes his eyes. When the side finishes, he opens his eyes and sees Jonny Beck standing just inside the flap of the tent. Jonny lifts the needle off and stops the turntable.

'Mozart.'

'Yeah.'

'That last part, it sounded military.'

'It's a sort of march. He called it *Rondo alla turca*.'

'Must be a bugger to play.'

'Get your fingers in the right places and it's easy.'

'I hate to say this but listening to that is like watching you fly.'

'Are you taking the piss?'

'It's a compliment, Jochen.'

'Right. I'm not used to that.'

'How do you do it? I'd caught you up, gone past you and now you're way ahead of me again. How do you do that thing when they're in a circle?'

'I don't know. Just point in the right place, I suppose, fly at the right speed, shoot at the right moment, get the deflection right. I don't think about it.'

'Lucky bastard.'

'Being the head murderer around here?'

'Being our leading expert.' Beck picks up the record. 'Schnabel! That Jew again!'

'So?'

'Where did you find this?'

'A stall in the market.'

'The Italians should run the man who sold you this out of town.'

'They're too busy making ice cream. Sensible chaps, the Eyeties.'

'Huh! Anyway, day off tomorrow for you.'

'I don't want a day off.'

'Winter's orders. Take it easy, build yourself up, he said.'

'That's your chance then.'

'Don't worry. A day's no good, I'd need a month.'

He hangs about with Jurg and Hans, inspects the repairs to his Friedrich's starboard wing, listens in at the command tent to the patrol Beck leads, searches out Gerhard and gets a haircut and has a good old natter about Berlin. Then he goes back to the tent and plays records and frets about Ilse and Lotte. He gets out paper to write and smokes three cigarettes while he stares at it. He writes to his mother and separately to Bauer at police headquarters. He feels shivery and goes to bed. Franz and Wolfie and some others come round and he gets up, pours brandy and feels better. He plays *Rumba Azul* and other dance tunes.

They're up early the next morning. Black smoke belches from their Friedrichs one after another as the ground crews start them up. Stukas again. Some don't like this duty but not Jochen. Stukas always attract Hurricanes. Over the ships, the Stukas tip up one after the other.

'Indians! Two o'clock level,' he calls, and puts his nose down at the Hurricanes diving from land towards the sea and the Stukas queuing up over it to bomb. There are two Hurricanes in front of him. He puts cannon shells and mg rounds into the cockpit of the nearest and it turns on its side and falls in a spin.

'One!' he hears Franz call.

A nudge on the stick puts him behind the second, who's broken to the right. His rounds and shells move from the wing root to the engine. It smokes as the propeller stops. It turns upside down and the pilot falls out. Jochen reverses bank and turns tight to port.

'Two!' from Franz. 'All clear behind.'

There are two more trails of smoke and one, two, three parachutes. There are no Hurricanes in sight. The last of the Stukas pulls up. There's a white splash next to a ship. The Stuka hares towards the land.

'Indian!' he calls as he spots a cross of shadow on the blue of the water. He puts his nose down. He's approaching the Hurricane at 500kph. The Stuka is weaving. He sees spurts of tracer from the rear gunner's machine gun. He fires as the Hurricane fills his windscreen. Its engine smokes. It turns on its back and hits the water with a tremendous splash. He pulls up and puts the stick over as Franz calls out, 'Three!'

He swoops round in a wide circle and pulls in alongside the Stuka and gives the crew a wave. They wave back.

At dinner, they celebrate his fiftieth victory. Hans has already marked it on the tail of his Friedrich. No one's got more in Africa. There's a signal of congratulation from Rommel. Jonny Beck proposes a toast but is very stiff and Prussian about it and doesn't smile.

In the night he feels ill. It isn't the alcohol. He gets another blanket and lies there shivering. As the light begins an orderly brings him coffee.

'Ask Oberfähnrich Dietrich to come and see me,' he says.

'I'll tell Jonny,' Franz says when he gets there.

The doctor comes and gives him something to get him to sleep. The last thing he hears is the staffel taking off.

He wakes in mid-afternoon. He shaves and dresses and wanders off to find some food. He eats an egg, drinks some coffee. Wolfie is there. He and Franz got a Tomahawk between them. No one else got anything.

Winter comes in.

'I heard you were up. Come over to the office.'

He wobbles the twenty yards and finds it full of pilots ready for the next flight.

He looks round. There are mechanics gathered at the open flap, Jurg and Hans at the front of them.

'What's going on?' he says to Winter.

'Leutnant Murville. Do up your collar and come to attention!'

He obeys, more or less.

Winter leans forward and hangs the Knight's Cross around his neck. Everyone yelps and cheers. Jochen grins. He grabs the back of a chair. His head is swimming.

'Even if you seem to be better we're going to keep you here for at least two weeks. You've been ill too often. We need to get you properly well.'

Jochen nods. The doctor passes Jochen's notes to a nurse and leaves. He's in the Luftwaffe hospital in Munich. He seems to live in hospitals. He turns to the window; a scrubby grey sky. He closes his eyes.

After a few days he's out of bed, visiting other patients, playing cards, playing the dayroom piano. There's no booze. He begins to eat; three substantial meals a day. His weight rises. He writes to his mother, finally writes to Lotte.

He pays an orderly to get his uniform cleaned, buy him a couple of shirts, some underwear. The day he leaves, he looks the part, worthy of his Knight's Cross.

He gets a tram from the station. He's early. His mother's out, that's good, she's living some kind of life. He has to go next door to borrow a key from the neighbour he's known since he was three. Inside at last he takes off his cap and tunic and falls asleep on the sofa. His mother hugs him when she gets back, fusses around him in almost her old way, manages to admire the Knight's Cross, although they both know the futility of his having won it.

He waits up for Bauer. His mother's gone to bed.

'It's not evidence,' Bauer says when he's poured them a brandy each.

'But she saw him.'

'She saw a reflection in a shop window and a view of someone's back walking away from her.'

'She was sure.'

'A hysterical woman, delusional about an ex-boyfriend.'

'Is that what you think?'

'It's what they'd say if we put that letter up as part of a case.'

'But you, what do you think?'

'I believe her. I knew her quite well, didn't I?'

'You know, she never took to you.'

'Yes. It's natural.' Bauer smiles. 'Stepfather. Why wouldn't she prefer her own father?'

'She was furious with him.'

'That was quite clear, too. These things are tough on kids. Grown-up things.' He laughs. 'Grown up!'

'What happens now?'

'They're still asking around in Vienna. We need a witness who could identify him there. A hotel register, a desk clerk.'

'What about the scratches on his face?'

'The cuts from flying glass, you mean. They'll be gone by now.'

'You didn't get a photograph of them, did you?'

'You need a reason to photograph someone. If we'd brought a charge, we could have.'

'So it's just like the letter.'

'I'm afraid so.'

'Do you think he did it?'

'Definitely. It turns out he's got some history. I put the word out around town to see if anyone knew him and someone said they remembered questioning him over a possible assault on a petty criminal found beaten up in the street. Did a real job on him apparently. The guy wouldn't talk about it but they'd been seen arguing together a short time before. And there was another one turned up, too. A prostitute. He'd made a real mess of her face. She lost teeth. Quite brutal. And there was a sexual assault. But of course with a prostitute that's a difficult thing to prove anyway. It was dark and though she said it was him there was no other evidence. Both times he said he was somewhere else and he had witnesses. If only I'd asked around sooner. When she started going out with him. Before.'

They're both silent for a while.

'Can't we do anything?'

'We can wait. We're looking. They're looking in Vienna. We do know what we're doing. Everyone wants to sort it out. His brother being in the Gestapo is the problem. If we did get it cut and dried, they still might be able to kill it.'

'So he can do what he likes.'

'Wait. Just wait.'

He can't sleep. Not after that conversation. He goes into Ilse's room, sits on the bed, puts on a light. Her books are still on the shelves. There's the Grimm Brothers that they read as kids; a book of English exercises that he passed on to her. He looks away. Her dressing gown hangs on the back of the door. He gets up and buries his face in it. He can just detect the scent she used to wear. He opens a drawer, underwear. Opens the drawer next to it, a bowl with coins in it; a purse. He opens that, Austrian schillings. Next to the purse is her identity card. Fräulein Ilse Bauer. There's powder, lipstick. His mother must have put it all away when it came back. Bauer must have brought it all with him when he brought her home. There are letters, too. Lots from him and four or five others. From whom? A postmark on one is Cologne. Harri. He hasn't heard back from him yet. But, what do you write? Of course a letter from Harri might well be following him around. He opens her wardrobe: coats, dresses. His mother hasn't given them to the church yet. How will she ever bring herself to do that? That would mean she's gone. Gone for good. Gone for ever. He falls on the bed and puts his face in her pillow.

He hears a step. Raises his head. His mother. She comes in and puts a hand on his shoulder.

'Go to bed, darling.'

He pulls himself up.

She sits next to him on the bed. 'You can't do any good here.'

'Mummy,' he says, and buries his face in her shoulder.

He goes to a studio for his photographic appointment. Picture postcards of him will soon be on sale. Knight's Cross recipients all go through this. There was a letter waiting for him when he got home. He sits on a chair, stands to attention, stands relaxed, half sits on a table, stands and laughs at some crack by the photographer, faces forward and looks off to the side, stands sideways and looks ahead, holds a cigarette, smokes a cigarette, cap off, cap on; the guy seems to have an endless supply of instructions to hand. Pictures will appear first in *Luftwaffe*, the Air Force magazine. As Jochen is at the door to go, the man calls his name. He swings round and there's another flash.

That evening at Lotte's her parents are out, her sister is a distant chaperone still at her books in her room. They sit close on a sofa.

'You'll have girls writing to you.'

'Don't be silly.'

'I've read about it. That's the effect of those postcards. You with sacks of mail; that'll be the next photo.'

'Well, I'm the best in Africa.'

'How many?'

'Fifty-two.'

'So that's forty-eight, really, then, with the four of yours you've crashed.'

'Bookkeeper! There've been two more since then,' he says, and from her face knows at once he shouldn't have.

'Oh. You didn't say in your letters. What happened?'

There's nothing for it. He has to tell her.

'A parachute?' Her eyes have gone wide. 'That's terrifying.'

'No, it's quite nice, really, when you consider the alternative.' He doesn't describe the alternative and she doesn't ask.

'I thought you'd stopped writing to me.'

'We were busy and then I was ill and I couldn't find the way to write. Your letter seemed different. I was confused.'

'I was horrible when you proposed. When I remembered what I said, I was mortified.'

'I think you were really saying you didn't want to end up like my mother. And you didn't trust me.'

She looks down at her hands clutched in front of her.

'Look at me.'

'I'm too ashamed. Poor Ilse spoke to me.'

'About me?'

She nods.

'She was right to. She was always better than me. We were both brought up in the church but she believed it all.'

Lotte looks up finally. Her eyes are full. 'What now?'

That face, looking at him; so close, such an intimate moment. If only he could have her now, here, right now.

'That's up to you, Lotte.'

'If you wanted to, you could ask me again.'

'Could I?'

She nods.

'Will you marry me?'

She gazes into his eyes for long moments. 'Yes.'

He laughs. 'Fifty years?'

She laughs, too. 'More.'

He holds her shoulder. It's so warm through her dress. He kisses her.

There's a noise and they spring apart and look up.

'Oh, sorry,' her sister says, and leaves at once.

'I've got all this time and you're working,' he says. 'Couldn't we manage to go away somewhere? Just us.'

He calls in at the whisky bar. No Gerda, of course, and only Otto at the piano. He takes a brandy over.

'I'm engaged. You're the first to know.'

'Congratulations! Prost!'

'Where are the others?'

'Called up.'

'I thought they'd be too old!'

'Apparently not. I'm just hoping I am. I was old the last time. I saw the widow, if you still want to know.'

'Of course. How is she?'

'Pale, a husk. When you think how she looked that first night after you'd been in with your sister. You don't ever bring her in.'

So he tells him, having avoided it before. Otto's jaw drops. He manages to move it to say, 'The poor girl! Your poor mother! And you.'

'You'll have me in tears again. Tell me about the widow. I'm glad you've found her.'

'She denied it but I could see it was her. I gave her the money. She said she'd save it for an emergency. She was anxious about being seen with anyone. If anyone did see us, I think they'd have taken me for a client.'

'A client! Where is it she's living? Her husband was a tank commander. She had a pension but they took it away.'

'Just one of our new enlightened policies.'

'Tell me the address.'

'I don't think you should go there. Someone would smell a rat. It's not somewhere a Knight's Cross hero pitches up at. I'm just a shabby white-haired old git so I don't stand out.'

'I won't go there. I just have to know, in case there's an emergency. I won't be in Berlin anyway, will I?'

Otto writes it down.

'I'll do another envelope for her.'

'Don't get too close, Kid. What would your Mrs-to-be say?'

'She'd understand.'

'She'd be the first girl who ever did, then.'

He spends his days brooding about Heinecke. One day he sees him in the distance and feels a physical shock. Bauer has nothing new to tell him. He goes to Tempelhof to cadge a flight but there's nothing available. He asks to be sent back, says he feels fine now, but the doctors say he needs longer for a real recovery. He didn't last three weeks out there last time. He was in hospital for two weeks and now he's been at home for three. He feels a fraud. They're dying out in the desert. He does his sit-ups morning and evening to get his stomach muscles back in trim.

He goes to the club, plays a few times. He meets three Luftwaffe guys who are impressed by the Knight's Cross. They want him to move on with them. They're going to find some girls. His Knight's Cross will help. He sends them on their way. Lotte has organised three days off to add on to a Saturday and Sunday and he's found a place in the country where Leutnant and Frau Murville can stay to relax and walk and talk and laugh and all the rest.

8

Shoeshine Boy

WINTER'S ON LEAVE. JONNY BECK'S IN CHARGE. He hasn't caught up with Jochen's score yet. Wolfie is dead. A Hurricane sent him straight into the sea like Renate's Kurt just after he'd shot another Hurricane off the tail of a Stuka.

Hans has got sand-fly fever. He's under a blanket shivering. Jochen slides the brandy and cigarettes he's brought back beneath Hans's bed.

'Thanks, boss,' Hans manages to say. Jochen sits and talks about Berlin and what everything's like now at home until he realises Hans has fallen asleep so he leaves.

Franz slaps his knees and doubles over with laughter when he tells him about Lotte. They agree to be each other's best man if they can manage to make their leaves coincide. Jochen and Lotte are thinking of Christmastime for their wedding. Jochen has no idea where they'll live. Lotte will probably stay on at home while he's on active service.

He takes his Friedrich up. Other people have flown it in his absence but it feels all right. He rolls and loops above the field. He taxis up and hands it back to Jurg and the guy helping him pro tem, Gunther.

Everyone comes to his tent as night falls. He plays his new music and they drink.

'How do you like being in charge?' he asks Jonny.

'It's bloody awful. I'm not in charge, the job's in charge.'

'Only two, then, while I've been gone?'

'There's no time to get up there. Forms, rotas, memos, reports. You wait.'

'They'll never give me a gruppe, Jonny.'

He waits but Jonny doesn't deny it.

The Mills Brothers are on the gramophone. *Tiger Rag*.

They all sing along in English. 'Hold that tiger, hold that tiger, hold that tiger, hold that tiger.'

'Well, Jonny. Four black men singing, no instruments, they make the sounds of the instruments themselves. What do you think?'

'Gibberish!' Beck says.

He smokes a last cigarette before he crawls in under his mosquito net. What's Lotte doing now? He sees her again that first morning holding her dressing gown to her breast, revealing her beautiful back and lovely rear as she flings open a shutter to let in some light then drops the dressing gown to cross the room and slide in under the covers next to him again.

They have Stukas to escort. Who'd want to fly one? He's full of admiration. They are entirely vulnerable as they queue up to dive on their targets. And they dive so slowly! 150 with their airbrakes open. There are two tankers in the harbour.

'Indians!' he calls out. 'Three o'clock high!'

Hurricanes are pouring down on the Stukas. They climb towards them. He fires at the leader as he climbs. Two hundred metres away at least. The Hurricane's engine smokes and flames appear. He can't wait there to watch. He moves the control column over to follow another, much closer now. It turns towards him. Jochen follows it in a left-hand circle. He cuts the throttle, lowers the flaps and begins to turn inside the Hurricane. The engine disappears beneath his nose and he fires. The Hurricane's propeller stops and its nose goes down. He fires again. Pieces fly off the starboard wing; half the wing snaps off and hurtles back towards him. The other wing flips the Hurricane over and over. It goes down.

'Two!' Franz calls out. 'All clear behind.'

A parachute is going down. And another. A Stuka splashes into the sea, an eruption of white against the blue. Another Stuka far below is zig-zagging above the sea to escape a Hurricane.

'Indian, two o'clock low, chasing a Stuka,' he calls as he tips his nose down. There's no time to get behind it. He goes directly to cut the Hurricane's path. He's doing 550 now. He fires ahead of the Englishman, almost at the Stuka. It looks right. Hits spark all around the cockpit. The Hurricane pitches forward, goes down fast, turning towards the land. He pulls up out of the dive. He's pushed down into his seat and he can barely move his hand to the throttle it's so heavy as the Friedrich continues up into a climb. The Hurricane's shadow appears on the sand and rock. Shadow and aeroplane merge and the machine is sliding across the land throwing up a rising trail of dust.

'Three!' Franz calls.

The Stukas are forming up to go home. They stay above and watch. There's nothing more.

Three hours later, they're up again. They catch Tomahawks that go at once into a circle. A Friedrich goes straight in. Number '7'. He doesn't know who it is. Unlucky number '7'. A Tomahawk pulls out of the circle and fires into it. The Friedrich goes down vertically and doesn't come out. Jochen dives straight through the circle, firing at the Tomahawk filling his windscreen.

'One!' Franz calls.

He pulls up and fires at the belly of another. It smokes and goes down.

'Two!'

There's nothing coming towards him so he carries on up into the blue and pulls into a stall turn, skidding across the sky and down towards the earth again and fires at the Tomahawk nose that appears in front of him. Bits fly off immediately. He carries on down and dives clear, nothing but the ochre land in his view.

'Three!' Franz calls.

He pulls up. The circle is split and Tomahawks are weaving about, two or three with Friedrich's behind them. He sees Franz shoot the tail off a Tomahawk as he follows Jochen down.

Jurg paints six more bars on his rudder.

It was a new guy, of course, Busch, who went down and smashed a hole in the desert in number '7'.

'Come with us next time, Jonny,' he says while he's reporting.

'I'll try,' Beck says. 'Meanwhile, get that out of here!' He jerks his head to one of the corporals who lugs out a mail sack the size of a large suitcase from behind a desk.

'What the fuck is that?'

'Your bedtime reading.'

Franz follows him but can't help him carry it back to his tent; he's too busy laughing. Jochen drops the sack on the bed and flops down next to it. He could take the photograph Lotte predicted now.

'Open it up, then,' Franz says.

He does and strews letters on the bed and floor.

'What am I supposed to do with this lot?'

'Answer them, every one.'

He picks one up and pulls the envelope open. Scent, purple ink.

'Christ!' He passes it over to Franz. 'Stop grinning.'

'I can't, "Dear Jochen,"' Franz reads. '"I may call you that, mayn't I? When I saw your picture, I was suddenly all of a flutter. How wonderful that we have such handsome heroes protecting us! How I would love to meet you!"'

'No, no, no!' Jochen puts his hands over his face.

Franz picks up another. 'This one's fat.' He opens it. Cream silk spills out. He picks it up. 'A pair of knickers!' He catches their aroma. 'Phoar! You'd think she'd have washed them first.' He holds them up and looks at them.

'Or perhaps that's the idea.' He throws them at Jochen and they land on his face.

Jochen brushes them off onto the ground. 'I need a drink.'

They leave the letters where they lie and make off for the mess.

The next morning they fly a patrol and see nothing. Beck comes, too. They land trailing the usual clouds of dust. When they come out of the command tent, a water truck is just pulling up. The driver opens his door and jumps down but one foot lands on a fair-sized rock he hasn't noticed. He falls and sits up clutching his ankle and looking as if he would like to yell out in pain but doesn't want to with an audience of officers. They stare at him, Dietrich, Lehmann, Beck, Jochen. He's in similar khaki drill to all of them but is clearly a British prisoner of war and he's black.

After a moment, Jochen strolls over.

'All right?' he says in English.

'Yes, Leutnant,' the man says. He puts his hand down to push himself up but when the injured ankle takes the strain he cries out.

'Here,' Jochen says, and holds out his hand.

The man stares at him.

'It won't bite you.'

The man takes hold and Jochen pulls him up. He holds the man's arm and helps him hop the two metres back to his truck where he sits on the running board.

'Cigarette?'

'Thank you.'

They light up.

'What's your name?'

'Private Sibeko, Christopher.'

Jochen smiles. 'Christof. Good name.'

The man smiles, too.

The others have taken water from the truck. Franz hands Jochen a mug of it.

He passes it to the black driver. The man stares at him for a moment.

'You first, sir.'

'You're the injured one, Christof.'

Christof raises the mug and takes a sip while still staring at Jochen over the rim. After that first sip, he gulps the rest of the water down and holds the mug out.

'Another?'

Christof nods. Jochen pours another mug full.

'What are you doing, Jochen?' Jonny says.

'Shut up, Jonny.' He passes the mug to Christof, who drains it. 'More?'

Christof shakes his head.

'You're a German officer!' Beck says.

'I wondered what this uniform was.' He fills the mug for himself and drains it in one go.

'You used the same mug!'

'Well?'

'You didn't wash it out.'

'It's had a lot of water in it.'

'You know what I mean.'

'I refuse to know what you mean.'

'Give us a hand, Franz.' Franz joins Jochen at the step. One each side they pull Christof up and support him as he hops between them.

'What are you doing, now?' Beck says.

'Medical tent.'

'You can't do that!'

'Jonny, this man's just driven forty kilometres to bring us water and now he's hurt himself. What's he supposed to do?'

'He's a prisoner and he's black!'

'He hurts just the same, Jonny.'

Christof can't drive, the doc says. He needs to use a crutch for a while. The office finds another driver to take the empty truck back but Christof doesn't go with him.

Jonny Beck is furious.

'He's under the doctor, Jonny, and the doctor's here.'

'Where's he going to sleep?'

'There's a lot of floor space in my tent.'

'What if he attacked you in the night? You're a valuable asset of the Reich.'

Jochen laughs.

Jonny takes him aside and talks to him quietly. 'I should have you arrested.'

Jochen holds out his wrists for the handcuffs.

'You make life very difficult for me, you know. Why don't you ever do what I want?'

'Because most of the time, Jonny, you act like a complete knob.'

They fly again after lunch and spot a group of Tomahawks disappearing into the distance over British territory. He picks one off at an outrageous range. It spirals down to the desert trailing smoke as a parachute spills out. They fly back chattering about it. Hans has recovered. He paints up another bar on the rudder.

Jochen stops at the flap of his tent. Has he come to the right one? The bed is made, the mosquito net pulled back neatly. The scattered letters have been picked up. Records are in a tidy pile by the gramophone. The rucked-up tarpaulin on the floor has been stretched taut. There are no clothes thrown around; on the bed, on the floor. The airman assigned as a servant to him and the occupants of the next five tents must have had a brainstorm. He goes to see Franz.

'Has…?' But he can see that no one has. 'Come and see my tent.'

'Must be the tent fairy,' Franz says.

He goes off to investigate and meets Jurg and Christof.

'I took Chris off for some grub. He hadn't eaten all day, boss. I thought I'd better when I saw how he'd tidied you up.'

'Nothing else to do,' Christof says when asked why.

They speak a mixture of English and German. Jochen's English is passable. Christof's German less good.

'Put a record on.'

'Which one?'

'You choose.'

'Fats Waller. He's very good,' Christof says.

They listen. *Ain't Misbehavin'*.

'He's a funny man, you know. Makes faces at the audience, tells jokes.'

'Have you seen him?'

'Before the war. In New York.'

'New York?'

'I was in the Merchant Marine.'

'Did you see anybody else?'

'Louis Armstrong, Duke Ellington.'

'In clubs?'

'Theatres.'

Jochen puts on *Rumba Azul*.

Christof grins and sways around to it.

'Why are you driving for us?'

'They asked for volunteers. Better than a camp.'

'But we're the other side.'

'You're both the other side. It's a white man's war. Nothing to do with us. We lost all our wars in Africa long ago.'

'Where are you from?'

'Kenya.'

Jochen remembers Kendall, the flight lieutenant. 'I know someone from Kenya. His family have a coffee plantation.'

Christof laughs. 'I don't know anyone with a plantation. I know sailors and day labourers and such like.'

'Listen,' Jochen says, and tells Christof the plan he's just come up with.

In the morning, he gets through to the officer in charge of transport and water trucks. Jochen agrees to send two bottles of brandy back to the officer with the next empty truck. Christof's records will be lost. Jonny storms off when he realises what Jochen's arranged.

Jochen begins to look smarter. Christof cleans shirts and shorts in petrol every day and hangs them on a guy rope to clear the smell. He pours the drinks in the evening. He puts the music on in Jochen's meticulously tidy tent and chats to everyone who turns up.

'Indians! Twelve o'clock high!'

He pulls the stick back and opens the throttle. They're at a disadvantage. How did the English get above them? One of the attackers banks a little and its wing shape appears. Spitfires!

'Spitfires!' someone calls out. Jonny? Jochen fires before the approaching Spitfire can pass. There are tracers flashing past him but he sees his own shells strike home with sparkles at the wing root and into the rear fuselage.

'Going right, Franz!' he calls to give a warning.

The sky swings onto his left side and the ground appears to his right. He pulls hard on the stick and tenses his stomach muscles tight. The world goes grey at the edges of his vision. Chasing the Spits, he tears towards the ground.

'Break right, Jochen!'

He does. He assumes there's a Spitfire behind him. Franz might get him but he cuts the throttle and drops his flaps and pulls as tight a turn as he can while staying conscious. Still nothing visible.

'Still there, Jochen.'

He lowers the undercarriage and keeps pulling the turn, his speed edging towards the white mark. There! Behind him. He turns and turns but doesn't get closer. Time to go.

He reverses bank and raises the undercarriage, opens the throttle, raises the flaps. He puts the nose straight down. Thank God Spitfires can't do that with their carburettors that flood if they do. The Spitfire pilot will have to do a wing over to follow him.

'All clear, Jochen,' Franz calls.

He pulls up and sees a Spitfire behind a Friedrich.

'Break left!' he calls. The Friedrich does. The Spitfire follows. He can't see who the Friedrich is but he slides in behind the Spitfire and fires as it fills his sight. His shells hit the wing root and move on to the engine. It burns. The Spitfire pulls round right in a tight turn and fires. He puts his nose down and gets out of the way.

'He's baling out,' Franz calls.

Beck isn't back. Lehmann is anxious. He feels responsible. Somehow after months of tailing his boss he's lost him at a crucial moment. They talk about the Spitfires. Life will be more difficult now. Jochen has a .303 bullet hole through his starboard aileron. Several others have been hit. Franz saw smoke beginning from the first Spit Jochen fired at but couldn't watch it any longer. Only Jochen got one. It must have been Jonny it was behind at the time. He didn't see the Friedrich again.

They split the desert up on their maps and take off in pairs. A kübelwagen is ready with two mechanics, petrol and water, waiting for a position to be radioed in. Pretty soon, they spot a thin trail of smoke rising vertically. It's from a pulverised aeroplane, black and burnt, half buried in the sand. They swing in a wide circle and spot the pilot. Khaki shorts and shirt. He's walking towards the British lines. Jochen swoops down and rocks his wings; the pilot waves and keeps on walking. It must be the Spitfire pilot. Franz radios the position in. They hear Lehmann calling back, too; a position a couple of kilometres away. Franz circles the British pilot while Jochen goes to take a look at Beck. He's down on his belly, propeller blades properly bent back and the tail snapped halfway back and at right angles to the rest of the fuselage. They won't need the mechanics. Beck waves back. Lehmann continues circling while Jochen climbs and joins up with Koehler, the other half of Lehmann's pair. Together they fly sentry duty above the circling Friedrich's below.

'Thanks,' Jonny says when he's back and learns it was Jochen who called the Spitfire.

'Just like the old days,' Jochen says, 'shooting Indians off your tail.'

'Is it?' Jonny isn't smiling.

He tells Christof to lose himself. There's a British officer around the place, a New Zealander actually. The pilot of the Spitfire Jochen got. He's at the medical tent when Jochen finds him, having a burnt arm bound up.

'Bob Barker,' he says at once, and sticks out his hand when Jochen introduces himself.

'Is your arm bad?' Jochen says.

'It's fine. I must have nine lives.'

'Nine lives?'

'Like a cat.'

'That's seven.'

Barker laughs. 'Not in New Zealand. Cats must be luckier in English.' They have a large mug of tea each. Barker makes a face.

'No good?'

'I thought our tea was bad but this! Still, beggars can't be choosers.'

Jochen's never heard that expression. He makes Barker explain.

Barker's from Auckland. He shipped as a deckhand to join the RAF in England before the war. What is it about Britain that produces these feelings in young men? 'It's the home country,' Barker says. Jochen gets another address for his post-war visits. Barker writes a short note.

The next morning, Jonny sees him getting into his Friedrich.

'What would you do if I forbade you to fly over there?'

'Oh, don't do that, Jonny.'

He and Franz deliver the note and bring down a Tomahawk each on their way back.

He lands and taxis up into the line, undoes his safety belt but doesn't answer when Jurg says, 'Any luck, boss?' He's asleep. It's his fourth flight of the day. Rommel's big attack starts tomorrow. Jurg hauls him out and he shambles over to report. Two Tomahawks shot out of a defensive circle and a Spitfire from the group they managed to bounce. He's got sixty-three now. He and Dietrich walk back to their tents. He puts on *Rumba Azul*, knocks back a brandy and lies on the bed to listen to the song. When Christof comes in, he's fast asleep. Christof pulls off Jochen's boots and takes the needle off the record. He doesn't wake. Later Christof arranges the mosquito net around him and he still doesn't wake.

Lotte seems to write every day. Letters arrive in every post bag. He can't keep up with her. There doesn't seem to be enough time. There are three or four flights a day and when he gets down, there are reports to make. The flying makes him sleepy and he naps often. He's got to eat and he's got the guys to natter with as Christof passes round the drinks and puts the records on. If Jurg and Hans have been working on 'Fourteen' then he has to test it, and he still practises shooting on the range three kilometres away. He goes up often, too, with new guys to show them around and give them tips and check out their flying skills and demonstrate that even the most successful need to stay on top of things.

Now and again he gets a day off, though, and drives into town with whoever is around for couscous and whatever else is available. He comes back one day with a parasol, very gay, red and yellow.

'I thought you were engaged,' Franz says.

'It's a present, not a trophy.'

He takes it to the flight line and puts it up over his open canopy when they have to sit in their cockpits ready for a scramble order. The temperature inside the cockpit drops to the almost bearable. He sees Beck staring at him.

'Jealous, Jonny?' he calls.

They bounce across the field, pushing opposite rudder to the propeller's torque, and lift off. Wheels rise, the right never quite in unison with the left. One circuit to join up and Jonny leads them off. The British are strafing the trucks and tanks of Rommel's advance.

They catch them flying home and fall on them. They're Tomahawks or perhaps Kittihawks; a little heavier; almost identical and faster but crucially not fast enough.

Jochen gets one, two, three straight off almost before the British are aware of the Friedrichs, then they break into the Friedrichs' attack. He fires ahead of the one turning to get at him and it flies into the shells. The engine burns and it goes down.

'Break right!' Franz calls. 'Indians, six o'clock high.'

Stick over and back before he straightens and climbs. Nothing but sun glare and blue ahead of him. In the glare he can just make out black specks that quickly become solid lumps with wings. He fires at the one head on in front of him before he races past. There are no more specks in front. He pulls a turn so tight that his vision begins to grey despite his tensed stomach muscles. The ground appears ahead of him. There's a huge plume of smoke going down. From his Spitfire or from a Friedrich? Machines are turning not far below. There's no future in that with Spitfires. He puts his nose towards one that's turning behind a Friedrich and fires ahead of it. The Englishman flies into the shells and burns at once. He continues his dive and gets another as he passes, sparkling hits that stop the propeller. The Spitfire turns upside down and the pilot falls out. The sky looks empty.

'Any more, Franz?' he calls.

'Isn't seven enough?'

They fly home one short. It's another new boy who's gone, Weber. No one saw anything. Refuelled and rearmed, they parcel out the desert and fly off in pairs. No one spots a Friedrich broken by a forced landing. There are several wrecks where planes have drilled into the desert. Weber is missing in action. Frau Weber will get one of those dreaded letters.

Christof teaches him to sing *Shoeshine Boy*. It's a number the Mills Brothers sing, as do many others, but Jochen hasn't got a record of it. Jochen holds a bottle upside down as a pretend microphone and sings.

'Shoeshine boy, soon the day will come.'

Christof does a soft shoe shuffle to it around the tent.

'Shoeshine boy, soon a tune you'll hum.

Every nickel helps a lot, So shine, shine, shoeshine boy.'

Guys gather at the tent flap.

'Encore!' someone shouts. They do it again. Beck pokes his head in over a shoulder, watches for a moment or two and then leaves without speaking.

He gets two Kittihawks in the morning, one after lunch and a Hurricane in the early evening. The next day, another one of cloudless bright blue sky, the ochre land beneath, he sees the glint of sun on perspex and leads them down on the Indians. Another defensive circle forms, the British slowed up even more by the bombs they carry. He gets one on his dive through and one on his climb back up, a wing over at the top and he gets a third which explodes as he's already past. Franz circles above, protecting him;

one hawk above, one hawk down among the pigeons. They fly home. How many Tomahawks and Kittihawks have the British got? Why can't the U-boats send the ships carrying them to the bottom before they reach Africa? And where do the pilots keep coming from?

More bars appear on his tail. Seventy-seven now; now eighty-two. He flies, plays his music, holds his parties, torments Jonny Beck and reads the letters that continue to arrive. Christof glances through them for him, looking for Berlin postmarks.

'You can't look them all up when you get home,' Franz says. 'You're engaged.'

'It's just out of interest.' But actually he doesn't want to miss anything that might come through from Gerda, who doesn't have his correct address and might well just write 'Leutnant Murville, Luftwaffe', as she did once before.

He picks one letter at random from each batch and writes an answer. The letter is more or less the same each time. He's always kind in tone and thanks the writer for getting in touch, is grateful for the good wishes and sends his own back and, a little cruelly, perhaps, adds those of his fiancée Lotte as well. Christof has a bonfire once a week when everyone else has read as many as they want to.

Jurg is painting up bar number ninety-four when Beck calls him over. Jochen's swapped his boots for some sandals Christof's made him from an old tyre. They've become a new fashion item on the field. Christof has an order list of six to complete.

'There's a new command in. It's strictly forbidden to fly messages over to the British.'

'Who's that from?'

'Reichsmarschall Goering.'

'How does he know about that?'

'It came to his attention, he says.'

'But how?'

'He takes a keen interest in his boys' doings. It was in a report.'

'Whose report? Yours?'

'Yes.'

'Christ, Jonny, it's simple humanity. Then their mothers know.'

'English mothers!'

'Wouldn't you want your mother to know what had happened to you?'

Winter is back. Everyone's glad to see him. He mingles with the guys in Jochen's tent, meets Christof, tries one of his cocktails. Winter goes up with Jochen to get his hand in again. Despite Winter's best efforts, Jochen sits unmoving on his tail.

Ground crews start betting on when he'll reach a hundred. Jurg puts on a cap, goes to Winter directly, salutes like a Prussian automaton and states his anxieties.

'It's bad luck, sir. He's got enough to worry about without people opening a book and bringing a jinx down on him.'

Winter keeps a straight face. 'Quite right.' He issues an order forbidding the betting. Jurg's name is mud with his mates for a day or two.

There's talk of when he'll get his Knight's Cross with Oak Leaves and Swords and whether he'll be called back for Hitler to present it. He starts getting worried about Christof's position as a black British prisoner of war if he's not there to protect him and begins to ask around and get promises from the guys to look after Christof.

There are Stukas to escort against a convoy. The ships' wakes seven thousand metres below are artist's brush strokes, ivory white across aquamarine. There's a flash to their right.

'Indians! Three o'clock high.'

As the Hurricanes hurtle past them towards the Stukas far below, they put their own noses straight down after them. Friedrichs dive faster than Hurricanes. He catches one and puts cannon shells all along the fuselage. The pilot bails out over the water. He's after another but leaves it instantly and turns as Franz calls, 'Jochen, break left!'

He tenses his stomach muscles and holds the stick right back, keeping his vision despite its grey surround.

'Keep going! I'm behind him,' Franz calls.

He stretches his neck back and round, searching between the canopy's glazing bars. Nothing! Then he sees it. A Spitfire. They were following the Hurricanes. They should have waited. But then the Hurricanes would have had a free hand with the Stukas.

He puts the nose straight down, knowing the Spit can't follow immediately and that if he does follow, Franz will have an easier shot.

He counts to ten slowly and then pulls up vertically. As his speed bleeds off, he rolls into a turn, reverses direction and puts the nose down again. A Spitfire flashes past followed by Franz. He takes a snapshot at the Spitfire following Franz and smoke billows out of the engine followed by flames. The pilot heads for land but almost immediately gets out. Jochen circles to see what's going on. There's nothing above or around. White splashes surround the ships as the Stukas go in. One ship has great billows of black smoke rising from it.

'Red one at five thousand metres,' he calls. A Friedrich pops up beside him. Number '4'.

'Any luck, Franz?'

'Got him. How many?'

'Two.'

Franz yelps into his microphone.

They fly back. Near home, they catch a Kittihawk low down. Jochen hits it with a short burst. It goes down trailing smokes and lands on its belly. They circle and watch the pilot get out. Franz radios the position. They'll have a guest for dinner.

When he lands, guys gather round, shouting congratulations. Jurg and Hans carry him on their shoulders to the squadron office. Winter is beaming. Jochen makes his report.

'101, then,' Winter says. 'That makes forty-nine in the fifty-four days you've been back here.'

The Kittihawk pilot's name is Winton. It was his first operation. He'd got separated and didn't know where he was. He's from Budleigh Salterton. Jochen gets him to write it down. He loves the sound of it. He collects Winton's address for his 'after the war tour'. They get onto cricket. Winton describes it and his audience is soon laughing.

'When the side that was in is out, the other side goes in, till they're out.'

'Then?' Jochen says.

'They do it again.' More laughter.

'How long does all this take?' Beck says, looking down his nose.

'Three days.' Peals of laughter. 'Or five if we're playing Australia.'

Franz is holding his side. 'Stop! Stop!' he says but Winton is enjoying himself.

'In 1914, we'd been playing South Africa for eleven days but the match had to stop because the war started and everyone had to go and fight.'

Amid the laughter, Jonny Beck shakes his head and mutters, 'Playing a game for days on end! Madness!'

In the morning, the sound of Daimler-Benz engines brings Beck out of his tent in time to see Jochen and Franz take off and head for the British lines. Beck is there when they land and watches Jochen taxi back to Jurg and Hans. He waits until Jochen has got out and had a word with his guys about the engine.

'Have you just dropped another note?'

'Yes.'

'It's forbidden.'

'Yes, you said.'

'Don't you care about that?'

'Not much, obviously.'

'You do just what you like, don't you, Murville? You've got no discipline!'

'And you have, I suppose.'

'Yes.'

'I didn't see you at first light checking your kite with your guys when I was checking mine.'

'Mine didn't need checking.'

'You don't use it enough.'

'What do you mean by that?'

'If you'd flown four operations, it might need checking. If you went up and practised your shooting it might need checking and you might hit one now and again.'

'You can't talk to me like that. I'm your superior.'

'Yeah, pull that one, Jonny, but remember, a superior is supposed to be superior.'

'You've got a nerve! You're a disgrace to the Reich!'

'I'm a good German.'

'A good German? Look at the state of you! Look at your boots! Don't they ever get polished?'

'In the desert?'

'Mine are clean.'

'Polishing boots in the desert! Hey, after the war, get a pitch at Berlin Terminus. You'll make a good living shining shoes there.'

Jochen turns and walks away singing, 'Shoeshine boy, soon the day will come, shoeshine boy, soon—'

'Murville!' Jonny sounds furious. 'I haven't finished yet!'

Jochen swings round. 'What now?'

'Consider yourself under arrest.'

'What charge?'

'Insubordination. I'll think of some more later. And you're grounded.'

Jochen goes straight to the command tent but Winter's gone off to HQ.

Back at his tent, Christof's got hold of some eggs somehow and he cooks Jochen and Franz an omelette.

'Get some sleep,' Franz says before he goes off on a job. Jochen watches them all take off, the long lines of dust slowly settling as they climb away. It's like seeing your friends running off to play in the park when you have to stay in bed with chickenpox.

He lies down and closes his eyes but only Jonny Beck arrives. Perhaps he shouldn't taunt him so much but Jonny seems to generate taunts and Jochen just can't help himself. He gets up. Write to Lotte. Nothing comes. Gerda. How is she? He could write to her but he doesn't want to bring anyone from the state into contact with her. Not even a postman.

The staffel lands back. One missing; Franz's wingman, Udo, only with them for two weeks, this was his third job. They jumped some Hurricanes. Franz got one, Jonny hit one, no result. Udo lands ten minutes after the others. He's got back on petrol fumes.

'Sorry,' he says, 'I got lost.'

'Can't you find someone else to fly with you?' Jochen says to Franz.

'He'll be all right.'

With three hours' daylight left they're off again. Udo is still flying with Franz. Winter is due back before dark. Everyone thinks Jochen will have to go home to be presented with his Oak Leaves and Swords, though nothing's in about it yet, so he finds Gerhard for a haircut. Gerhard is miserable but philosophical. After four months he's finally had a letter. His girlfriend has ditched him. For twenty minutes they smoke and debate the mystery of women.

He lies on his bed. Christof is outside, cleaning shirts and shorts with petrol. What are they doing in Berlin? It's a Tuesday. Lotte's probably on her way back from school. His mother is queuing or cooking. Bauer is having a first dinner or perhaps there's new information about Heinecke to collate. Gerda. What's Gerda doing? Probably stirring sheets in a copper or mangling them or hanging them out to dry in a hospital basement. She didn't say which hospital's laundry she worked in.

Unless she's moved. She worked in a factory making switches first, she said. She might have changed again. Once he'd have wondered about Ilse, too, but he knows exactly what she's doing now and where she is. Ilse and Gerda. And Lotte. He couldn't help Ilse. Could he help Gerda? And Lotte? What about her?

They've been gone an hour. He wanders up to the command tent to listen in. There's just the usual crackling from the radio.

'Anything?'

'There was contact a couple of minutes ago,' one of the typing clerks says, 'but nothing since.'

'Break left!' Lehmann's tense voice shouts through the crackling. Then come the sounds of panting breaths.

'Two behind you, Jonny!' Lehmann again. 'They're gaining.'

'Dive away! Dive!' Jonny's voice.

No sound of Franz or Udo. Where are they? There are no sounds from either of them and neither Beck nor Lehmann call them up.

'Home,' he hears Beck say. The English will be following or perhaps, left far behind by the dive, not bothering.

Where are Franz and Udo?

He has a sick feeling; a terrible feeling that spins, collects force and becomes anger; a fury that in a flash occupies every part of his mind, every part of his body. He knows. They were bounced by Spitfires and Udo and Franz have gone straight down into the desert floor, buried three metres into it, because Udo on his fourth job couldn't see anything in the sky and shouldn't have been up there flying wingman to Franz. But it isn't Udo's fault. It's Beck's fault, that stupid ramrod Nazi. If Beck hadn't grounded him, Jochen and Franz would have been up there together and Franz would have spotted them and they'd be flying home now having got two or three between them.

He stares across the field in the direction they'll come from. The sun is low. There's an hour of light left. There's nothing. No, there's the distant sound. It grows and the two Friedrichs appear. They swing into the circuit and land, billowing dust behind them as they taxi to their dispersal points. Beck and Lehmann climb out. Beck goes straight to the command tent. Lehmann sees Jochen and comes over. He tells him. It's just as Jochen imagined. Spitfires. Lehmann saw them just in time but too late for Franz and Udo. They were gone in one pass. They went straight down, Udo in flames, Franz not but probably dead already. He didn't see them hit the ground but he's sure they did.

Jurg and Hans have come over. Franz and Udo's guys are there, too, awkward, listening in to officers' talk. He sees Beck come out of the command tent and walk towards his own tent. His head is down. He doesn't look over to the group. He isn't coming over to tell Franz's guys what happened. Ten months out here. Up there every day. And not a word now Franz has gone. Jochen is trembling with rage.

He sets off towards his Friedrich. He calls over his shoulder, 'Jurg!'

He climbs onto the wing and swings himself into the cockpit.

'Start her up!' he calls to Jurg. He does up his straps.

'Where are you going, boss? You're grounded.'

'Start her up!'

Jurg obeys. The propeller turns two or three times; the engine explodes and belches black smoke. He waves the chocks away, taxis out and hammers across the field. He climbs quickly to five hundred metres and circles. Jonny's tent is clear to see at the end of a line of three and from way across the field he puts his nose down. The tent grows as he gets lower and closer. He's at a hundred metres now and must be doing 350. He pulls back into level flight as he crosses over the tent at about ten metres and blasts it with his slipstream. He pulls up in a stall turn and sees

Jonny's tent leaning to one side with guy ropes separated from their pegs. Jonny seems to be struggling out from the collapsed canvas. Back on the other side of the field, Jochen turns again and dives for the tent. Three hundred metres away, he fires his machine guns. The spurts of the bullets in the sand race towards the tent. He takes his thumb off the button and the last spurt kicks up sand fifteen metres from the tent. He turns away, circles the field and lands. He's taxiing back when Winter's Friedrich arrives over the field. Jochen rips off his straps and jumps out.

'Boss!' Jurg calls, but Jochen's past him and running for Beck's demolished tent. Now he's frightened him, he's going to kill him. He's wearing his pistol. He'd like to beat him to death, but Jonny's twice his size and he wouldn't last thirty seconds in a fist fight but a bullet makes him Jonny's equal. 'Boss! Stop!' Jurg is chasing him but can't get close.

Without warning, a shape appears to the right of his peripheral vision and he's thumped in the side. All the breath has gone from him as he hurtles down to the sand. He lies on his side gasping for air. Half a metre from his face is Christof's face also on its side, staring with wide, anxious eyes into his.

'Enough, boss. That's enough.'

9

The Entertainer

Berlin is sweltering. The windows hang wide. He moons about the apartment in his corduroys and old white shirt. His mother's forbidden him to put on his newly pressed uniform until it's time to leave. The Führer doesn't keep military hours so Jochen's not expected to arrive until the afternoon.

Ghosts fill his mind: Ilse, Renate, Franz. He touches his side. His ribs are still sore where Christof slammed into him. Later, in the tent, Christof told him that in Kenya someone would have shot him on the spot for assaulting a white man in that way, hammering him into the dust like that, but everyone was pleased he had and Jochen himself was grateful. He'd been deranged for a while, unable to see past that view of Beck walking head down towards his tent, not acknowledging Franz's death. But Christof shocked him out of his madness. Lying in the dust, he saw himself riddling Jonny's tent with bullets, shooting him in the forehead; saw the enormity of what he'd just done, the irrevocability of what he was just about to do.

Beck ran up shouting, 'You'll be court-martialled for that. You're a madman.'

'And you're a murderer, sending Udo up to look after Franz!'

They might have come to blows, with Beck destroying Jochen, but Winter was finally there and he settled everything with a couple of crisp commands. 'Jochen, get a bag together. You're out on tonight's transport. Jonny, come and have some coffee.'

Through the window he watches an old lady in black with a laden string bag hobbling slowly down the street under the lime trees. A horse, just skin and bones, trudges along dragging an empty cart. It'll never move the cart when it's been loaded up but the driver looks too ancient to load it anyway.

When he goes back, what? Will they send him to a different unit? To Russia? Or post Beck away? Franz won't be there, so he doesn't much care what happens. Except he cares about Jurg and Hans. And Christof. It would be impossible to take him somewhere else. And what *would* happen to him if Jochen wasn't around?

He must write to Franz's fiancée. But what is there he can say? He was as good as murdered by his superior officer? It will come out as the usual bland clichés. A quick death, no suffering. A wonderful guy. But it *was* a quick death. Violent but quick. And he *was* a wonderful guy.

Hitler's breath stinks. Jochen has to force himself not to recoil. It distracts him from the glory of the moment: Hitler hanging the Knight's Cross with Oak Leaves and Swords at Jochen's throat. The teeth are brown and stumpy he sees as Hitler congratulates him. He follows him into another room where they sit in adjacent armchairs. An orderly offers coffee but Hitler will have none so Jochen refuses. He knows Hitler doesn't smoke so he doesn't either.

'Very hot and the flies are terrible,' he says when Hitler asks about the desert.

'And the English?'

'Worse than the flies. We swat them but there are always more.'

'They're a persistent race.'

'And patient. They have a sport that takes five days to play and sometimes no one has won at the end. It wouldn't suit Germans.'

'I never wanted to fight Britain,' Hitler says. 'We're too similar. We should be dividing the world between us.'

It's a strange interlude with Hitler. He's weird to be with but has undeniable charm. The invitation to a private interview is highly flattering and his sincerity is obvious.

'I've met one or two Englishmen as prisoners and men from their Empire, too,' Jochen says. 'On the whole they seem very likeable.'

He'd like to pass on Kendall's opinion that the Reich has no chance now the Americans are in the war but knows it wouldn't go down well.

Hitler asks about Luftwaffe equipment in the desert.

'We need radar out there,' he says, 'then we could fly straight at the enemy instead of wasting time patrolling, hoping to come across them. And we need faster and more heavily armed fighters.'

'We have a lot of calls upon our resources.'

'Of course, Herr Reich Chancellor.'

'You've done exceptionally well, Murville. The Reich will have need of men like you after the war.'

'I don't imagine I'll still be around, though.'

There's a reception later. With whisky. He has one, then another. Goering enters, looks around the room and storms over, red in the face.

'What do you mean by telling the Führer what you need in the desert?'

'He asked for my opinion.'

'Leutnants don't have opinions. Your answer should have been, "Everything is more than satisfactory."' Goering stomps off.

At dinner, Goering seems to have forgotten his anger and pulls Jochen over to sit next to him. Jochen continues with whisky since it's disappeared from his favourite club. He's astonished to see that Goering's fingernails are shiny. Nail varnish? And when he leans his head towards Jochen's to speak, a definite flowered scent comes off the Reichsmarschall.

'Murville's an unusual name for a German,' Goering says.

'It's Huguenot. The Prussians gave us refuge in the seventeenth century when the French were intent on massacring us all.'

Goering is beaming. 'Goering is a Huguenot name, too. We share the same heritage.'

There's little sign of the war at dinner; steak with excellent wine, and afterwards, Goering lights a cigar and waxes lyrical about his time as a chase pilot on the Western Front. Everyone listens. 'Oh, it was fun, the camaraderie, the thrill of the chase. How I wish I could be up there with you hunting the British again. What do you think, Murville, could your unit spare a 109 for me?'

Jochen looks at him for a moment, at the stomach resting against the table's edge, at the extra-sized chair that Goering fills. 'It might be a bit of a tight fit, Herr Reichsmarschall.'

Goering's eyes pop. One or two at the table glance at each other. But Goering gives a snort of laughter and cuffs Jochen round the head. 'You cheeky young bleeder! Well, all right, I might need to lose a kilo or two but it would be fun.'

At Lotte's he's feted. Her father opens a brandy hoarded for a special occasion and they all toast him. Anna kisses his cheek and calls him brother. Her mother kisses him on both cheeks and then lightly on the lips, which disturbs him. When they're alone together, Lotte kisses him properly.

'What's that?' he can finally ask. She's wearing a small badge pinned above her left breast. There's a swastika on it below a German eagle.

'The National Socialist Teachers' League. I'm a member now.'

'Why?'

'The headmaster said I should join. He said it was my duty as a German teacher.'

'I don't like to see you wearing a swastika.'

'You do.'

'It's my uniform.'

'This is part of my uniform. As a teacher.'

'So you're almost a National Socialist.'

'Of course. What do you think I teach but National Socialism?'

'No. Of course.'

But he hasn't thought that. He's imagined Lotte teaches her kids history, geography, sums, spelling and all that, as he was taught. But she's telling them about Jews and their evil ways and Aryanism and all the rest of it. He feels winded. Jonny Beck would laugh at his naivety.

'I should go home and see my mother.'

'Oh.' Lotte's face has fallen.

'I've barely spoken to her since I got back.'

She recovers and smiles. 'Yes, you must.'

'How many?' Bauer says.

'A hundred and one.'

'Good grief!'

Jochen laughs but his mother has an anxious look. 'And they all thought they were invincible.'

'I suppose so.'

'Are they all dead?'

'Christa!' Bauer says.

'Not all. I've met some of them. Got their addresses. I'll go and visit after the war. New Zealand, Kenya, Budleigh Salterton.'

His mother has a cherry brandy but it goes straight to her head and she turns in.

'Heinecke?' Jochen says when they're alone.

'It was him, for sure,' Bauer says. 'The Vienna police found a hotel clerk who recognised his description so we pulled Heinecke in and questioned him again, and lo and behold the next day the clerk turned up at Vienna police HQ and begged to change his statement, said he'd been confused, said the man he'd seen had been much shorter and limped and only put spectacles on to sign the register. And of course, Heinecke didn't use his own name.'

'How did he come to change his statement?'

'Heinecke phoned his brother, I expect, and he got on to someone in Vienna who paid a visit to the clerk, who then realised his error. You can't blame him.'

'Fingerprints. Isn't that what the police always use?'

'We would but there weren't any to find. You need shiny surfaces.'

'No other Sherlock Holmes stuff?'

'No. We're not going to get him into a court, Jochen.'

'But he had that bandage afterwards. Ilse must have scratched his face to shreds.'

'He had an explanation for that.'

'He was out of circulation for days.'

'Ill. Doctor's certificate.'

'Although there was no reason to have a doctor's certificate.'

'He'd find a reason.'

'You know his address, I suppose.'

'Yes, but I'm not telling you. I don't want you doing anything stupid.'

'It wouldn't be stupid.'

'Go out and have a drink, it's early yet. Take your mind off it.'

'Not called up yet?' he says to Otto when he takes him a brandy during the break. Otto moves over and Jochen plays lounge music in his place while they talk.

'They must have forgotten about me.'

'Have you seen her?'

'She's still about. I had a word with her the last time. She's frightened but I think she trusts me. She said if only she could get out of the country. She's saved your money for that.'

'I've got some more for her.'

He slides an envelope from a pocket and holds it at his side. Otto takes it without looking down. Jochen carries on playing.

'Getting out? Switzerland? All those mountains. She'd never make it. And two borders to cross.'

'No. She'd need a guide. Same language, though. That would help.'

'She speaks some Polish. She said she has some relatives there,' Jochen says.

'Poland wouldn't really be an escape, would it? And are the relatives still there?'

There's a new photo session to mark his Oak Leaves. The photographer remembers him. It's the same routine. He feels like a prize poodle. He attends several parties; many officers in splendid uniforms and women in gowns that just about cover them. Where is the war here? There have been no proper raids on Berlin this year, just half a dozen alerts that came to nothing and one or two raids by ineffective Russian bombers. He feels out of place at parties and even more uncomfortable than he does at large in Berlin, so far from his unit. Several times he's about to ask when he's going back but there are constant suggestions of plans for him.

He visits a Messerschmitt plant with Willi Messerschmitt himself and talks to men on the assembly line, thanks them for their hard work. Wendel the test pilot is there. To Jochen's amazement Wendel tells him how envious he is of Jochen and his success in Africa. After a quick introduction by Wendel, Jochen takes up the latest 109, a Gustav. Faster but heavier than a Friedrich, a slower turn, too, but no 109 can turn with a Spitfire anyway.

At another party he meets Leni Riefenstahl. He's seen her Olympics film and the one about Hitler and the National Socialists. He agrees to meet her again and do some filming. They dance and she folds herself against him.

He talks to schoolchildren and has many photographs taken which will appear in magazines. He sits among a sea of boys in their Hitler Youth uniforms. Is he joining the circus? He can't see how he can refuse the invitations; they're really commands rephrased without an imperative.

At night he takes to sleeping in Ilse's bed. He feels calmer there. He lies wide awake in the dark for hours it seems, tapping the ash from endless cigarettes into the ashtray on his chest. Heinecke he thinks about, always Heinecke, unless it's Gerda. He sees her stumbling in driving snow across a mountain pass to reach Switzerland.

He receives a couple of invitations to bring Lotte along to parties. He doesn't pass the invitations on. He doesn't know what to make of her now. He's glad they have no opportunity to sleep together. He would feel dishonest doing that now. He doesn't know if he can marry her. How could he live with someone who teaches children all that vile muck about people like that good man Herr Walter and Herr Gold, who tuned the pianos of Berlin and would sit in the Murville living room pressing piano key after piano key in a dream of sound? But of course, he thinks at three o'clock one morning, he won't be marrying Lotte. He won't be around to marry her.

He sees Leni Riefenstahl again at the next party. When he wakes between her silk sheets, she's sitting in an armchair staring at him. A lamp in the corner throws shadows over her bare body. Her legs are crossed. The smoke from her cigarette trails up across her breasts and then her face.

'I want to make an aviation drama with you,' she says when she sees his eyes are open. He pulls himself up in the bed. 'It will take three months. I'm sure the Führer will allow you the time.'

'I can't act.'

'You won't have to act. Just be yourself. The public will go wild for you.'

'Do you think there'll be a market for your film in a year or two when the Americans are in Berlin?'

She laughs. 'How can you say that?'

'Don't you think they will be?'

'Be careful who you say that to. You could get yourself shot.'

'I don't want to be in your film, Leni. I need to be at the front. Find someone else.'

Goering invites him to his hunting lodge; boar and deer. He can't shoot deer, they're too magnificent. What is the point in shooting them unless it's to eat? Four go down to other guns. One would be enough for twenty dinners. He shoots a boar. Boar are ugly enough.

Goering has a change of clothes for every occasion. Hunting clothes, a feather in his hat; a white uniform for ceremonial parades; field grey with gold everywhere for meetings with subordinates. Who is running the Luftwaffe while Goering is changing uniforms and shooting wild animals and enjoying large and long dinners, smoking cigars and drinking schnapps?

He's been back two weeks and been too busy to see much of Lotte. Her school year is coming to an end.

'I'll be off with the children in the countryside again soon,' she says. He plays chess with her father, has more discussions with Anna about the physiological effects of flying and avoids being alone in the room with her mother.

He relents and one Saturday evening takes Lotte to a party at the Goebbels'. Lotte spends all afternoon getting ready with her mother in attendance. A car arrives for them. Lotte is very nervous and clutches his hand.

'They're just people,' he says, to reassure her. 'You were fine with the Goebbels at that concert.'

'I had no time to think about it that evening.'

He brings her in; marble steps, a marble floor. He hands over his cap. Magda Goebbels sweeps Lotte off. Jochen gets a drink and takes a cigarette from a limping army leutnant that he's seen at parties before. He nods to Leni across the room. She nods back and swings her head towards Lotte, smiles and nods her head in appreciation. He smiles back. Food appears, more drink. A small band plays. There's dancing. He takes Lotte around the floor. She dances well but Ilse danced better. An SS hauptmann interrupts and takes Lotte off. Leni comes over. They dance. 'Not too close,' he says. Lotte and he are back together when the music stops and heels click and salutes are thrown up. Applause begins as the Führer moves further into the room. He greets several people, kisses a hand here and there, and Goebbels takes Jochen and Lotte over to him. He kisses Lotte's hand. 'My dear,' he says. Lotte is unable to speak.

'Didn't I tell you they are the perfect Aryan couple?'

Hitler nods.

Later, Goebbels says, 'Leutnant, the Führer has heard that you play well. Would you play for us?' Another order phrased as a request.

He sits, plays a note to check the tuning, the sound is impeccable, and plays *Fur Elise*; Beethoven, a safe choice and short. Hitler is beaming at the end. He plays Chopin, not quite so safe but Poland is German now so presumably acceptable. He spots the score of Schubert's *B Flat Sonata* on a pile by the piano. It's too long to play complete at a party so he plays only the exuberant movement. There is loud applause led by the Führer and Magda Goebbels. Jochen grins around at everyone. Lotte gazes at him with shining proprietorial eyes. Leni is standing just behind Lotte. He sees her lean forward and say something in her ear. Lotte turns and smiles. He pauses for a moment running tunes through his head, has an idea, thinks no, but then, why not?

The first notes confuse the room. People look from one to another. After a few syncopated bars Hitler stands up, says something to Goebbels and moves off towards the door. He nods to Jochen on his way out. There are horrified looks on some faces; others are trying to hide grins. Magda Goebbels is laughing.

'What is that?' he hears a woman behind him ask.

'Ragtime,' a man says.

Jochen keeps his eyes down and plays to the end when he stands with a flourish and announces the piece to the room. 'That piece is called *The Entertainer* and was written by a wonderful American composer, Scott Joplin.'

There is only a smattering of applause but Magda calls out, 'Bravo,' and Jochen bows to her.

The SS hauptmann who danced with Lotte is nearby and he smiles at Jochen while shaking his head. 'I don't know, you Luftwaffe types!' he says.

'Why did you play that? That jungle music?' Lotte asks on their way home.

'I wanted to suddenly. It's a cheerful entertaining melody.'

'But it's by an American.'

'And he's black.'

She gasps.

'That doesn't make it bad.'

'Doesn't it?'

'It's music, Lotte.'

They go on in silence.

'Will you come in?' she says at her door.

'It's late.' They peck each other on the lips and he leaves.

The bar is about to close and Otto is putting the lid of the piano down. They have a brandy together. Jochen tells him about the party.

'That thing won't keep you safe forever,' Otto says. He means the Knight's Cross at Jochen's throat. 'What would the general say?'

'"Don't join the circus."'

'Good advice.'

'It was only Scott Joplin.'

'You don't have to be naïve, Kid, just because you're only twenty-one.'

He leaves with Otto and goes his way. Otto responds to his questions.

'I was in the States before the last war. Came home in '14, thought I ought to. I was in Russia six months later. Afterwards I went to Paris for a few years. I said I was American; it went down better. It was only Americans who could tell I wasn't. Paris was nice. It always is. Did you get there?'

'Passed through. I didn't have time to really see it. Later.'

'Take Lotte when we've won.'

'Huh!'

'Oh, dear.'

He tells Otto everything.

'Don't be too hard. She's only a kid, too. She's immersed in it. And the headmaster told her it's her duty to join that mob. She hasn't got your distractions. I expect the last thing you and your mates think about is National Socialist doctrine when you're dodging the English and wondering when the next drink's coming along.'

Jochen laughs. 'You must have been a chase pilot, Otto.'

'I wish. Stuck in the mud, I was. You'd better leave me here or you might see where the widow lives.'

'In my head she's always shambling through the snow over a mountain pass to Switzerland.'

They stop. Otto will go no further with Jochen.

'Look,' Otto says, 'there might be another way.' They talk for several minutes more and then part. Jochen hurries home in the dark.

He drives around with Leni to various places. She films him. It's never intimate. There are always camera and sound men there. She's quite imperious in her manner when filming. She get shots of him chatting to a ground crew, climbing into a Friedrich and taxiing out of shot. She enthuses to him afterwards about his naturalness on camera but he says he's still not interested in her aviation film.

A letter arrives from Harri. Jochen's letter finally got to him and after weeks, Harri's has reached Jochen. Harri was very keen on Ilse and he's heartbroken. As Jochen imagined, he'd had hopes, all gone now. There are thoughts for their mother and for him. Harri knows Ilse was like his other half. He says there's nothing to do now but their duty, nothing to hope for but to get through this horror, what for, he isn't sure, except that the alternative is worse.

Franz's fiancée Irene writes, too, also heartbroken. She thanks him for his thoughts and the several little stories of Franz he included in his letter, things about their lives in the desert that she would never have known otherwise. She tells him how highly Franz thought of him, what a good friend and comrade he was. Though he won't now be their best man, she hopes one day to meet him. She prays for his safety. The letters bring him down very low.

Despite the Scott Joplin, he's still invited to parties. He doesn't take Lotte. He plays once or twice but he sticks to Beethoven and Schubert. He drinks, smokes and dances with whoever's around. One evening, at nearly midnight, he leans against a wall with a cigarette and a spritzer to cool him down. A couple of chairs close by are occupied by an oberst and a general. The alcohol has made them loud. He can't avoid hearing every word they say.

'January the twentieth it was, at a villa on the Wannsee.'

'And everything's decided?'

'Yes.'

'Is it all of them?'

'All of them. There won't be a single one left in a year or so, all shipped east and disposed of.'

'It'll come down to the railways then. Timetable work.'

'The tracks run straight into the camps.'

'Most convenient. Very efficient. No wasted effort.'

'Very German.'

They both laugh.

'Think of the saving in food.'

'And yellow cloth. There'll be no more need for it. What a splendid solution.'

'And there'll be so much salvage. Shoes, clothes, glasses.'

'Gold teeth!'

'They won't be needing them any longer!'

They laugh again.

Jochen is rigid, staring ahead at the chandelier in the middle of the room. He forces himself to move, takes a sip of his spritzer. Disposed of. Saving in food. Gold teeth. Yellow cloth! He closes his eyes.

'Are you all right, Leutnant?'

They've stood up, the general and the oberst. They're in front of him. The general has a caring voice.

'Yes, thank you, sir.'

'A drop too much, perhaps.'

'Probably, sir.'

'Take more water with it,' the oberst says.

'Go and stick your finger down your throat, son,' the caring general says. He and the oberst move off towards the bar.

He has a vision of hundreds of ragged people shuffling down ramps from cattle trucks; they'll surely never supply passenger carriages for those who are to be disposed of, ragged people like the woman, the child and the old man hustled onto that truck in the street that day, supervised by the SS leutnant, fingered by Heinecke. Herr Gold, Herr Walter, his overcoat flapping around him like wings that are unable to fly him away from this scene of horror. And then what? Machine-gunned? But they won't want those precious clothes to have bullet holes or be stained with blood. Strip! Clothes in piles! Strip! Men, women, children, all together, shamingly, moments before death? Machine-gunned bodies everywhere, scattered around, all to be buried. But first to be gathered up. Not very efficient, the oberst would say, not very German. Get them in a pit first. He feels suddenly sick. None of this is very German. None of it is at all German. He puts his glass down and hurries out. He gets there just in time, but with no time to close the door, just to fling up the seat as his gorge rises and hurls the drinks and his dinner out of him and into the lavatory pan. He crouches there, still retching, his mouth bitter with bile as the general walks by.

'You've got rid of it then, Leutnant. Excellent. I'll be at the bar. I'll buy you a drink.'

Jochen leans against the tiled wall with a hand to his cheek. He feels weak. 'I think I should go home, sir.'

'You youngsters! No bottom. As you like.'

Jochen flushes the pan, closes the door and lowers the seat. He sits and leans over to cool his forehead on the tiles to his right.

Thousands and thousands. How many are there in Germany? Millions? And will it be just from Germany or all the occupied lands? So many lives snuffed out, families destroyed. Names that have lived over hundreds of years, gone forever! How many composers, artists, engineers, mathematicians, good family men and women will die? He imagines all the families and the children's families who will never be, all wiped from the pages of history. How right Gerda was to hide. Gerda! In all these thoughts of horror, he hasn't remembered her. She won't be safe in hiding when this new plan gets into its stride. That oberst who loves efficiency or someone like him will root her out, force her to strip on a railway siding and shoot her down where she stands.

He leaves the cubicle and washes his face, washes his mouth out. He picks up his cap at the door and hurries down the marble stairs, so many marble stairs in Berlin, and makes his way to the club and Otto.

In the morning when he's alone in the apartment, he takes Ilse's identity card from her handbag in the drawer their mother put it in when Bauer brought it back from Vienna. Her travel pass to Austria is also there. He takes that, too, just in case. He writes a note to Gerda explaining everything, signs it 'J' and puts some money in with it. He gives the note and the cards to Otto that evening. His promotion to oberleutnant is through and he wears the new insignia.

'General before you know it, I suppose,' Otto says.

'Not many in the Luftwaffe live that long,' Jochen says. 'Look, I could be posted back any day, so tell your guy to be as quick as he can.'

'He knows it's urgent but he can't rush it. What he's going to do needs care.'

His mother's in bed. She's far better during the day than she was but takes early refuge in a pill and sleep when the sun goes. He waits up for Bauer. They talk over a couple of brandies.

'You ought to go easy on the sauce at your age,' Bauer tells him.

'The doc says it thins the blood and that helps me stay conscious in tight turns.'

Jochen tells him about the conversation he overhead at the party. Bauer looks shocked.

'Could you have misunderstood them?'

'I really don't think so.'

Bauer stares at him. 'A Jew saved my life in Belgium. He pulled me out of a shell hole when I'd slipped off the duckboards. The mud had got hold of me. Another ten seconds and I'd have been begging him to shoot me before I drowned. You know, Jochen, I get these orders across my desk sometimes; pick someone up. It's not really our job but it happens. We can't avoid it. It's an order. There's one of our guys who'll tell people to run if he can get there before the pick-up squad. I make sure he knows when an order's come in. Then I look the other way. He's braver than me. You can't talk about it. You never really know what anybody thinks, how they'll react. It's an individual thing. You might be picked up yourself. So this is where it all ends, is it? A railway truck and a machine gun. God help us all!'

Jochen tells him what he intends to do but without any details. What Bauer doesn't know can't be beaten out of him.

'Just in case you think all this is normal,' Bauer says, 'this is not what things are supposed to be like, you know. When I was your age, life was good. No rationing, no war, no blackout, no looking over your shoulder all the time. 1912. It was a nice summer: beer to drink, girls to dance with, work to go to in the morning. But all right, I'll do what you want.'

'And,' Jochen goes on but Bauer refuses again and again. Jochen has to keep on at him, badger him. 'It has to be done and it's my place to do it,' he says. 'Just help me out a bit.'

Bauer gives in.

'I will keep investigating him,' he says.

'I know. But it must happen now.'

He and Lotte finally go to another party together. She beams as their picture is taken. He hears his father's disapproval in his head. They dance, eat a buffet supper. Lotte glances over her plate at him often and smiles each time. Afterwards in her living room, she asks why he has changed. He doesn't know how to reply. 'Your swastika,' isn't a sufficient answer. He can't tell her about the conversation he heard and therefore everything he sees hidden behind the swastika that he'd imagined she was innocent of. What can he say?

'I suppose it's my fault,' she says. 'I went to bed with you so now you don't want me. You're a man like all the others.'

He shakes his head. 'No, no. Not that.' He honestly doesn't know what it is he's feeling. Lotte's joined this teachers' organisation, but really how could she not with the headmaster telling her to? She's just a kid like him. How can she say no to the headmaster? She doesn't even have Jochen's arrogance to help her.

'It's me. I'm stupid. I'm naïve,' he says. 'I was always thinking of you in your classroom teaching those kids of yours sums and spelling and folk songs. But actually you're teaching them how bad the Jews are and what makes a perfect Aryan.'

'It's the curriculum.'

'Yes. I realise that now. I hadn't thought before. It's years since I was in a classroom. What else can you do?'

'But what else would I do? I know those pictures we use to show how debased Jews look are all exaggerated, but only to make the point, to make it clear to the children how bad Jews are, how evil.'

'Evil.'

'Yes.'

'And Aryans are tall and slim and fair?'

'Yes.'

'Like Hitler and Goering and Goebbels.'

'What are you saying?'

He looks at her. So beautiful. 'I don't know. I really don't know, Lotte.'

'Don't break us up, Jochen.'

'No.' The war will do that. 'I have to go. Riefenstahl wants more pictures of me tomorrow.'

'Be careful of her. Don't let her steal you. She thinks you're remarkable. She told me. But you should do that film she wants you for.'

'My friends are dying in the desert, Lotte. How can I?'

When he gets to the club, Otto shakes his head and says, 'Not yet. Patience.'

Leni films him talking to ground crew again, walking across tarmac, then doing it again because the light was wrong or some such nonsense. How could anyone bear to spend three months at this sort of malarkey? You stand around chatting and smoking most of the day and then do something for fifteen or twenty seconds and then do it twice more and then once more for luck. You'd want to shoot yourself.

That evening, Otto nods to him when he comes in. He takes two brandies over when Otto has his break. Jochen plays. To any observer they're discussing music and musicianship.

'They're ready. I'll get them to her. But are you sure,' she says. She's worried it's too dangerous for you.'

'What are they going to do? Send me to Russia?'

They talk details; when and where to meet. It's months since he saw Gerda. He's excited. He'd like to talk to someone about her. But there's no one.

He waits up for Bauer and tells him he's ready. On his way to the bank the next morning he posts a letter to Franz's mother. At the bank counter he slides three thousand Reichmarks, nearly a year's pay, into an envelope and the envelope into his inside pocket. He's got about RM500 left in the account. He walks to Berlin Central, warming himself under admiring glances and smiles from girls, and checks departure times. There's a train in the morning and one in the evening.

At home, there's a small bundle on the table in his room. He lifts back the flaps of the cloth wrapping and checks out what's inside. Then he wraps it again and puts the bundle in a drawer together with the envelope of money. He rings Leni and tells her he can't manage the filming scheduled for two days' time. He meets Lotte from school and walks her home. He joins the family for dinner. Anna is working. He plays for them afterwards, Chopin and Schubert.

'Play that thing that Lotte says you played at the Goebbels', her mother says.

'Mother!'

'Oh, Lotte, it's all right. It's only us.'

He plays *The Entertainer*. Her mother smiles at him all the way through.

'Charming,' she says. 'I've never heard it before. I like it. The rhythm is captivating and it's so cheerful. We can all do with a bit of cheering up. Thank you, Jochen.' She puts her hand on his cheek.

When her parents have gone to bed, he tells Lotte he'll be gone for a couple of days. He's going to see Franz's family.

'Can't I come? I'd like to meet them. You've told me so much about him.'

'I need to go now and you're still at work. I can't wait. I might be posted back any day. They don't consider anyone's arrangements. And anyway, I'd hate to turn up with you, all happy and with a future, and make them think again about what might have been with Franz and Irene.'

'Oh, of course. That's very sensitive, Jochen.' He leaves, feeling like a heel.

At home, not knowing his plans, his mother has left him some soup. Handy. He goes to his bedroom, takes the gun from the bundle in the drawer, puts it in his pocket just in case and goes to the club. When it closes, he walks back with Otto.

'I live up there,' Otto says, and points, but they turn right and then left, enter a building and go up some stairs. Otto taps on a door. They hear steps on the other side.

'It's us,' Otto says.

The door opens. 'I'm ready.'

Gerda comes out. She's carrying a large bag. She gives him her wide smile. It's as exciting as ever. They go down the stairs as quietly as possible and into the street.

'I'm going this way,' Otto says.

'Thank you, Otto,' Gerda says.

'See you in a day or two,' Jochen says.

'Of course, Kid.'

They start walking. The moon pops out from time to time and that makes walking easier, but anyway, Gerda takes Jochen's arm. That's exciting, too.

'Why didn't you want to go straight from where I'm living?'

'You need to make a good impression. From what Otto said I thought that might be difficult if we went straight off. You're travelling with a hero of the Reich, remember. You have to look the part.'

'Am I that bad?'

'You're as beautiful as ever.'

The streets are empty. It's a half-hour walk. The trams have stopped. There are no taxis. They talk quietly.

'Why are you doing this, Jochen?'

'I can't bear the thought of your being taken away. The whole thing is… inhuman. Do they know you're still around?'

'Before I left the flat you came to, the postman turned up with another letter for me. It looked the same as the one that told me to report. He didn't know me so I told him that person wasn't around; she'd already reported. He wrote "gone east" on the letter and took it back with him.'

'So they think they've got you already.'

'I hope so.'

He opens the door, glances around. His mother is still asleep after her pill.

Gerda puts down her bag and takes her shoes off to be quieter.

'Lovely place,' Gerda says.

'Hungry?'

'Always.'

'This way.' He leads her into the kitchen and heats up the soup.

'Ooh,' Gerda moans at the first mouthful. 'Sorry, it's so lovely.'

He watches her eat. She shuts her eyes with each spoonful she puts in her mouth.

She looks at him finally and realises something. 'Is this your soup?'

'Mother made it for me but I had dinner. It's all for you.'

When the soup's gone, he gets out some bread and cheese. She has a slice of each. He enjoys watching her eat. Her hunger is very sensual. He imagines her teeth moving behind her closed lips. She stops.

'More?'

'I'll be ill if I have more. I've forgotten what good food is like. I'm not used to it now.'

They look at each other.

'Where is it?' she says.

He points down the hall. 'Second door.'

When she comes back, she says, 'Everything's so lovely here. You can't imagine how wonderful it is to use a civilised lavatory. That hole I've been living in!'

'We'd better go to bed.'

She follows him to his room and glances round it, takes in its look. 'But this must be yours.'

'I've been sleeping in my sister's room.'

'Oh.' He hasn't mentioned Ilse but he knows Otto told her. 'I suppose you feel closer to her there.'

'Something like that.' He turns to go.

'Won't you stay?'

'I'm engaged, Gerda.'

'Oh.' This must be new information. 'Does she know I'm here?'

'No.'

'Does she know about me?'

'No.'

'Can't you stay? For a while. I'd like you to.'

He follows her in.

His mother shakes his shoulder to wake him. He's in Ilse's room now.

'Jochen, there's a girl in your room. I went to ask if you wanted coffee and there's a girl there in your bed. It isn't Lotte.'

'I'll be out and explain,' he says. He pulls on some clothes and joins his mother in the kitchen. She's poured out a cup of the muck they drink now but still call coffee. He tells her briefly.

'A Jew! What are you thinking of bringing her here? Does Lotte know?'

'Only you and Rolf.'

'Rolf knows? What's he thinking of?'

'He's being a human.'

'But he's not here!'

'I told him to make one of his trips. He shouldn't know anything about it in his position.'

'So the pair of you are in cahoots! And what about my position?'

He feels bad, springing this on his mother, as he imagined he would. But he didn't want to give her time to think, to worry, to argue.

'Do you love her?'

'I don't know.'

'What about Lotte?'

'I don't know.'

There's a step at the door. Gerda is there. Bare feet, bare legs, her shabby coat pulled quickly on; above it, unkempt dark hair around her bare and beautiful face.

'Frau Bauer, excuse me. I feared this wasn't a good idea. Give me a few minutes and I'll be gone.' She turns.

'Gerda, stop,' Jochen calls but she doesn't. He goes after her, turns at the door, 'Mother, pour some more coffee, please.' He brings Gerda back, sits her down, puts the coffee into her hands.

'Mother,' he says, 'if we don't help Gerda, they'll find her and put her on a train somewhere, to some hell-hole no one returns from. She was married to a panzer commander. He died for the Reich. She had a pension but they stopped it when they discovered she's a Jew. And what's her crime? Being born to her parents? We're all guilty of that.'

His mother is staring at him. 'We couldn't save Ilse,' he says, 'but we can save Gerda.' His mother stands and walks out, goes to her room. They hear the door close.

'I must go,' Gerda says.

'No.' He gets her bread, margarine, cheese, conserve. 'Eat. Have some more coffee.' He drinks his own. They sit in silence, drinking and eating.

'Your poor mother,' Gerda says after a while, 'you shouldn't put her through this. Let me go.'

He shakes his head. She puts their plates and cups together in the sink to wash; Jochen puts the food away. They don't hear his mother come back.

'There's a bath running, Gerda. And you should wash your hair. Jochen, clear out of Ilse's room. You use it, Gerda.

Have a look in the wardrobe; there are lots of things to wear. You're about the right size. There's underwear, there's make-up in a drawer if you want it. Use anything you like.'

They leave as darkness is falling. Jochen carries Gerda's bag. It belonged to Ilse. He has a bag, too. His Swords and Oak Leaves is in his pocket. There are so few of them around that if he wore the decoration, it would make him too easy to recognise. The two Iron Crosses are enough to gain immediate respect. Gerda is used to skulking in shadows. Now she's hiding in plain view at Jochen's side. She's very nervous. She wants to walk in the dark and not take the underground or a tram.

'No one will notice you,' Jochen told her. 'They'll all be looking at me.' He humours her, though, and they stride out arm in arm while the light is good enough for speed. He's just got his torch out to help them along when a siren goes off. They continue on their way, ignoring the people hurrying for shelter. They're not far from the whisky club. Searchlights play across the black sky. There are no engines to be heard, though.

'Another false alarm, I expect,' Jochen says.

A policeman suddenly confronts them. 'There's a public shelter over there.' He points.

'We need to get on.'

'Don't be foolhardy, sir. Think of the young lady.'

Jochen gives way. He's wary of making a fuss that might be remembered.

He leads Gerda down the dark steps to the shelter below. A bare lightbulb hangs by a wire and gives a poor light. The seats along the wall are largely occupied by women. Chivalry still exists. Men and some women stand around, talk, smoke, stare over shoulders at nothing. He keeps hold of their bags; the floor is too filthy to put them down. People continue to arrive.

'We'll stay a few minutes,' he says. 'That cop will have gone soon, I expect.' He flicks his eyes around the room and with a shock catches sight of a figure he recognises facing away from them. He turns away himself. He doesn't want to move now. It might attract attention. But it doesn't work.

'Leutnant,' he hears above the conversation of the shelter. He turns. Heinecke is there and has a shocked expression, too. He's staring at Gerda. 'I thought for a moment you were someone I know.'

'Used to know,' Jochen says. 'My mother's passed Ilse's coat on. And it's oberleutnant, now.'

Heinecke continues to stare at Gerda. He'll certainly remember her face. 'Congratulations. But where's your Knight's Cross?'

'It can be embarrassing to wear it in public. People sometimes stare.'

'The price of fame. Aren't you going to introduce me?'

'No.'

'Why ever not?'

'We have to go.'

'During a raid?'

'A false alarm, I'm sure. The British have other targets at present.'

'It might be the Russians up there.'

'Anything's possible. Let's go,' he says to Gerda.

She takes his arm and they move towards the door. People shuffle out of their way.

Heinecke creeps out beside them. On the pavement, Jochen stops for a moment to get used to the darkness. Gerda still clutches his arm. Searchlights cross the black. They shed little light on the streets far below them. There are engines now in the sky whose sound he doesn't recognise. Perhaps it *is* the Russians. Here and there the skyline lights up instants before the sound of the explosions arrive. Guns are firing. There's a constant faraway crump, crump but occasionally a much louder crack comes from somewhere nearby.

Jochen is struck by the moment. It will never be better. He makes an instant decision as he might in the air.

'Stay here, in that doorway,' he says to Gerda. He pushes the bags into her hands. 'I'll be back very soon.' He's moved away before she can protest. His right hand is in his tunic pocket holding the Beretta .32 automatic that Bauer got for him.

The bullets, if ever examined, will be clearly different to those of his Luftwaffe issue Walther .38. His left hand takes Heinecke's elbow. 'Let's have a private word.'

'What about?' Heinecke says as Jochen guides him on and around a corner into a side street. The distant crumps from the flak still come every few seconds, together with the sharper cracks from the guns that are closer. Explosions and searchlights throw just enough light down into the street to illuminate each face from time to time.

'Just a word about my sister.'

'A lovely girl.'

'Then why did you kill her?'

'What?'

'You were recognised at a hotel in Vienna. And Ilse wrote to tell me she'd seen you in the street. She scraped your face with her nails and I saw your cheek all plastered up, remember.'

'Is that supposed to be proof?'

'Good enough for me.'

'Wouldn't I have been put on trial if this proof was so good?'

'These are bad times for justice. Think of this conversation as your trial.'

'Very interesting, Oberleutnant, but I have things to do.'

'Jochen!' Gerda calls from the doorway.

'Interesting girl,' Heinecke says. 'Interesting face. A touch degenerate-looking, though, wouldn't you say? Very unlike your own dear Lotte.'

While speaking Jochen has realised his sudden decision was an error. His hand is on the gun in his tunic pocket. He can shoot Heinecke now as he's planned to; stick the Beretta in his stomach and fire, then a bullet to the brain when he's down. The explosions and the flak will cover the sound of the shots. But the body will be found at first light before Gerda's safely out of Germany and people in that shelter have seen him talk to Heinecke, seen them leave together. Someone might have recognised him from one of those postcards, even without the Knight's Cross. He can't endanger Gerda's escape. He'll have to use the gun when he's back.

'Goodbye, Heinecke. On your way.'

Heinecke spins round and disappears into the darkness. Jochen walks back to Gerda. 'We'd better step out. You never know, it might leave on time.'

'Where's your friend?'

'He had to get on.'

Gerda doesn't speak again. The sound of her heels marks the speed of their walking. He can hear her breathing.

'Too fast?'

'No.' She's quiet again for a while. 'Who was the man in the shelter? He had a strange manner.'

'Well.' He pauses for a moment then tells her what he knows and what he suspects.

She looks around, looks behind as they walk. 'Are we safe?'

'Of course. Don't worry. We're fine.'

Jochen feels almost light-headed. He's told Gerda they're safe. Are they? He should never have started talking to Heinecke if he couldn't shoot him afterwards. Everything's at risk now. He's no good on the ground. His element is the air.

The all-clear sounds as they reach the station. There seem to be police everywhere and there's a pair of threatening-looking men of military age in suits and dark hats. He decides he'll feel more secure wearing his Swords and Oak Leaves. He turns to face a wall and puts it on.

'Half an hour late,' the woman who checks their tickets says. They find a bench and sit to cool off.

'Do you think that man followed us?'

'No,' Jochen says with confidence.

She lays her head on his shoulder.

'We're not lovers here, remember, I'm your dead fiancé's friend.'

'I want to rest my head.'

'Close your eyes, then. Pretend to be asleep. Then your head will just have flopped.'

A policeman salutes him as he passes. Later, another does, too. He nods to them. His exalted status must be protecting Gerda, who would surely have been questioned without him there. After a while, they drink foul coffee in the bar. The train is announced.

Jochen looks right and left down the length of the train as they get in. No one he sees looks like a threat. He puts Gerda in a corner seat and sits next to her. In the old days they could have stared into the back windows of houses and apartment blocks, at gardens, at the beautiful pattern of streetlights extending away from them across Berlin. Now the compartment is blacked out and quickly fugged with tobacco smoke under the weak bulb in the centre of the ceiling. On the walls above head rest height are country views of Northern Germany from the days when people had time to explore outside the town. The compartment is old and the worse for wear, like its occupants: an aged couple in shabby clothes with what could be their dinner in a paper parcel on the woman's lap; a middle-aged woman in glasses, whose clothes have seen better days; a leutnant, no longer young, passed over for promotion and slumped in a far corner on his way back to his unit with a few more than one drink taken.

The train starts and stops. A hundred metres then a wait; a steady pull for twenty minutes, another wait; half an hour of speed when the wheels clackety-clack in a merry way on the tracks; a slowing and another wait. The hands on his watch seem never to move. One hour passes, two hours, three, four, normally enough to have arrived but they haven't. Gerda sleeps. Jochen nods off, wakes, nods off again. No one attempts conversation, thank God.

It's the middle of the night when they slow and pull up.

'Stralsund!' the call goes up. 'Stralsund. Change here for Sassnitz.'

Jochen takes their bags from the rack. He nods at the leutnant as he follows Gerda from the compartment. They climb down from the carriage onto the platform. A white line painted for safety along the edge is just visible. The night air is chilly. The train pulls away as they look around for someone to give them information. They're left in silence.

He finds a man in uniform behind the door he knocks on. Three hours till the first Sassnitz train. Someone selling coffee and rolls should be there half an hour before they leave. They find the lavatories, then the waiting room. It's empty. They have a little bread left and some cheese. They share it and take a sip of brandy. Jochen sits in the corner of one of the solid oak benches and Gerda rests against his side, her head on his shoulder.

'Don't snuggle,' he says. 'I'm just a friend, remember.'

'It's nice to travel with you,' Gerda tells him. 'If I wasn't so anxious, I'd be enjoying myself.'

Time passes slowly.

'Tell me about your fiancée.'

He does.

'But she's a Nazi,' he says finally, and explains.

'What will you do?'

He shrugs. She squeezes his hand.

Once or twice they sleep until discomfort wakes them. They're pacing the platform when the coffee seller arrives. It's not light yet. The coffee and the warm fresh rolls revive them.

A policeman strides up the platform. He salutes Jochen. 'Papers, please. Forgive me, Oberleutnant. I am required to.' Jochen feels a frisson of nerves as the policeman studies Gerda's papers, glances up at her face to check the photograph is correct for Fräulein Ilse Bauer and then hands them back. The rubber stamp outline hand painted by Otto's connection across Gerda's photograph has passed its first test.

The train pulls in. Several more people have arrived. Jochen gets a glance from some but it's far too early for anyone to take an interest in them as they find seats. They soon leave the outskirts of the town and move onto the causeway where the train runs along a few metres above the sea. The water is grey, the sky not much lighter. For a few seconds he watches two Friedrichs cross the width of the window. They leave the causeway and almost at once there are platform railings and signs for Sassnitz and they're pulling up.

Outside, he finds a shadowed corner, moves behind a luggage trolley, takes off his cap and pulls on the old brown overcoat he's brought in his bag. He does the button up at the neck, takes Bauer's shabby fedora from the bag, punches it into shape and puts it on. His boots emerge below the hem of the coat but many men wear similar boots. Gerda looks at him and gives him that smile.

Following Otto's directions they head straight for the sea past the large grey-painted town hall. He glances round to check for anyone trailing them. There's little traffic and just a handful of people on the streets. The main sound is the cries of the gulls that circle and swoop over the quays by the sea. It's strange to imagine Otto growing up in this place and becoming such a musician. They turn left and then right and knock on the door of an old cottage that stands on its own set back a little from the road with a garden full of vegetables in front.

Uwe, who opens the door, has more hair than his brother Otto although he's older. He almost buries his face in the package of real coffee Jochen's brought him. He closes his eyes and breathes in the aroma. 'So lovely,' he says. 'We'll have some.' His wife smiles but says little. She takes Gerda off. He hears their voices. Gerda comes back washed and brushed up. Jochen washes, too, and they drink coffee and eat. There's an upright piano in the corner. Jochen plays a Chopin nocturne. 'Otto said you were good,' Uwe says. He plays a Beethoven bagatelle and then a couple of dance tunes. Gerda laughs. 'What a waste that you're in the Luftwaffe.'

Uwe has a visit to make and his wife goes shopping but first Uwe takes them upstairs to a bedroom where they can wait out of sight of stray callers. Jochen feels suddenly anxious for Gerda's safety after he's left her. He pulls the

Beretta from his tunic pocket. 'I think you should take this, Gerda.'

She stares at him as he goes on.

'Look, you can carry it with a bullet up the spout so all you have to do is take the safety off and it's ready to fire.'

He flicks the safety catch off and on with his thumb to demonstrate. He holds it out and she takes it. It looks much bigger in her hand. She flicks the safety off and then on again but hands it back to him. 'What would I do with it, Jochen? My husband showed me how to shoot with his pistol once but I doubt if I could shoot a person and if it was found on me, how could I explain it?'

Uwe comes back. 'Have you got the money?' he says to Gerda.

She takes it from her bag.

Uwe counts some out and hands the rest back. 'No one's doing it for money, Fräulein, but there are expenses. Have you got enough left?'

Gerda shrugs. 'Who can say?'

Jochen wants to get some air but Uwe thinks they should both stay indoors out of sight. Uwe and his wife have their lives to live, so Jochen and Gerda are alone most of the day in their upstairs room.

'I don't know where my parents are,' Gerda tells him. 'When I got married they didn't want to see me. I think my mother did but my father forbade her. It shocked him that I married outside the faith. A friend of mine used to write with news of them but then she stopped. I think they've probably all gone east.'

Gerda has taken a notepad and pencil from her bag and as she talks, she makes a sketch of Jochen. 'When I left my apartment, I had to move around often but there were people who helped me and I worked in a Daimler factory and for Siemens and that laundry. People go along with the Nazi line but when they see a girl on her own struggling to get by I think it feels different to many of them, even if they still call her a kike. And I tell everyone I'm a war widow. That helps the sympathy along.'

He tells her about seeing the Jews carried off in the street, about Feinstein and Gold and Walter disappearing, finally about the conversation he overheard at the party. She listens to that in rapt horror.

'So I was right to run.'

He nods. 'I was so busy training and flying, for years, really, and so pleased with myself, that I didn't see anything that was going on. I asked some old guy in Walter's building why he'd gone and he said, "Where have you been? The moon?" Otto calls me "kid". I think I am.'

She squeezes his hand again and leans over and kisses him.

'Oh, God! I look so sad!' he says when she shows him her sketch.

'I'm afraid you do a lot of the time. Poor Jochen. Your friend, your sister. And now Lotte. There isn't much to smile about, is there?'

Uwe and his wife are back. They all eat. Soup, sausage, bread. They have to wait for dark. Jochen plays more

Chopin then turns half round to face them and plays and sings *Shoeshine Boy*. They applaud.

Uwe goes off to meet his friend Herbert to prepare the boat. They're fishermen and if anyone asks, it's a normal fishing trip they're making, so everything must be as usual. When it's dark, Uwe returns. He and Herbert entered the port through the gates, past the guard, showing their passes and ID. Uwe has returned via the hidden way in and out that the fishermen use when they bring in clandestine cargoes from Sweden.

Following Uwe, and staying close in the dark, they pass the final fisherman's cottage. Gerda is in borrowed rubber boots; Jochen wears the brown overcoat and fedora and carries their bags. Jochen is agitated and often looks back, searching the darkness for a trailing figure. He'd feel less nervous with six Spitfires after him. Gerda seems calm. But then Jochen probably seems calm. A cold breeze from the sea chills his face. Far distant sounds of boat engines reach them, probably Uwe's and Herbert's fellow fishermen. Herbert has feigned engine trouble to delay their departure so that Gerda can get aboard unspotted on an empty quay. They cross low grassy dunes and reach a wire mesh fence that appears to head into the water. At a fence post, Uwe removes a bolt and pulls a section of the fence back. They creep through and Uwe replaces the fence and the bolt. He ties a rag onto the fence so that Jochen can find the right place in the dark when he returns alone. They cross more sand until the sand gives way to concrete. They've reached the quay and the boat.

Uwe goes below and Jochen and Gerda are standing in silence not quite knowing how to say goodbye when Heinecke appears out of the dark, gun in hand, and steps over the side of the boat. Jochen can do nothing but think, 'How? How did he get here?' And ransack his mind for some way of reacting. There are loud noises from below, coughs and chugs and small explosions as Uwe helps his friend Herbert get the engine started. Jochen can only take his pistol from its holster and hand it over to Heinecke. How did he get here? Did he track them all the way? Is there anyone with him?

'Surprised, Oberleutnant?' Heinecke says in a triumphant tone. 'I followed you. Don't blame yourself. I *am* trained to do it.'

If only he hadn't finally managed to persuade Gerda to take the Beretta, it would be sitting in his tunic pocket ready to pull out! What can he grab? What is there lying around? There must be many potential weapons on the deck of a fishing boat. There's an intermittent moon but he can't see much in the shadows when he looks down. He could dive straight at him. Knock him over, snatch the gun. But Heinecke has two guns now.

'I look forward to having a good talk with you and with your friend. Such a lovely if degenerate young woman! Now if you'll call the men below up on deck, I can march you all down to the gate and have the guards put you safely in custody.'

He'll just have to get the gun from Gerda's bag as they go down to the gate.

'And be careful, won't you? You're a hero but I will shoot if necessary. After all, you're attempting to flee the country with a Jew, and in that overcoat and that very non-military hat some might say you're dressed as a spy.'

He can only obey. He turns away from Heinecke and makes out a coil of rope by the hatch. Grab it and straight at his face with it! He takes two steps towards the hatch as if to call below. He realises an instant later that his movement has hidden Gerda from Heinecke's view so that her hand can dart into her bag, pull out the Beretta and all in the same movement fire it past Jochen. Heinecke gives a gasp and falls to the deck. Jochen takes the gun from Gerda's hand and goes over to Heinecke. He's moaning horribly with both hands clutched to his stomach. Small explosions and sounds like coughs are still rising from the engine below. There is no benefit to anyone aboard in treating Heinecke's wound. He bends down with the pistol and does what he wanted to do in that street in Berlin. The bullet to Heinecke's head stops his moaning.

10

Appassionata

HE OPENS AN EYE. A SLICE OF LIGHT IS FALLING through a gap in the shutters and onto the beautiful cherry wood of the wardrobe. He twists and picks up his watch from the bedside table. Twenty to seven. He's ravenous. Coffee and some of those eyetie pastries! He turns his head back. Rosaria is still asleep. A bare shoulder and her face turned towards him. He shouldn't have. But it seemed like the only thing to do when he met her at that party they threw for him. And really, why not? She wanted to and he won't last long when they catch up with him. Unless they just send him off to the Urals to slaughter commies until he's overwhelmed. He slips out of bed, pulls on his trousers and shirt, and creeps out to the bathroom. He pees, washes his face and armpits, and stares at himself in the mirror. Sometime his beard will catch up with his age and he'll have to shave every day but not yet, thank God.

Back in the room, he dresses properly, puts on his last clean shirt, hangs his Swords and Oak Leaves at his throat and runs a comb through his hair from front to back. The decoration that he was sent to Rome a week ago to receive from Mussolini is on the table; the 'order of magnificent airmen' or some such twaddle. He can't wear it. Not next to his others. He slips it in a pocket. Rosaria hasn't stirred; black hair across the pillow. Should he wake her or just sneak out for breakfast? He nudges the shutter a little wider and leans against the wall to look at the dusty lane below and the shadows of olive trees across it. This house is on the edge of the village. The bar they bought the wine at last night is about a hundred metres away.

Sassnitz was twelve days ago now. For the umpteenth time he wonders if Gerda got to Trelleborg. Did they dodge the patrol boats? But why would they be stopped? It was just a fishing boat and she'd be out of sight. But it was a hundred kilometres. In the dark. And then the daylight. Did the fog come up as Uwe hoped? Has she found the Jewish family Otto and Uwe spoke about? Is she hiding, terrified or sitting in the Swedish sunshine trying out her first words in her new language?

He can't wait any longer. With the pencil he always carries he writes on the corner of the paper that wrapped the salami they bought with the wine, '*Vado per caffe. x.*'

He's turning for the door when there's the sudden noise of a car driving up and stopping in a shower of grit on the lane below. Her husband or the SS? He looks out. Black uniforms. At least he won't have to fight an angry cuckold.

Rosaria wakes. She turns, sits and pulls the sheet up over her breasts.

'*Che cos'e?*' She's barely awake.

'*Non e tuo marito, cara,*' he says. There are loud German voices below. '*Sono venuti per me.*' He throws his few things in his bag, straps on his pistol; something to surrender in a little ceremony before they arrest him, and bends to kiss her.

'*Devo andare,*' he says.

'*Che peccato.*'

There is hammering from below. He smiles, kisses her again and goes to the door. '*Ci vedremo, Rosaria.*'

The hammering continues as he goes down the stairs preparing mentally to lose his freedom, to be hauled off to stand trial. He creaks the door open and sees a leutnant of the SS on the step with two troopers with machine pistols slung ready. The leutnant salutes.

'Oberleutnant Murville?'

He nods.

'I have orders to take you' ...into custody... 'to Fiumicino and your transport to Africa, sir. You are officially absent without leave. Five days, sir.'

AWOL! That's what they want him for.

'Five days! How time flies! Leutnant, have you and your men had breakfast?'

The heat is a shock. He's had sixty-three days of calmer summer temperatures. Most of the others have been there flying and fighting all that time. Someone crashed his Friedrich but Jurg and Hans have another ready. He flies with Bubi Schuster as his new wingman. He isn't Franz but he'll be fine after a couple of fights. 'Just keep your eyes peeled,' he tells him.

The first job is escorting Stukas.

'Hi, fourteen,' one of them breaks radio silence to call. 'Good to have you back.'

The sea is a ravishing turquoise as it spreads to the horizon. He's missed it.

When the Hurricanes attack the Stukas, the Friedrichs tear down after them. He gets two very quickly with shots from astern. Both pilots bale out, tumbling and flailing around until their parachutes jerk them upright and they hang like puppets. He shoots another Hurricane off the tail of a Stuka. It goes straight down trailing smoke until it bursts into flames. He sees Schuster get another.

'Saw it, Bubi,' he calls.

The Hurricanes have gone. A Stuka is spinning down, trailing smoke. It straightens into a shallow dive and one after the other, two men jump.

In the afternoon they bounce Kittihawk fighter-bombers and he gets three. One explodes; another spins into the desert floor; the third flies towards home, trailing smoke but then puts down, wheels up, in British territory.

Christof has been looking after Lehmann and Winter in Jochen's absence and they swear by him. Their tents have never been so tidy, their clothes never so clean. Jonny Beck is on leave, but five days after Jochen gets back, he climbs down from the evening transport; short haircut, spotless uniform, dazzling boots. Jochen opens a bottle to make peace and they all drink his health sitting in a circle outside Jonny's tent. There is no mention of Jochen's attack on Jonny. Winter has worked his customary magic and calmed Beck. Christof has got hold of some olives and they spit the stones into the sand in the middle of the circle.

'So what's new, Jonny?' Winter says. 'Getting married? Met Leni Riefenstahl? Dinner with Fatty?'

'I've joined the party.'

'What party's that?' Lehmann says.

'The National Socialists, of course.'

'Fuck!' Lehmann says.

'Why fuck?'

'We're soldiers,' Jochen says. 'We serve the nation.'

'The National Socialists are the nation.'

'Will you be reporting back on us all?' Jochen says.

'Don't be absurd!'

The party's over. They drink up and go to bed.

They fly three or four times a day. There are always British to attack but because of all the Hurricanes and Kittihawks and Spitfires they have to get rid of first they rarely get through to the Blenheim and Maryland bombers which are their real targets. One morning he manages to ignore the fighters and shoots the port engine off a Maryland which then loses its wing and goes straight down. He's turning towards another when Schuster shouts, 'Break left!' and he's at once into a turning match with a Spitfire, which he wins by dropping his flaps and slowing right down. He fires when the Spitfire's nose disappears under his own. Bits fly off it and then the engine is smoking and the pilot jumps.

He lies on his bed for an hour. He does that after every flight if there's time. He's prey to ugly thoughts, and nightmares if he sleeps. He'd like a letter but he hasn't been back long enough. He listens to the recording of the *Appassionata* that he found in a shop in Rome. He hasn't managed yet to tell Beck that he has a new record by Schnabel the Jew. Always in his mind is the conversation he overheard at that party, and memories of looking for Herr Walter and Dr Feinstein, and the old man he helped to his feet in the street, the woman and her child being put on the truck: 'State business,' the trooper said. And National Socialists are the state, Jonny says.

'Do you know what's happened to the Jews?' he says to Lehmann.

'What do you mean?'

'There aren't any in Berlin.'

'Aren't they being moved east to be put to work?'

'Weren't they working before? Our family doctor was. What could he be given to do that's more important than being a doctor?'

'Don't ask me, Jochen. I've got a Friedrich to test.'

He tells Winter what he overheard; that the Jews are being removed from history, rubbed out, will exist no longer.

'You must have misheard or misunderstood.'

'Because that's unthinkable, you mean. It would be wrong, wouldn't it? A crime. An obscenity, right?'

'Jochen. Don't get distracted from your job. You have to concentrate up there. You haven't got time to think about things like that; none of us have. Put it out of your head.'

The British are always there. So many of them. He knocks down two or three every time he goes up; the dive, the short burst, the Kittihawk or Hurricane falling away, the zoom, the short burst, another one falling away and Bubi circling above watching for attackers, calling them out as they fall, 'One, Jochen.' 'Two.' 'Three.'

He slays so economically that anyone he flies with becomes just a bodyguard watching his back. Winter orders him to have a break every three or four days. He drinks, plays his records, wanders around the field in his shorts and the sandals Christof made him from the old tyre. He's still got the colourful parasol and he carries that to aggravate Beck. He reads letters from the sacks that still arrive for him. He finds it grotesque that people do this. Some of them are love letters; some are ideological rants about the might of the Reich, appreciations of Jochen's own personal splendour or descriptions of the enormity of the crimes of the Jews. The letters sicken him.

He's been back nine days and he's already got twenty more. Jurg paints them up on the rudder each evening when flying has finished for the day. One night he wakes and finds himself standing under the stars by the tail of his Friedrich. He turns his head and sees Christof.

'What am I doing here?'

Christof shrugs.

'Have I done this before?'

'A couple of times. Don't worry about it. You won't hurt yourself. I follow you.'

'Don't tell the boss.'

'I won't. But he knows everything, doesn't he?'

Back in the tent, he lies down again. Christof is quickly asleep. Jochen hears his breathing from near the tent flap. His head is elsewhere as he waits for sleep to arrive. When he got back from Sassnitz, his mother looked at him. He smiled and nodded his head. She asked no questions. When she'd gone to bed, Bauer said, 'Where's the gun?'

'In the Baltic.'

Bauer raised his eyebrows. 'A good place,' he said. 'A couple of people said they saw Heinecke leave a shelter. With a Luftwaffe officer.'

'Oh.'

'And a woman. No one's seen him since. I didn't think you had it in you.'

Winter summons him to the command tent. As he goes in, the corporals leave. Jochen turns to watch them go and sits down.

'What's up?'

'Listen, Jochen, there's no easy way to say this. There's a message in. I'm afraid your father's been killed.'

'Oh.'

'He was ambushed by Russian irregulars. Three of his staff and his driver were killed, too.'

Jochen remembers the driver slumped asleep in the Mercedes outside the restaurant in Berlin that night. Was it him?

'When?'

'Two days ago.'

'He didn't think he'd be coming back.'

Winter pours two brandies and raises his. 'General Murville.'

They both drink.

'I didn't really know him. I used to think he was a shit but I saw him before he went out there and when Ilse died and he didn't seem so bad.'

Winter pours another drink.

'He knew your father,' Jochen says. 'Said he was a good guy and a good soldier.'

'He knew more than me then. They rounded up fifty people from the nearest village and shot them.'

'Ten each.'

'Yes.'

'Is that how we do things?'

'It seems to be.'

The news gets around. People clap him on the shoulder and say they're sorry. Jurg and Hans seek him out with a bottle and insist on drinking a toast to the general with him. He must write to his mother but he can't think of what to say so he puts it off. Having a general as a father is unusual, so over dinner people ask about him and Jochen tells them what he knows. Jonny Beck is pompously solicitous. He probably wishes he had a general for a father, so Jochen sings the song in English that his father sang him in the restaurant: 'Hitler has only got one ball…' Everyone bursts into laughter but Jonny jumps up. 'Degenerate!' he says and stomps out.

'It's your family now,' Christof says. 'You're the head.' But there's only his mother. He must write to her. An ambush! Did he have a chance to fight back? Did he have time to draw his revolver, to die with a weapon in his hand?

He puts Schnabel and the *Appassionata* on and listens to it with a last cigarette. It *is* passionate. But who knows whether Beethoven thought it was. It was someone else who named it.

He gets four the next morning and three in the afternoon. In the evening they see nothing. The day after, they're up early with the Stukas, who always attract the British. They fly above them at six thousand metres. To one side as usual, is the solid blue of the sea, to the other the buff-coloured land with long shadows thrown by the barely risen sun.

'Indians!' he calls. 'Three o'clock low.'

They turn and dive on the Hurricanes, which turn into them and fire as they close. He fires far ahead of one, which flies into the burst and starts burning.

'One,' he hears Bubi call.

'Break left, Jonny!' he calls, and shoots the two chasing Beck, one in the engine, one in the tail, which snaps off. Both pilots jump.

'Two, three,' comes Bubi's call.

He shoots another off the tail of a Stuka and as Bubi calls, 'Break right,' does so and, using the throttle, slows right down to turn onto the tail of another Hurricane and send it spinning down with a short burst into the cockpit.

'Four, five,' Bubi calls. He spots shadows on the land below and goes after them; Hurricanes low down. One is hit in the engine and cartwheels across the stony ground to burst into flames. He sees his bullets sparkle around the cockpit and wing root of the other and it noses down to an immediate belly landing. The pilot climbs out.

'Six, seven.'

Flying home, he and Bubi get a Blenheim each. Winter is grinning as they enter the command tent. He's heard it all on the loudspeaker. He's sent a report to HQ already. 'No one's ever got eight in one operation before.'

On their afternoon escort, Hurricanes attack the Stukas and they dive down on them. He hits three in their engines. Each smokes and the pilots jump before their machines burn. Coming back they find Kittihawk fighter-bombers which straight away go into a defensive circle. Dive, fire; zoom, fire, and he has two more. The circle scatters and he chases another until it turns. He circles two or three times until the Kittihawk's nose slides under his own. He fires and the Englishman goes down as smoke pours from his engine.

'Fourteen,' Bubi calls out.

Winter tells him to have a rest but Jurg and Hans have got his Friedrich ready so he goes as usual with the early evening patrol.

'Indians!' Lehmann calls. 'Eight o'clock low.' Bombed up Kittihawks looking for convoys of trucks.

They're spotted at the last moment and the British turn towards them but Jochen's exposes his belly and the short burst of fire hits him there and probably the bomb, too, because the aeroplane explodes. He moves in behind another which has jettisoned its bomb and is turning slowly and tightly. Jochen slows on the throttle, drops his flaps and, on the verge of unconsciousness from the tightness of the turn, despite tensing his stomach muscles, stays with the Englishman. His nose nudges up and up along the fuselage until it covers the Kittihawk's nose. He fires and the Englishman flies into the shells and bullets. The engine burns, the aeroplane turns over and the pilot drops out. As Jochen completes his turn he sees the parachute open.

He sees a Kittihawk on his right about to flash past his nose. He kicks the rudder and the Friedrich skids left. He takes a snapshot. There are sparkles around the cockpit. The propeller stops and the machine goes straight down.

'Seventeen!' he hears Bubi screaming.

'The rest of us might as well stay at home,' Lehmann says in his ears.

As he taxis up, Winter is waiting. Jurg and Hans are grinning. Jurg holds his paint pot ready. Winter grabs him round the waist and lifts and twirls him. 'That's 150,' he says.

Jochen grins. 'The lads are looking after me.'

'We're not,' Lehmann says. 'We just can't get near them, you're always in the way.'

'You're a lucky bastard, Murville,' Beck says, 'but I have to say you're a brilliant lucky bastard.'

'Thanks, Jonny.'

Bubi grins, just glad to be associated.

'Get yourself scrubbed up. Rommel's coming to dinner. He wants to meet the "boy wonder". His words.'

Jochen goes to his tent and flops on the bed. His eyes are sore and he closes them. He and Gerda are running. It's an alley in Berlin. In the blackout. Heinecke is after them. It's a dead end. Gerda clings to him and cries, 'Jochen, Jochen, keep me safe!' She's hugging him tight. She's very soft against him. He pulls a gun from his tunic pocket. Heinecke is in front of him. 'What can you do, Leutnant?'

'Oberleutnant,' he says. He pulls the trigger but nothing happens. Heinecke laughs and reaches out to pull the gun from his hand but Gerda has it. There's a loud bang as she fires. He opens his eyes.

'Sorry, boss.' Christof is reaching down for the enamel bowl he's just dropped onto the ammunition box that's there to sit on.

'Seventeen in a day! That's a miracle,' Rommel says. 'That deserves the Diamonds on its own. You'd better get him on a transport, Winter. Fatty will want a picture with him.'

'I can't leave, sir,' Jochen says. 'I've only been back a couple of weeks. I need to put some time in.'

He can't go back now. He feels safe out here with his unit, with his comrades, with Winter looking after him. He'd be on his own back in Berlin. The SS or the Gestapo would be sure to track him down. There were loose ends left that must be flapping in their faces. His visit to Franz's family after Sassnitz doesn't cover the time he was out of Berlin. And who knows who saw him in Sassnitz? A man in an old brown overcoat with a young woman on his arm. And Christof! The more he thinks about him, the more anxious he feels. Would they protect Christof if Jochen weren't here? And Rommel's bound to start losing soon.

The Americans are on their way, and Jochen and his mates so rarely get through to the English bombers that they can't stop them pounding Rommel's tanks and trucks. What would happen to Christof if there were a surrender? He'd be a traitor in the eyes of the English. He's been doing their washing for them, pouring their drinks, tidying their tents, cooking omelettes.

Christof offers Rommel a cognac. He takes it. 'Who's this?' he says to Jochen.

'A friend of mine. He goes where I go.'

Rommel laughs. 'Funny old things, wars,' he says.

And Lotte! If he went back now, he'd have to do something about her, make a decision. Fix a date or break it off.

Rommel is good company. He tells stories of life in the Great War, his memories of Jochen's and Winter's fathers; he knew them then.

'How did you find our Great Leader?'

'His breath stank. It was difficult to sit there.'

'It's his teeth. They're rotten.'

'Sir,' Beck says, 'should we be talking about the Führer like this?'

'It's all right, son,' Rommel says. 'We're all friends here, aren't we?'

Beck looks grim.

'What about Fatty and Goebbels?'

'A bit peculiar. I swear Fatty was wearing nail varnish and every time I saw him he had a different uniform on!'

'They are strange. Perhaps you need to be to take control of a country. To even think of doing it.'

Jonny Beck looks as if he's going to explode.

'Jonny,' Winter says, 'you may be excused if you'd prefer.'

Beck stands, nods to Rommel and leaves.

'What's up with him?' Rommel says.

He's awarded the Knight's Cross with Diamonds. A signal comes through about it. Hitler will present it; so few are awarded, that Hitler has each one made up personally. Jochen refuses to go back before Christmas. He tells Winter he feels like a fraud having so much time off.

He writes to Lotte; just news; Rommel, the seventeen, the Diamonds. She'll like all that. She'll be excited, probably her face will flush as she reads it; as a proper National Socialist fräulein's face should flush to hear of great success for her man. What a dreadful thought to have! But forced to think about Lotte as he writes, he realises that his feelings for her have changed so much that he almost doesn't recognise them as feelings. Ilse would have smiled and made a crack to hear about his success; Gerda would laugh and ask if she had to pay a fee now to talk to the great man.

Winter gives some of them the day off and goes with them to the sea. Christof drives their kübelwagen. Another kübelwagen follows them with six troopers carrying machine pistols and rifles. They lie on sand near some rocks, a bit of cover in case any Indians spot them and come strafing. He closes his eyes against the blaze of the sun. He's hot. He shouldn't stay too long like this but it's delicious to laze. Where is Gerda and doing what? 'Stay alive,' they each said to the other. And 'One day,' she said. He could just see her smile in the low light from the bridge house on the fishing boat. 'One day,' he said, too, and squeezed her hand before he left. She'd amazed him that night. He and Gerda were still clutching each other when Herbert came up from below with the engine chugging nicely and said, 'What was that?'

There are shouts. He sits up. Something's wrong. Far out to sea someone's waving and calling. He looks around at who's on the beach. It must be Winter out there! He runs to the sea. Jonny Beck is in front of him. Jonny swims quite well but Jochen won't be able to help; he can barely stay afloat in water. Winter is still waving. Beck is fifty metres out, past the breakers, when a brown head with brown arms moving like paddle wheels goes past him and on towards Winter. Jochen joins Bubi in jumping up and down and shouting encouragement to Christof, who must be two hundred metres out now and still going like a torpedo towards the boss.

The two heads, close together, bob slowly back through the sparkling waves towards the shore. Beck joins them, three heads now. Jochen and Bubi wade in and slide Winter's arms over their shoulders to relieve the swimmers. They walk Winter out onto the sand where he collapses and sits, coughing and spluttering. Beck and Christof throw themselves down on their backs on the sand, their chests heaving.

Beck is still gasping in air when Christof gets up and goes over to Winter.

'Are you OK, Major?'

Winter looks up. 'Where did you learn to swim like that?'

'At the pictures. *Tarzan*, Johnny Weissmuller.'

'I'm glad you did. Thanks.'

'Thanks is no good, boss! Have you got a sister?' Jochen says to Christof.

'Three.'

'There you are, boss,' Jochen says with a laugh. 'You've even got a choice.'

Bubi has a brandy bottle out. It passes among them, including Christof. Beck gives the top an exaggerated wipe before drinking.

Jochen feels suddenly light-hearted. The SS and Gestapo may still want his head and every Spitfire pilot he meets in the air may want him in flames but Winter will surely find a way to look after Christof now even if Rommel has to surrender.

Jochen sits under his parasol and lays it on a rock when he goes to paddle about in the sea. When he comes back, he's just in time to see Beck, who's clambering down the rocks, step on the parasol and snap the wooden shaft in two. Beck stumbles and half falls to the sand.

'Who left that there?'

'Are you blind?' Jochen shouts.

'I could have broken my ankle!'

Winter groans. 'Do I have to be the referee forever?' he calls over.

Christof takes the parasol away to see if he can mend it.

'Sorry,' Beck says after a moment, 'but that parasol is inappropriate kit for a German officer.'

Jochen blows a raspberry.

Christof brings the parasol back. He's found a driftwood stick and tied it as a splint onto the broken shaft. It'll do for now. Jurg can probably repair it properly when they're back.

Jochen sits down next to Beck on the sand, holding the parasol over his head.

'Why did you join the Nazis, Jonny?'

'I don't like that abbreviation. The National Socialists.'

'OK, them. Why?'

'I believe in what they want to achieve. It's what we're fighting for.'

'You know they're working on exterminating every Jew in the country and in the occupied lands?'

'I know you're telling everyone that.'

'I heard a general talking about it.'

'You were probably drunk.'

'I was definitely drunk. But that doesn't affect my hearing. Assume it's true. What do you think about it?'

'Damn good idea.'

'Millions of people.'

'Of Jews.'

'Don't they count?'

'No.'

'Would you shoot them yourself?'

'If I were given the order, it would be my duty.'

'But if you kill all the Jews, why stop there?'

'Yes, why?'

'So who's next? Gypsies, queers, cripples, negroes?'

'Yes. The lot.'

'Christof? The man who's just saved the boss's life?'

'I was only a moment or two behind him.'

'You were nowhere near. I was watching.'

'What are all these questions for, Jochen?'

'I was just wondering if our leaders were the only lunatics around but I see they're not.'

'You'll need to be careful, Jochen, when we've won this war.'

'If there's any justice, we won't win it. What will the world be like if we do? We don't deserve to win.'

Beck leaps up. 'If there was any justice, you'd be arrested for saying that.'

The next morning when he wakes up, his feet are covered in sand and there's sand on the bed.

Gustavs have arrived for them. It's not thought that they need a conversion course this time. Jurg and Hans are working on Jochen's. While they do so, he flies his Friedrich on a high patrol. They bounce some Hurricanes. He gets one immediately from behind. It turns on its back and goes straight down trailing thick black smoke. He clenches his stomach muscles hard to stay behind another in a tight turn. He fires and the bullets sparkle around the cockpit and move towards the engine. The propeller windmills and slows. He stops firing as the pilot turns the machine and falls free.

'Break right!' Bubi shouts in his ears. He pulls the stick into his stomach and a Spitfire shoots past him. There's another behind Bubi.

'Break left, Bubi!'

Bubi's turn brings the chasing Spitfire towards him and he fires as they approach each other. He isn't conscious of aiming but he hits the engine. The propeller disintegrates. The pilot puts the nose straight down. Jochen puts his down too and fires again, hitting the tail. The Spitfire drops towards the desert.

He gets three more Kittihawks in the early evening then sits with a lamp and finally writes to his mother about his father. He tells her he came to know him a little at the end and valued the advice he gave him and that he'd learnt how his father had stayed in touch with her about him and Ilse. He's sorry he won't have the chance now to get to know him better. He seals the letter, realising how inadequate it is, but he's powerless to write more. That night he wakes up standing by his Friedrich again, staring up at the multitudes of stars in the moonless desert sky. Christof walks back with him to their tent.

'You'll look after Christof if I'm not here, won't you, boss?' he says to Winter the next morning before he goes off to test his new Gustav.

Winter laughs. 'I'm not marrying any sisters, though.'

The Gustav is heavy. It's faster than his Friedrich but does nothing more quickly, except dive. He's not sure he likes it. 'Keep the Friedrich going for the time being,' he tells Hans and Jurg. Then he remembers something that Gerda said about her time making components in the

Daimler factory. There were many Polish and Jewish girls working with her.

'Someone told me there's a growing problem with deliberate sabotage of engine parts. Can you check what you can?'

'We always do, boss, but a lot are well buried. We have to rely on factory quality control.'

They're rested until the evening. He lies on his bed and listens three times to *Rumba Azul*. Such an addictive tune. He gets up and puts on the *Appassionata*. With its strong melodies and breathtaking rapid sections it's like an air fight where things sometimes happen so fast that there's no time to think. He imagines playing it, almost feels his fingers on the keys, an audience spellbound in silence before him. What a different life he could have had. He might have met Schnabel in that different world. What a master he is! Why can't Beck and his vile crew see that Schnabel and all those others like him are the instant and undeniable refutation of Nazi doctrine?

They take off in the late afternoon. It will be nearly dark when they land. Shadows are spreading below. They climb. His shirt, damp with sweat at take-off, cools rapidly. The sky is a deep azure, the sea a glorious aquamarine but golden towards the west as the sun begins its descent. His eyes continue their constant trawl across the sky, up, down, left, right.

'Indians,' he calls, 'dead ahead.' They're flying at eight thousand metres. 'Bombers! Anyone see an escort?' He looks higher.

'Above, just behind!' Lehmann shouts.

He pulls the nose up to meet the fighters which are coming down on them now. They get bigger. They're Spitfires.

He has one dead ahead of him as he climbs. He's about to shoot when it flicks aside and is gone. Clever! He pulls the stick into his stomach and clenching the muscles turns to the right as tightly as he can. He sees a Spitfire also turning to get back at him. There's no future in turning with a Spit but he continues. He lowers his flaps. So does the Spit pilot. Tracers fly past on his right. He slams the stick over to the left, pulls up his flaps and puts the nose down. He should be clear. With no fuel injection, the Spitfire can't follow that manoeuvre instantly. He pulls up and to the left. There's a Spitfire behind a Friedrich. Number nine.

'Break right, Bubi!' He does and Jochen is behind the Spitfire, which is now turning to follow Bubi. He shoots and hits the outer port wing. The Spitfire instantly breaks off and spins round in a tight turn to starboard. Jochen follows, clenches his stomach muscles, lowers his flaps and turns, turns, turns with the Spitfire. He forces his head against the turn to try to see behind, past the cockpit glazing bars. Oh, for a nice clear bubble canopy with a handy mirror to glance up into like the Spit has! Where's Bubi? He turns, the Spitfire turns, the sea keeps appearing and disappearing from view. Go home, he thinks to the Englishman. I won't follow. Honest. Suddenly he's had enough and pulls straight up into the sun, hoping to disappear into it and become invisible to the other pilot. He climbs till he loses speed and flicks over in a stall turn and dives back the way he came. There's the Spitfire climbing blind into the sun after him. He fires and hits the engine and all around the cockpit. Black smoke gushes and billows as the Spitfire stops momentarily before flopping over to hurtle downwards on fire and corkscrewing out of control towards the distant desert. Poor devil!

'Seen it!' Bubi calls.

He looks around. Once again they haven't got any of the bombers, so Rommel will lose more tanks. They land in pairs. He taxis over to Jurg and Hans, swings around to point out onto the field and cuts the engine. The cockpit feels like home. He could go to sleep here. Hans opens his straps. Jochen rubs his shoulders, pulls himself up. The air is still hot. He climbs out onto the wing. He can feel the heat of the engine from here. It ticks and clicks as it cools. He jumps down, walks away ten metres and lights a cigarette.

'I'll fly the Gustav tomorrow, Jurg,' he calls, and goes off to report. Winter is coming towards him with a big smile. What now?

'Jochen, it's just in. You're Hauptmann Murville now. The youngest in the Luftwaffe. Signed by Fatty himself. You'd better slow down or you'll have my job.'

They swarm around him, shouting, slapping his back. What does it mean? More pay? He can't spend what he earns now. More papers to read and sign probably. He outranks Jonny Beck now. He can tell him to stuff himself. But he already does. They toast his new rank.

Jonny Beck nods to him over his glass although he can't raise a smile.

'Congratulations, boss,' Christof says at the tent flap, then leaves to let him rest. He puts on Schnabel and lies down. That playing! Still no letters. Has a transport gone down? No news from Gerda.

'My God!' Herbert said on the boat after, 'What was that?' when he and Uwe came up from starting the engine, now puttering away below. 'Who is he?'

Jochen told him then described how Gerda had saved them all. Herbert took charge. A communist since the naval rebellions of 1918, Herbert told them, he'd lain low since Hitler came to power. He'd longed to see a Nazi dead at his feet, he said, and now that day had come to pass. He slung a tarpaulin over the body.

'I've got some chains over there I can wrap around him when we're out to sea. We'll drop him over the side, right, Uwe? We should get going. Do you think he had anyone with him?'

'He said he followed us,' Jochen said. 'Sounded pleased with himself and he was going to get the guard at the gate to hold us. I think he was on his own. He must have been behind us as we went over the dunes and through the fence. Unless he left someone there and I run into them on my way back.'

'Let's hope not. Keep your gun out. Say goodbye, Oberleutnant, we'll be up again directly.' He and Uwe went below, leaving the deck to Jochen and Gerda.

'Thank you for my life,' Gerda said.

'Thank you for *my* life. Do you want the pistol?'

'No more pistols. I don't think I could do that again.'

'We never had dinner.'

'We didn't have time.'

'We didn't have time for a lot of things.'

'One day, Jochen.'

'Send me a postcard. From Trelleborg.'

'Wish you were here?'

He laughs.

'Come with me,' she said.

He had the flash of a vision of them as a couple, struggling with Swedish, growing potatoes in a back garden, Gerda doing washing, him doing odd jobs for cash or teaching the piano, together in bed under a threadbare blanket. But together. Then, his mother alone and weeping, Bauer trying to console her; Winter trying to puzzle it all out.

He smiled. 'You know I can't.'

'You could.'

'Gerda.'

'One day, though, Jochen darling.'

'One day.'

He heard Herbert's feet on the top step.

'We're going.' Herbert cast off at the bow and started for the stern.

Gerda threw her arms around his neck and kissed his lips. He hugged her to him then let her go but squeezed her hand.

'Stay alive, my love,' she said.

He turned and stepped ashore. The fishing boat bobbed free. Herbert swung the wheel and the boat moved out in an arc away from the quay. Gerda held on to the side of the wheel house with one hand and with the other waved and continued to wave as the sound of the boat's engine diminished and until she disappeared in the darkness. Jochen looked down at the Beretta still in his hand. He swung his arm back and, as if throwing a grenade, swung it forward again and let the gun go. It was too dark to see it flying towards Sweden but after a moment or two he heard it splash into the water.

It's time to fly the Gustav. But can he keep his Friedrich if he doesn't like the Gustav?

'Jochen, you're a Hauptmann with the Knight's Cross with Diamonds, you can do what you like,' Winter says.

Back in his tent to put on his boots and pick up his helmet he sees letters on his bed at last; Lotte's handwriting and underneath that, his mother's. Only the two.

Was it all for nothing then? Was there a storm? Did she drown? Or was she captured by a patrol boat and taken east to a camp and shot in a pit? He sits on the bed next to the letters, kicks off his sandals, pulls on his dusty boots, and stares at their scratched and scuffed toes. He buries his face in his hands. Gerda! Gerda!

'Boss,' Christof's voice from the tent flap, 'this one got mixed up with Fähnrich Schuster's.'

Jochen takes the postcard with its message in Swedish across the corner that he realises can only translate as, 'Greetings from Trelleborg.' A sepia print of fishing boats tied up at a quay, really boring but quite, quite beautiful to him as he grins down at it; he'll keep it all his life: 'Greetings from Trelleborg.'

He turns it over.

'Wish you were here. Gerda.'

He jumps up, grabs the bemused Christof by the shoulders and dances around the tent with him, still holding the postcard, the beautiful postcard from Gerda. She will have a life! He might just possibly see her again one day. One day, as she said. One day. But anyway, whatever, she will have a life and her sideways smile will carry its charm on in the world.

It's early but quickly warming up. He can't stop grinning. He feels it on his face. Their 109s glint in the sunlight. Their metal skins are already hot to the touch. 'Good hunting!' they shout across to each other as they climb onto their port wings to reach the cockpits.

'One more!' he calls to Bubi. Bubi has four. The next one will bring him an Iron Cross. Not bad at nineteen.

In the command tent Winter has the tannoy on to keep track of the patrol.

'Straight up to eight thousand,' Beck says. He's still leading for today but Jochen will have his own staffel from tomorrow.

They leave long trails of dust behind them as they take off. Christof turns from watching to pick up clothes from Jochen's tent.

In the air, the 109s climb at forty-five degrees towards the British line. Jochen leans forward to check his straps are tight. He swings the stick left and looks down past the wing, then does the same to the right. All clear. He moves his eyes constantly up and down, left and right. Seven thousand on the altimeter. Nothing visible so far. Is it the British weekend? They level off and fly on for ten minutes. Bubi is two hundred metres to his left, fifty metres behind. Something grey drifts across the windscreen. What? There's smoke entering the cockpit from under the instruments.

'I've got smoke in here,' he says. 'Am I on fire?'

He sees Bubi pull up alongside.

'Can't see anything,' Bubi calls.

In the command tent, Winter stops reading and puts down his pen. He takes out a cigarette and holds it to his mouth. Christof is walking to the command tent to check if Winter needs anything cleaned.

The smoke in Jochen's cockpit turns from grey to black.

'I'm going home,' he calls. He swings the stick to the right.

'We'll all come,' Beck calls.

'There's a flame, low down,' Bubi calls. 'Get out, Jochen.'

'I'll get a bit closer.'

Back in the command tent the NCOs have stopped typing. Winter still hasn't lit his cigarette. Christof waits for Winter. He's realised what he's hearing.

'Get out now, Jochen,' Beck calls. 'That's an order.'

'You can't order me now, Jonny,' he says, but coughs into his mask straight afterwards. Why is he on fire? One of Gerda's saboteurs? A damaged part not properly checked in the factory and broken now, deep inside the engine?

'Here I go,' he says.

He switches off the engine and gets rid of the canopy. It flies away and air rushes into the cockpit. The smoke is gushing around him now.

'Au revoir, lads.'

He slips his straps, checking first it's the seat straps and not the parachute. He pulls the mask off from the poppers on his helmet, drops it at his feet and pulls out the radio lead. This is his seventh life. Curtains for a cat.

In the command tent Winter's cigarette is still poised before his lips. Christof still waits.

'There's no chute! There's no chute!' Bubi yells over the intercom.

BRUCE FELLOWS has written a novel, *That Quiet Earth*, as well as plays and performance pieces for Brass Works Theatre, Theatre West and Show of Strength Theatre Company.